DEADLY

Coincidence

BRANTLEY WALKER:
Off the Books

By Nicole Edwards

THE WALKERS

ALLURING INDULGENCE

Kaleb
Zane
Travis
Holidays with The Walker Brothers
Ethan
Braydon
Sawyer
Brendon

THE WALKERS OF COYOTE RIDGE

Curtis
Jared (a crossover novel)
Hard to Hold
Hard to Handle
Beau
Rex
A Coyote Ridge Christmas
Mack
Kaden & Keegan
Alibi (a crossover novel)

BRANTLEY WALKER: OFF THE BOOKS

All In
Without A Trace
Hide & Seek
Deadly Coincidence
Alibi (a crossover novel)

AUSTIN ARROWS

Rush
Kaufman

DEADLY *Coincidence*

BRANTLEY WALKER: OFF THE BOOKS, 4

NICOLE EDWARDS

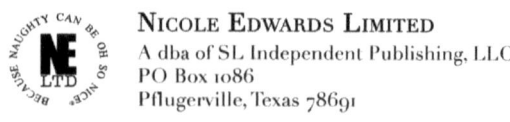

NICOLE EDWARDS LIMITED
A dba of SL Independent Publishing, LLC
PO Box 1086
Pflugerville, Texas 78691

DEADLY COINCIDENCE
Brantley Walker: Off the Books, 4
Nicole Edwards

COVER DETAILS:
Image: © Lario Tus (68715560) | 123rf.com
Design: © Nicole Edwards Limited

INTERIOR DETAILS:
Formatting: Nicole Edwards Limited
Editing: Blue Otter Editing

IDENTIFIERS:
ISBN: (ebook) 978-1-64418-041-9 | (paperback) 978-1-64418-042-6 | (audio) 978-1-64418-043-3
BISAC: FICTION / Romance / General

Chapter One

Wednesday, December 23, 2020

REESE TAVOULARIS STARED OUT THE SECOND-FLOOR window, his binoculars bringing the monstrosity of a house across the street into sharp focus. It was still dark outside, the sun not quite coming over the horizon, but the vast estate was lit up like the surface of the sun, making his job easier.

Just shy of forty-eight hours on this painfully boring stakeout and they hadn't seen a single person at the Prince residence. No one had so much as poked their head out. Not Nicholas Prince, not his new young wife or his daughter. Hell, not even the maid, the butler, or the pool cleaner. And Reese expected that would continue to be the case, no matter how long they remained here, because this was what they referred to as a total bust.

Then again, the Prince family was out of town for the holidays. And by *holidays*, Reese was referring to the entire months of December and January, starting, of course, back in November because, hey, why the hell not?

Who took a vacation for two solid months? In France?

Apparently the uber-rich, that's who. The one-percenters. One of the many who lived in this ritzy neighborhood with its palatial mansions and luxury cars, kids who went to fancy boarding schools, and pets who had not only groomers but massage therapists.

Yep, it was a thing. Ask Evelyn "Just call me Maude" Montgomery, the seventy-two-year-old randy widow who lived here in this four-thousand-square-foot stately abode with her ninety-six-year-old mother, who could give Betty White a run for her money, as well as Maude's best friend, Maxine. Sound familiar? If not, think a live version of *The Golden Girls* off in here, because that was exactly what was going on.

If Blanche and team had a miniature poodle named Snookums, that was.

And like the promiscuous Blanche Devereaux on *The Golden Girls*, Maude did have guests of the male variety on occasion, she had happily told them, but for the duration of their stay, she would ensure her many suitors were kept at bay.

Nice of her.

"Anything?" the deep, rumbling voice sounded from behind him.

Reese lowered the binoculars, scanned the yard and street one final time. "Nope."

"I think it's time to call it," Brantley said in that sexy, just-woken-up, gravel-laced voice.

"I agree."

Reese hadn't been keen on the idea of spending the few days before Christmas camping out in some old lady's second-floor spare bedroom just so they could keep a close eye on the house where they *thought* Juliet Prince *might possibly* appear, but he'd been overruled by Brantley, as well as Brantley's cousin Travis, who was insistent they would find Juliet if they just looked hard enough. Didn't seem to matter that they'd been dedicating a tremendous amount of time and effort the past few weeks to finding the woman and still nothing.

Of course, Reese didn't have much say in the matter. After all, he worked for the Off the Books Task Force that Brantley spearheaded, and if Brantley wanted a stakeout, Brantley would get a stakeout.

Not that Reese had put up much of a fight. Not after Brantley had sweet-talked him with a blow job followed by breakfast in bed. Initially, Reese had figured the extra attention was his reward for finding a significant lead in a cold case they'd been sweating for the two weeks prior to this impromptu trip.

Oh, how wrong he'd been.

Brantley had given Reese the news of this supposed lovers' getaway *after* that intimate massage with his lips and tongue, assuring Reese this was a chance for them to enjoy some downtime—a vacation if you will—before the chaos known as Christmas with the Walkers.

Teach him to give in to that wickedly skilled mouth, because this most certainly was *not* a vacation.

But Brantley had been right about needing some downtime. It would be scarce, because once the holidays were over, they were dedicating the first few weeks of the new year to doing interviews for the task force vacancies, and if he was being honest, despite knowing they needed the help, Reese wasn't looking forward to it. He'd mastered many things in his life, but interviews weren't on that list.

He was, however, looking forward to going home to see Tesha, his four-legged, furry partner, who was spending the weekend with JJ.

"So when do you wanna leave?" Reese asked, glancing back at Brantley.

Ho-ly.

Fuck.

That was not what he'd been expecting to see, but he wouldn't deny he was intrigued.

Setting the binoculars on the window ledge, Reese turned around fully, taking in the sight of the naked man currently propped up on a stack of pillows, his cock in his hand.

And just like that, lust burst into flame within him, making his cock pulse behind his zipper. Never in his life had he seen someone who could flip his switch so easily.

"I was hopin' this would do the trick," Brantley said with a grunt, his eyes hooded, mouth lax.

Sexy. As. Fuck.

"You think I'm that easy?" Reese asked, crossing his arms over his chest and watching as Brantley stroked himself. Up, down, up, down. Slow and easy, his thick, heavy cock gliding through his fist.

"Come here," Brantley groaned, his fist pausing at the base. "Put your mouth on me."

A few months ago, before Brantley had come into his life, Reese would've been taken aback at the thought of having a cock in his mouth. Then Brantley Walker had appeared, and life as he knew it had fluttered off on a breeze. It hadn't taken long before Reese realized he wasn't as straight as he'd thought he was. Not when it came to the ridiculously attractive former Navy SEAL who'd somehow managed to shift Reese's way of thinking entirely.

Brantley resumed stroking, several grunts escaping as his hips began to pump upward. And yes, that was sexy as fuck, too.

Damn but the man was so fucking hot. All that hard muscle packed on a six-foot-four-inch frame, a head of dark hair that had gotten a little too long, steel-blue eyes that glittered with desire. Needless to say, Reese was a goner when it came to the man who was not only his lover but also his partner in every sense of the word.

Add to that Brantley's brains, his wit, and yes, that heart-stopping smile and the man had it all. No wonder Reese had fallen so damn hard for him.

"Fuck," Brantley growled, his eyes closing. "Lemme feel your mouth on me."

When he said it like that, as though Reese was the only thing in the world he needed right then, there was no way he could resist him. Even if it meant he would have to crawl up on that twin-sized bed and pray they wouldn't end up on the floor before they were finished.

Would've made more sense for them to push the two twin beds together, but Reese had resisted the urge. He didn't want to offend their gracious hosts, after all.

"Reese... damn it... your mouth. Now."

Oh, sure, he would oblige, but Reese wanted something more. Hell, it had been two days since they'd had sex, thanks to all the tiptoeing-around, careful-not-to-offend-anyone bit. And now his lust factor had surged well past maximum capacity, leaving him desperate and ready for an outlet. A blow job just wasn't going to cut it.

As he moved closer to the bed, he tugged his shirt over his head, dropped it to the floor as he toed off his boots. His jeans came next, along with his boxer briefs, both discarded behind him. Socks were the last to go, and then he was as naked as the man on the bed.

He paused long enough to grab the lube from the duffel bag sitting on the upholstered chair in the corner then resumed his prowl.

At this point, Brantley was watching him, and Reese had to wonder if the man realized he was about to change the agenda. Probably, if he had to guess. Brantley was good like that, always expecting the unexpected.

Reese crawled up on the bed, right between Brantley's spread thighs, moving slowly, his gaze locked on the wide, bulbous head glistening with anticipation.

When he was close enough, Reese leaned down, slid his tongue over Brantley's iron-hard length from root to tip. And that was a sensation he'd gotten familiar with as of late. All that velvet-soft flesh stretched delectably over an iron-hard shaft sent a frisson of heat down his spine. Considering, before Brantley, he'd never given a blow job in his life, turned out he was pretty good at it. At least if Brantley's reactions were anything to go by.

He swirled his tongue around the head before sucking Brantley into his mouth. He repeated the maneuver a couple of times, taking him as deep as he could, teasing Brantley's balls lightly on each pass.

But he didn't linger.

Straightening up, still kneeling between Brantley's thighs, Reese shot the man a smile as he flipped open the lid on the lubricant tube, aimed for his palm, and—

"I hope you boys are awake and decent," came a high-pitched voice from in the hall. "We'll be having pancakes. Thought you might want to join us."

Reese had just enough time to dive off of Brantley, stumble the few feet to the other bed, and fall into it, grateful he hadn't bothered making it, otherwise his dick would've been wagging in the breeze rather than tucked beneath the patchwork quilt he yanked over himself when Maude came strolling in.

Christ Almighty. Chills raced down his arms and his spine at the same time, and these weren't the good kind, either. They were the foreboding kind. The make-your-balls-shrivel-up-inside-you kind.

"Lazy if I ever saw one," Maude said with a smile, her poof of white hair perfectly helmeting her head.

Clearly she was oblivious to what she'd interrupted.

Thank God for that.

"You boys spend far too much time napping," she said with a slight shake of her head.

Napping. Yes. *That* was what they were doing.

Without a care in the world, their sweet, if not nosy, host was glancing from Reese to Brantley then to the mess of clothing Reese had left on the floor. She *tsk*ed them a few times as she began picking up his clothes.

As he watched, Reese's gaze snagged on the tube of lubricant he'd dropped during his hasty retreat.

Please, God, don't let her see it. Please, please—

"Just like my boys when they were your age," Maude said absently as she neatly folded Reese's jeans and hung them over the back of the desk chair. "Couldn't get 'em to be tidy no matter how hard I tried. They'd go out and play, come back all sweaty, and leave their clothes wherever they landed."

How old did she think they were?

"Now, come on. Up and at 'em. It's almost seven and I held off as long as I could. Breakfast'll be ready soon, and Mother's looking forward to sitting down with the two of you."

Reese waited for Brantley to speak up, to urge her to leave, but he remained completely silent. So silent, Reese heard only the rush of blood in his ears, felt the heat as it consumed his face.

Praying Brantley would say *something*, Reese peered over only to realize Brantley was pretending to be asleep.

Son of a—

"He's a late sleeper, huh?" Maude asked, glancing over at Brantley and shaking her head. "Well, wake him up and you two can join us in the parlor for coffee before breakfast is served."

Reese wanted to decline her offer, but his voice had vanished, embarrassment flooding him from the roots of his hair down to his toenails.

"Five minutes," Maude said as she stepped out into the hall. "I expect you both by then."

When the door closed behind her, Reese released the breath he'd been holding, overwhelmed with a relief so potent he was glad he was lying down.

The next thing he knew, Brantley was joining him, jerking the quilt back as he settled on top of him, the heat of his naked body covering him completely as Brantley stared down into his face.

"Now where were we?" Brantley leaned in for a kiss.

Reese glared up at him, still in shock because … *seriously?*

Rather than succumb to the kiss, he shoved Brantley off him and shot out of the bed. He didn't even care that Brantley's hard thump on the floor where his ass met the hardwood might possibly bring Maude back in.

"While you're down there, get the lube," Reese snapped.

"Oh, come on," Brantley grumbled, grabbing the tube and getting to his feet. "You're seriously not gonna choose breakfast over sex, are you?"

Reese yanked his jeans from the chair, jammed one leg in, then the other. "You pretended to be asleep."

"Well, yeah." Brantley laughed. "What else was I supposed to do?"

"Something," Reese bit out, angrily buttoning and zipping. "*Anything* would've been nice."

"It's not *my* fault she doesn't put locks on her doors."

A fact that had completely slipped Reese's mind, although he wasn't sure how. For the two days they'd been here, Maude had proven she cared not for their privacy, walking in uninvited whenever she felt the need.

"Come back to bed," Brantley urged. "Finish what you started."

Reese glared at him as he tugged his shirt over his head, then stabbed his arms into the sleeves. "Not a chance."

"Fine. What about on the plane?" Brantley asked, strolling toward the adjoining bathroom.

Reese shot him a *get real* look. "It's gonna take me some time to get over that."

Brantley stopped in the doorway, frowned. "Like what? A few minutes? Hours?"

Reese dropped into the chair to pull on his socks and boots. "Try *days*, Walker."

"*Days?*" Brantley's expression reflected his incredulity, as though Reese couldn't possibly hold out on him for a lengthy period of time.

Reese sat up straight, met Brantley's gaze. "Maybe weeks."

The look on the other man's face was absolutely fucking priceless, and seeing it made Reese feel a tad bit better.

But only a tad.

"Where the hell's the parlor?" Reese muttered, snatching his phone on the way to the door.

"Maybe weeks, my ass," Brantley muttered, walking into the bathroom and flipping on the shower.

He didn't bother with hot water, knowing cold would have to do the trick since the last thing he wanted was to go downstairs sporting a hard-on. Interacting with these women was awkward enough; no way would he add an internal struggle to the matter.

"Weeks," he snorted indignantly, stepping into the tiled enclosure. "I'd like to see him try."

After dunking his head beneath the spray, Brantley glanced down at his cock. For grins, he circled it with his fist, stroked firmly.

Okay. Not so bad.

He exhaled slowly, reaching for a sense of calm.

Closing his eyes, he took himself back in time to that moment when Reese had been kneeling between his legs, those full lips gliding effortlessly over him. Up, down, slow, easy. God, he fucking loved Reese's mouth. The hesitancy mixed with the eagerness... He wasn't sure Reese was even aware of it, but Brantley was, and he fucking loved that about the man. Yes, Reese was still unsure of himself in many ways, despite the fact he could so easily rock Brantley's world—sometimes with merely a look—but that only made their encounters even hotter.

For long seconds, he was lost in the fantasy, almost able to imagine Reese's mouth was still on him, so hot, so—

Up and at 'em.

Aw, fuck. The fantasy was obliterated by the sound of Maude's voice in his head. Always interrupting.

"For fuck's sake," he growled, releasing his cock as the damn thing deflated.

Although there was some discomfort from the lack of satisfaction, Brantley found he could keep the soft-on going as long as he thought about Maude, so he finished with the shower, dressed, and made a quick call to the pilot to confirm their flight back to Texas. As far as he was concerned, they'd wasted enough time here in Mississippi hoping Juliet Prince might emerge. The theory being the woman would come out of hiding to see her daughter at some point during the holidays, so they were keeping a close eye on things now.

Clearly she wasn't ready to poke her head out of the sand just yet. But Brantley had made a promise to his cousin Travis, and he fully intended to follow through until they found the vile woman who'd kidnapped Travis's daughter a few months back. Unfortunately, that wasn't going to happen right now. The woman was underground—rightfully so, since she was wanted by the FBI—and if he had to guess, she would remain in hiding for some time. At least if she was smart, anyway.

As for him and Reese, it was time to get back. They had holidays to celebrate, then it was back to the grindstone. Or it would be, right after he had breakfast with Maude and her mother, whose name appeared to be simply Mother.

When Brantley made his way downstairs a short time later, he found everyone had vacated the parlor in lieu of the fancy formal dining room with its heavy gold drapes and gilded-frame photos of people Brantley assumed were relatives. Now that he thought about it, it was creepy to have all those eyes tracking him.

And to think, these people had meals in there often.

He could hear the soft murmur of voices and the clang of silverware and wondered if he'd get a slap on the wrist from Maude for being late.

Running a hand down his shirt, he pulled himself together and resigned himself to joining them.

The chatter ceased almost immediately, all eyes shifting to him as he stepped down into the room.

"Good morning, sleepyhead," Maude greeted cheerfully, peering up at him with a glint in her eye before patting the chair to her right. "Please, join us."

If only he had another option.

It was slightly awkward that the chair she'd allocated for him was at the head of the table. Okay, a little more than *slightly*, but he solved that problem by taking the seat directly across from her, the one beside Reese.

"Mornin'." He acknowledged each person with a smile and a nod, pulling out the chair and easing into it.

He glanced over at Reese, waiting for him to look his way. He didn't.

Maxine spoke up from her spot beside Maude. "Reese tells us the two of you will be leaving today."

"Yes, ma'am." And not a minute too soon.

"Well, that's a shame. We were hoping to spend more time with you both."

Brantley liked the way Maxine spoke, her voice soft, her words dripping with southern sweetness, so prim and proper. A contradiction to Maude's loud and boisterous personality. But like they said, opposites did attract. Evidently that went for lifelong friendships as well.

"I assume you've got time for breakfast," Maude implored, her gaze pinned on him.

"Yes, ma'am," he said politely, then accepted coffee when the housekeeper offered. "We don't need to leave for a couple of hours."

"Vacations are never long enough." Maxine winked at him as she reached for her coffee, which he suspected was spiked with her favored Irish whiskey.

"No, ma'am. They're not," he agreed, letting them continue to believe they were here on vacation, mistaking Maude's house for the Airbnb they had thought they were getting.

Initially, Brantley hadn't been sure how he was going to insert himself into the neighborhood in order to stake out the Prince residence. He'd figured they would get comfortable in their rented SUV but learned that wasn't an option because the gated community didn't allow parking on the street and had twenty-four-seven security guarding the place.

At that point, they'd had to get creative. Hence the reason they'd ended up here.

"Well, that's a shame. I was enjoying your company." Maude fluttered her lashes then shifted her gaze to the woman pouring coffee into Brantley's cup. "Anna, have a seat. Stop fawning over these boys."

"I don't think I'm the one fawning," Anna muttered under her breath, offering a forced smile over Brantley's head.

"You know you're welcome to join us," Maxine suggested, evidently chiming in to get Anna on board.

"Not on your life," she said with a dramatic sigh, followed by an eye roll as she backed out of the room.

According to Maude, Anna had been with her and Mother for going on thirty years now, and the ornery woman with the hair-trigger temper—Mother's description—was more family than staff. She'd made it sound like they were close, but he wasn't so sure Anna felt the same. Then again, putting up with someone for thirty years did require some serious commitment.

"You're not eatin'?" Brantley asked Maxine before picking up his fork.

"Not this morning, no." She took a sip of her spiked coffee, smiled sweetly. "I have an appointment."

Mother snorted, a sound that made Brantley chuckle. He'd learned that Mother thought Maxine to be somewhat of a hussy. Her exact words, actually. Which an interesting twist considering Mother's own daughter was more than willing to talk about her midnight trysts. Yes, that was how Maude referred to her overnight guests, and in the short time they'd been there, Brantley had found himself on the receiving end of more than one of her many sordid stories. Not by choice, mind you.

"So, tell me," Maude prompted. "How long have the two of you been working together?"

"I wanna know how long they've been sleeping together," Mother blurted, her voice that of a two-pack-a-day smoker, although she swore she'd never smoked a cigarette in her life.

Maxine laughed.

Reese choked, then attempted to cover it with a cough. Based on how red his face was and how much he was clearing his throat, his toast had gone down the wrong way.

"*Mother*," Maude chastised, shooing her with a flail of her linen napkin. "I told you. They only work together."

"Like hell," Mother snipped, her blue eyes peering into Brantley as though she was searching his soul.

He offered her a wink, which earned him a thin, wrinkled grin in return. He liked the old lady. She had spunk. He figured she had been a spitfire when she was younger.

"The task force we manage is relatively new," Brantley informed Maude, setting down his fork and picking up his coffee. "We've only been workin' together for a few months."

"And you were both in the military prior to this?"

"Yes, ma'am. Reese was air force, I was navy."

"Don't ask, don't tell," Mother said under her breath, grinning at her plate.

"Mother." Maude sighed. "I told you—"

"Yeah, yeah. They only work together," Mother echoed, her sarcasm dripping like molasses. "Shows how perceptive you are."

Only because he didn't want to embarrass Reese did Brantley not clarify that, yes, they were, in fact, in a relationship. He wasn't ashamed of it, but it wasn't something Reese was comfortable discussing. Considering the man was still wrapping his head around the fact that he'd gone from believing he was straight as an arrow to learning he had the hots for a man, Brantley figured it would take some time.

"Tell her it's not true," Maude pleaded, wiping the corners of her mouth with her napkin.

"It's not anything to be ashamed of," Mother said, her attention on the glass of orange juice she was working to pick up with her gnarled hand. "My third husband was gay."

"Mother!" Maude huffed at her.

Brantley couldn't help but grin.

"What? It's true." Mother looked at him. "I didn't learn that until we were married. Back then, it wasn't appropriate to fornicate before the *I do's*."

She sure had a colorful way of explaining herself.

"Of course, I went against the rules after that," Mother continued. "No sense wasting anyone's time if my fertilizer wasn't gonna make the tree grow."

Brantley barked a laugh. He saw that Maxine was grinning but trying to hide it, while Maude was shaking her head. Clearly she was used to Mother being so illustrative.

"How many times were you married?" he asked, taking a sip of what he'd learned was coffee with something called chicory added to it. Not his favorite, but it was palatable.

"Six," Mother said proudly. "Married for money."

"Really?" He picked up his fork, poked at his eggs.

"*My* money." Mother grinned. "When you have it, they line up. Found love a couple of times even. I learned it was fun to make 'em work for it."

They came from old money, that was what Maude had said. It explained the enormous historical home, the elaborate grounds, and the framed photos of ancestors.

"It's more fun, Mother, *without* the marriage," Maude announced, this time laughing. "Either of you boys ever been married?"

"No, ma'am." Brantley glanced at Reese, who still wasn't looking at him but was politely paying attention to their hosts.

"Ever come close?" Maude was directing the question at Reese.

Reese met her eyes, looking like a deer caught in the headlights. He remained like that, on the spot as the silence became thicker. Brantley probably should've saved him, but he was curious as to the delay. How hard was it to say—

"Once, ma'am," Reese said softly.

Brantley's hand paused halfway to his mouth, his fork suspended, his breath suddenly lodged somewhere in his sternum.

He hadn't known that. Reese had never mentioned it before.

"What stopped you?" Mother inquired.

Yeah, Brantley thought. *What stopped you?*

"She did," Reese said, his attention diverted back to his plate.

There was a strange sensation filling his chest, one Brantley wasn't sure he'd ever felt before. Jealousy? Fear? Could've been either because he wasn't used to feeling such emotions. Until Reese, he'd never really known love, never taken a chance on it after his one and only serious relationship when he was a teenager.

Realizing he was staring at Reese, Brantley forced his gaze away. He noticed Maude was watching him, those light blue eyes fixed on him, and Brantley could feel the scrutiny. But like a true southern woman, Maude kept the question to herself.

As they said in the south, *bless her heart.*

Two hours later, once he was settled on the private jet that would deliver them home, Brantley was still battling the strange emotions churning in his gut. They hadn't abated, but they'd almost been drowned out by an overwhelming curiosity. He wanted Reese to explain, to elaborate, to tell him that his *almost marriage* hadn't really been anything, that he'd said it just to appease the women.

"First stop is to pick up Tesha, right?" Reese asked when he eased into the seat across from Brantley.

He answered with a nod, staring out the window as they taxied to the runway.

"I figured I'd run to the grocery store," Reese continued.

Another nod, his imagination threatening to run away from him with thoughts of Reese waiting for some woman at the altar, preparing to pledge his life and love to her.

"Thought I'd make lasagna for dinner."

He didn't even bother to nod this time, surprised that he'd been able to keep his thoughts to himself for this long. And he damn sure wasn't going to sit here and talk about what they were having for dinner when what he wanted to know was why the fuck he hadn't known Reese had almost been married.

Brantley turned his attention to Reese, cocked an eyebrow. "Engaged?"

"What?" Reese cleared his throat as though he was shocked by the change in subject. "No, uh… No, I wasn't engaged."

Patiently waiting for Reese to elaborate, Brantley continued to hold his gaze.

"Never made it that far," Reese added. "I asked. She turned me down."

Brantley swallowed the hot ball of emotion lodged in his throat, letting it sink in, hating that there was a gnawing jealousy in the pit of his stomach.

"It was a long time ago, Brantley."

Sure it was. "How long?"

Reese's gaze lowered. "Two years. Almost."

"Two—?" They'd been seeing each other for a little more than four months now, living together for the past two. And it had been *almost* two years?

"How *almost* is almost?"

Reese's attention remained on his lap. "Sixteen months or so."

Sixteen months? Sixteen. Freaking. Months. That meant—

Brantley swallowed hard. "A *year* before—? You were engaged a year before I met you?"

"A little more than," Reese countered, then sighed and added a subdued, "But no, I wasn't engaged."

Right. Because she'd turned him down. Otherwise...

"And you didn't think this was somethin' I should know?"

Reese's head snapped back like Brantley had slapped him, his eyebrows slamming down. "I don't remember you askin'."

Touché. "Who is she?"

"You don't know her."

Brantley waited for Reese to look at him, then hardened his stare. "Who?"

Reese sighed heavily, obviously resigned to answering. "Her name's Madison Adorite. We dated for a while. Long-distance. She lives in Dallas."

"How'd you meet her?"

"Through Travis."

Fucking figured. "And it got serious enough that you asked her to marry you?"

"No. It didn't."

Okay, now he was confused.

"That was the problem," Reese continued, his voice rougher. "She was breakin' it off because she needed to focus on … the family business." Reese stared at him for several long seconds before finally saying, "She's an Adorite. As in the Adorite crime family, also known as the Southern Boy Mafia."

Brantley had no idea what he was talking about, but it didn't actually matter who this Madison was. The simple fact that Reese had asked her to marry him was what he was hung up on. Not necessarily because Reese had had a near-miss with getting hitched, but more so that he'd been nearly engaged to a woman. Key word being *woman*. Brantley was used to competing for what he wanted, but when it came down to it, there was no competing in that arena.

And that fucking bothered him.

"And what? You panicked and asked her to marry you?"

Reese shrugged one shoulder. "Basically. Yeah."

Wow.

Just wow.

"Brantley?"

He continued to stare at the table. "What?"

"Say somethin'."

"What do you want me to say?"

"Are you pissed?"

"No." That much was true. He wasn't angry, he was confused. Worried, maybe. He'd go so far as to say he was hurt, even. Although the last one made no sense at all. It wasn't like they'd shared all their deepest, darkest secrets with one another. Hell, there were some big ones neither of them had revealed yet.

But for some reason, this particular secret felt … enormous.

"She's in the past," Reese stated. "I haven't talked to her since that day. The day she broke things off."

He glanced back at Reese. "Did you love her?"

"I thought I did. At the time."

Brantley nodded, but he looked away again.

How had he not known this? What else didn't he know about Reese?

More importantly, what other things in Reese's past would he have to compete with?

Chapter Two

SEVERAL HOURS LATER, AFTER A TENSE FLIGHT home, after they'd picked up Tesha from JJ's and returned to the house, Reese was doing his best to give Brantley some space. Not because he wanted to but because he could tell Brantley preferred it.

Ever since Reese had revealed that he'd been almost engaged, Brantley had been acting strange. And while he said he wasn't pissed, Reese wasn't sure he believed him. He'd seen Brantley angry before and the man didn't resort to violence. He was far too controlled for that. No, Brantley leaned more toward passive-aggressive, shutting down completely, closing himself off, pushing everyone away. Anything to avoid confrontation.

Which was exactly what he was doing now.

And Reese was letting him.

Because he preferred not to sit on his thumbs and wait for Brantley to come around, after a quick trip to the grocery store, Reese had made a call to Magnus Storme, the man they'd hired to handle Tesha's training, hoping Magnus could squeeze an extra session into his busy schedule, grateful when the trainer had agreed.

The owner of Camp K-9, a highly sought-after dog daycare and search-and-rescue training facility just a few miles down the road, was well regarded by his clients and came highly recommended. Kennedy, Tesha's veterinarian, had recommended Magnus to Brantley. In turn, Brantley'd done his research and decided to check him out prior to mentioning him to Reese. By the time Reese was officially introduced, Brantley had deemed the man capable and deserving of their business.

And by *business*, Reese was referring to his desire to train Tesha to assist with their cases. More along the lines of search and rescue—assisting with finding missing people—but also patrol training, which consisted of obedience, agility, tracking, and the like. And they were starting from the beginning with basic training and whatnot.

Now, as Reese waited for Magnus to arrive, he tossed the ball for Tesha, sat patiently on the step while she scampered across the brittle, dry grass, retrieved it, and returned. She was getting better, no longer wandering off aimlessly unless she'd already dropped the ball at Reese's feet, but they still had a long way to go.

"Tesha, here," he commanded, watching his four-legged friend as she trotted his way.

She came to a stop directly in front of him, plopping her butt on the ground and staring up at him with such hope in her eyes. Yeah, there was no doubt about it, when it came to this dog, he was a goner.

It'd only been a few weeks since, during a witness interview down in Houston, he'd found Tesha malnourished and chained to a stake with no water and no shelter in sight. Because her video-game-playing, chain-smoking, whiskey-chugging owners felt it was okay to ignore her, Reese had decided she deserved better.

Perhaps his actions had been technically illegal, but Reese hadn't lost a minute of sleep since he'd personally relocated her, carrying her right out of that backyard and putting her into their SUV. He could still remember the fury he'd felt that day, seeing her helpless and neglected. It had filled him with a pain he hadn't experienced before, and he couldn't, in good conscience, walk away from her.

So here she was. And under the close eye of the town veterinarian, he was happy to say Tesha had put on a solid ten pounds and sported a happy-go-lucky grin more often than not.

Reese found himself smiling. "I take it you were good for JJ while we were gone?"

Tesha's head cocked to the side, and Reese would've sworn she was smiling back at him.

"Maybe not *too* good." He reached down to scratch her head.

Tesha's tongue lolled out of her mouth and her eyes closed, making him laugh.

"Well, look at you."

Reese glanced over to see Magnus strolling toward them, his full attention on Tesha. She spared Magnus a brief look only to have her interest piqued. She barked once, stood momentarily, then sat directly in front of Reese, facing away from him this time, her tail thumping with barely restrained anticipation.

Magnus laughed as he neared. "Hello, Tesha."

Reese could admit he'd been skeptical upon first meeting Magnus when Brantley had dragged him over to the dog day camp to introduce them. It didn't have anything to do with the camp itself, which he learned was well maintained and well staffed. The five-acre facility held a single-story house, where Magnus lived, a decent-sized metal barn behind it, which was the main office, training room, and luxury kennels, as well as several outbuildings, a few penned-in areas, and a large swimming pool specifically for the dogs.

That didn't include the three hundred acres of rocky terrain the facility sat on that Magnus utilized for training search-and-rescue dogs.

Reese thought back to his first introduction to the twenty-four-year-old Magnus, which had been shortly after they'd happened upon a young woman—clearly rocking her going-out clothes from the previous night out—slipping out of Magnus's house and right into the backseat of an Uber as they were pulling in. He wouldn't have thought anything of it except it wasn't a drop-in type of meeting. Magnus had been expecting them, yet his flavor of the night had been lingering upon their arrival.

Turned out, if it hadn't been for the woman doing the walk of shame, Reese would've been highly impressed. He'd given Magnus the benefit of the doubt, and after a solid hour of Magnus working with Tesha, Reese's pessimism had been quashed. More so when Magnus had informed him that Tesha wouldn't be the only one undergoing training. Evidently, Reese and Brantley would learn just as much as Tesha, and they had been for the past few weeks.

The good news was, Tesha had taken to Magnus, something Reese had been worried about in the beginning. She still rarely left Reese's side when they were together, but she didn't cower or quiver when Magnus was around. In fact, he'd go so far as to say Tesha liked the man. Then again, it was easy to like Magnus. He was just … likable.

"Doesn't look like you partied too much with JJ," Magnus said to Tesha.

The man had been introduced to Jessica James, the Off the Books Task Force's hacker extraordinaire, several months ago, even worked with her a few times on how to handle Tesha in regard to training. Being a bit on the protective side where Tesha was concerned, Reese had asked JJ for her opinion of the man. Her honest answer: "He's got bedroom eyes and really, *really* nice arms."

Not exactly the type of feedback he'd been looking for, but that was JJ. Ever helpful if you were looking to date someone, but not necessarily when you wanted to utilize their professional services.

"Probably in bed by ten," Reese commented. Seemed to be what JJ did these days, ever since she'd broken things off with Baz.

When Tesha stood, Magnus held up one finger. She immediately sat again.

"Good, girl," he crooned, praising her with a scratch on the head.

"Keepin' up with the training, I see."

"It's our main focus," he admitted. "Now that we've mastered house trainin', anyway."

Magnus squatted down to get on Tesha's level. "Mastered, huh? Very impressive, Tesha."

It really was. For the first two weeks of her being in the house, Reese had felt as though he spent most of his time at the back door, urging her to go out in order to avoid any accidents. As time went by, she'd started announcing her need to go out until it was second nature. Then, like they'd done in the barn, once the fence had been put up, they'd installed a dog door, giving her free rein.

"And the leash? How's that goin'?"

"She has no problem with the harness," he admitted, remembering how Tesha had been terrified when he'd first started training her on a leash. He figured it had to do with the fact she'd been tied up for so long. Magnus had suggested trying the harness rather than the collar and, sure enough, no issues.

"And your bed?" Magnus grinned. "She still fightin' to sleep there?"

Reese chuckled. "No. Definitely not."

That had been the main thing Brantley had been focused on, ensuring they didn't have to share a bed with the dog.

Speaking of Brantley…

Reese glanced up at the house, wondering if Brantley was going to come out or if he would stay inside, hiding from the world. Last he'd seen him, Brantley had headed upstairs to his office, claiming he had things to catch up on. Reese wasn't buying it, but he knew better than to argue. That would come later, if and when Brantley's mood didn't improve.

No sooner had Magnus asked Reese to leash Tesha than his watch buzzed, signaling someone's arrival. Since he didn't have his phone with him, he had to wait for their visitor to stroll around. These days he had no idea who might be making an appearance. Could be JJ coming to work for a bit or Baz or even Charlie, for that matter. Those three were known to spend a day off catching up on email or researching a case they were working on.

But the new arrival was none of the above.

Reese watched as Brantley's older brother ambled over, Trey's focus on Magnus as he approached. He was wearing sunglasses, which shielded his eyes, but Reese knew Trey was watching Magnus like a hawk. Trey was like Brantley in that way, innately curious and inherently skeptical.

"What brings you by?" Reese asked when Trey came to a stop beside him.

"Thought I'd see how the trip went and tackle a couple of things," Trey answered, although his attention was still on Magnus.

"Trey," Magnus greeted with a smirk.

Trey removed his sunglasses, hung them on the neck of his dark blue Henley before tucking his hands in his pockets. The two men stared at one another, their eyes locked as though they were in some sort of battle for who would blink first. Reese watched with interest.

Rather than acknowledge Magnus verbally, something Reese had noticed Trey rarely did, Brantley's brother turned to him. "Any luck in Mississippi?"

"Nope. We staked it out for two days. Nothin'."

"But you didn't expect it, either."

Reese shook his head. "Couldn't be that easy."

"Never is." Trey gave a curt nod. "I'll be in the barn if you need me."

"Brantley's in the house," Reese told him. "If, you know, you wanna talk to him."

Reese was hoping someone would.

Once again Trey's gaze swung to Magnus as he said, "Yeah, sure. I'll go in, say hello."

And then Trey was walking toward the house and Magnus was watching intently.

"You two have a problem?" Reese asked, too curious not to.

"What?" Magnus's gaze slammed into him. "No." He shook his head. "No problem here."

"How's your … uh … girlfriend?" Reese inquired, referring to the woman who'd been with Magnus the last time they'd gone to Camp K-9. For the record, there had been a different woman there nearly every time Reese had stopped in for a training session.

Magnus frowned, his black eyebrows lowering. "No girlfriend."

"Oh. You were with… Sorry, her name eludes me." Only because he'd never gotten her name.

It was obvious Magnus was attempting to think back. It took a second before he smiled and shrugged. "That was … um … Mich—uh, Melanie. Yeah. I'd just met her. We're not a thing. Just a one-nighter."

Interesting.

More so when Magnus's gaze shifted to the house once again, as though he might possibly lure Trey back out that way.

TREY WALKER STEPPED INTO BRANTLEY AND REESE'S house, forced himself not to turn around and look at the trainer who for some stupid reason had snagged his attention from the jump. Since the day he'd met Tesha's trainer, he found himself fantasizing about him for no good reason.

And fine, Trey would admit there was something strangely appealing about Magnus Storme, with his closely cropped brown hair, hazel eyes, square jaw, and a nose that was slightly crooked. The previously broken nose didn't even detract, only lent a rugged appeal to Magnus's otherwise good-looking face.

Initially, he'd tried to tell himself it was a good thing that Magnus invaded his thoughts from time to time. That fantasizing about a man he wasn't intimate with, nor would he ever be, was no big deal. It didn't matter that the guy plagued his dreams, because Trey had no intention of acting on his attraction. And not only because he knew Magnus was straight.

No, Trey's biggest reason for not acting on his attraction was the simple fact that he was doomed to fail at his relationships, and after Cyrus had up and left for a job in California, Trey realized it was easier to give up altogether than to hope that one day he would find a man who'd give as good as he got. So, for now, he was abstaining. Indefinitely.

Heading for the stairs, he went up, proud of himself for maintaining his focus and not lingering on Magnus for too long. He even managed to avoid looking out the sliding doors that overlooked the yard to see if the man was in view. Just because the guy was good-looking, or because he could swear there was a mischievous gleam in Magnus's eyes when he looked at him, did not mean Trey needed to entertain—

"Why're you here?" Brantley asked, pulling Trey from his thoughts.

Realizing he was standing in the doorway of Brantley's office, he raised his eyebrows. "What?"

"You. Here. Why?"

Trey smiled, understanding why Reese had suggested Trey talk to his brother. "What's got your panties in a twist? Somethin' go wrong on your stakeout?"

"It's almost Christmas. Shouldn't you be at the mall gettin' those last-minute gifts?"

"Shouldn't *you*?" Trey countered.

"I plan to. Later."

"Me, too."

"Fuck you," Brantley bit out with a smile.

"Fuck you, too."

Then they were both quiet, staring at one another.

He knew Brantley had changed the subject for a reason, and while he didn't have a problem giving any of his brothers or sisters shit, Trey knew when to hold off. Right now felt like one of those times.

Trey jerked his chin in the direction of the barn. "Figured I'd follow up on a couple of things," he told his brother, leaning against the doorjamb. "You know, before everyone's out of the office for the long weekend."

Brantley was still leaning back in his chair. Every so often his gaze would shift to the window. Trey figured he was attempting to see Reese, but there was no way. Not from where he was sitting.

"You're comin' to Mom and Dad's for Christmas breakfast, right?" he asked when Brantley didn't say anything. "And gettin' with Reese's family for dinner?"

"That's the plan," Brantley muttered, and Trey could tell his mind was elsewhere.

He stood tall. "Well, then. I guess I'll leave you to it."

"Yep."

He paused for a moment, watched his brother.

"You sure everything's cool?"

"All good."

Clearly something was bothering him, but Trey couldn't bring himself to dig. At the moment, he didn't have the energy to shoulder the weight of anyone else's problems. Not with his own bearing down on him.

Trey made it back down the stairs and glanced at the front door, tempted to go out that way, hop in his truck, and head back to his house. He didn't really have anything pressing that needed his attention. Plus the thought of seeing Magnus didn't sit well with him, but he had no fucking clue why he'd even care. The guy might be a flirt, but he was harmless.

Okay, so he did know why he cared. Because he had sworn off men, dammit. Enacted a vow of celibacy. Abstaining. A born-again virgin. Just call him a monk.

No. Men.

And he was fucking lonely because of it. Dammit.

Trey snorted, then forced his feet toward the back door. No way was he going to run like a scared fucking rabbit. Damn sure not because of some … some … kid.

And that was exactly what Magnus was. At least compared to Trey. Thirty-six minus twenty-four equaled … hell, Trey was likely getting his first kiss by the time Magnus popped out of his mama. No fucking way would he even entertain the idea.

No. Fucking. Way.

But he wasn't a coward, so he marched his ass right out the back door, onto the deck, down the steps, and made a beeline for the barn. Trey forced his gaze to remain on his destination, doing his damnedest not to listen for the slightest sound that might tell him where Magnus was.

He was almost home free when the blasted man appeared on the other side of the barn, walking Tesha on a leash. Magnus lifted his gaze as he turned the corner, and Trey stopped mid-stride.

Like every single one of their previous encounters, Magnus's gaze raked over him slowly before stopping on his face.

It was the eyes. The hazel color was such a unique mix of brown and green and blue, it didn't seem real. Add in the fact they contrasted perfectly with the dark brown hair, the long lashes… Definitely fuckable.

No, dammit. Not. *Not* fuckable.

Not anything.

Trey realized Magnus was still staring at him.

"What?" Trey asked, frowning.

"I didn't say anything."

"But you were thinkin' somethin'."

"Was I?" Magnus's cocky smirk irritated the shit out of him.

"Where's Reese?"

Magnus's chin jerked in the direction of the house. "Went to grab his phone."

Remembering he was not going to see this guy as a challenge, Trey nodded, relaxed his shoulders, and closed the distance between him and the electronic panel that opened the barn door.

"Don't let me keep you," Trey said absently, glancing back over his shoulder just in time to catch the man staring at his ass.

He could've sworn someone mentioned Magnus had a girlfriend.

Right. Uh-huh.

"You can keep me anytime you'd like," Magnus muttered.

Before Trey could spin around and comment, the man was sauntering away. Trey was about to call him on it when he saw Reese walking toward them.

Grinding his teeth together, Trey forced himself to punch in the code to unlock the door.

After all, it gave him something to think about besides the fucking hard-on that damn man inspired.

BRANTLEY STARED AT THE SPACE HIS BROTHER had vacated, briefly wondering how long ago Trey had left. A minute? Ten? Considering how distracted he was, it could've been an hour that he'd sat staring into space, his brain twisting and turning the information he'd recently received.

Oddly enough, he wished he could've spent that time thinking about Reese's almost engagement but he hadn't. No, he'd been too busy processing the email he'd received from Governor Greenwood.

The email that informed him the task force would most likely be eliminated after the first of the year.

Eliminated.

Three months in, five cases closed, half a dozen more in the works, and they were going to be eliminated.

Fucking politics.

He'd read the email three times, remembered seeing something about budget cuts and fund allocation. Probably Greenwood's way of overwhelming Brantley with information so he didn't lock on to the fact that he'd created the team and eliminated it within a matter of months.

And he'd relayed all that information in an email.

A fucking email, not even a phone call.

Oh, but the good news was, the governor would take his time in picking up the equipment they were in possession of, but unfortunately, their access to government databases would be relinquished immediately.

Always a *but*.

So basically, it sounded like they wouldn't be looking to fill empty positions within the task force after the first of the year after all. Rather they'd be looking for jobs elsewhere.

Brantley massaged the bridge of his nose, fully aware of the headache that was looming. It was going to be a bad one. He could feel it already.

Two hours later, Brantley was still at his desk; however, he was no longer pretending to work. He'd given that shit up a while ago but hadn't found the energy to stand up.

"You comin' down for dinner?"

He peered up from his desk chair to see Reese standing in the doorway, his chest bare and a pair of black sweats hanging low on his hips. When he wore things like that—so casual, so very ... male—it made Brantley wonder how he managed to go a second without running his hands over every long, lean inch of him. Even now, when his thoughts were muddled and the pain behind his eyes was growing more intense by the second, he wanted to touch and taste, explore and ravish.

"Yeah," he answered but didn't move from where he sat.

He wanted to get up, but the headache that had started two hours ago had taken root. In no time, it would be a full-blown migraine, and he would do anything to keep it from intensifying. This was the first one he'd had in two weeks, and it dispelled his theory that they were possibly going away for good. Ever since the incident that ended his career as a SEAL, he'd been battling them, and each and every time, he prayed that one would be his last.

"You've got a headache," Reese said softly, taking one step into the office.

Brantley could see so much concern in those brown eyes, and it hit him somewhere in the center of his chest. It pissed him off that he'd spent the better part of the day sulking over the fact that Reese hadn't told him he'd nearly gotten married at one point in his life. It was a stupid worry, he knew. Something he had no business harping on. There were a lot of things they didn't know about each other, a lot of things they would eventually learn.

Yet it still made his stomach twist into knots.

Reese flipped off the overhead light, then pulled the cord to close the blinds. Even though the sun was still shining through, it helped. Some.

"Come on," Reese urged, moving over and holding out his hand. "I'll get your medicine."

Because he knew the migraine was inevitable and it would be a hell of a lot easier to be in his bed in a completely dark room, Brantley nodded and put his hand in Reese's.

When he stood, Reese stepped in close, cupping his cheek with his free hand before pressing his lips gently to his. Brantley felt some of the tension ease from his shoulders even as the shift in position made his head throb more.

Without another word, Reese led the way downstairs, through the kitchen, grabbing a bottle of water on the way to their bedroom. By the time he got there, Brantley had no choice but to ease down on the bed and close his eyes. The nausea always hit him when he walked, and the throbbing had increased tenfold in such a short distance.

He heard the click of the lamp when Reese turned it off, followed by the sound of the medicine cabinet in the bathroom opening, closing, then footsteps coming his way.

"Here," Reese whispered as something pressed against Brantley's lips.

He opened his mouth, took the pill, and accepted the water Reese helped him with.

"You want me to undress you?"

Brantley nodded, wishing like hell Reese would ask that question when he was well enough to come up with a quip to lighten the mood.

Unfortunately, that wasn't going to happen now.

When Brantley woke up, the pain was like a knife in his skull. The instant he was conscious, the nausea hit him like a freight train.

He groaned and managed to roll out of bed, stumble to the bathroom. His knees hit the tile floor with a thud, seconds before he heaved. This was the worst part. Wasn't the blinding headache enough? Vomiting only made it worse. A vicious cycle that he found himself in as he fought to breathe in slow and steady, willing the pain away enough to get him back to the bed.

Several agonizingly long seconds later, he stumbled to the sink to rinse his mouth out. The action took effort, but he managed. It wasn't until he returned to the bedroom that he realized Reese wasn't there. The clock on the nightstand read 0128.

He paused long enough to look at the door, considered going to find him, but gave up the ghost when his stomach pitched again.

The headache had to go before he—

"Let me help you."

Reese.

A foreign sense of relief swept over him as he crawled back into the bed. "I thought you were gone."

"Went to get this."

Brantley's eyes were closed, so he couldn't see what Reese was referring to. Then there was something cold against the side of his neck, and Reese's hand was curling beneath his head, lifting it and adjusting the pillow so he could tuck the cold can at the base of his skull.

Never had he considered using a cold can to alleviate the pain until Reese. Oddly enough, the home remedy did help. Some.

When he felt the mattress dip, he reached for Reese, sliding his hand over Reese's knee and exhaling slowly.

"Sleep," Reese urged.

The last thing he remembered before he drifted off was how good Reese's fingers felt as they massaged his temples.

Chapter Three

Thursday, December 24, 2020

THE FOLLOWING MORNING, REESE WAS UP BEFORE the sun. He managed to extricate himself from the bed without waking Brantley, hoping to give him a couple more hours of uninterrupted sleep. The migraine had proven to be brutal, which was par for the course, and Reese knew Brantley hadn't slept soundly because of it.

"You ready, girl?" Reese asked when he got to the living room to find Tesha curled up in her bed. "Wanna go for a run?"

That got her attention, and instantly Tesha was up, her entire body wagging with excitement.

She did love her morning exercise.

"All right. Lemme grab my shoes."

It only took a moment to pull on his shoes, tie them, get Tesha harnessed, and then they were out the door. The air was thick with humidity, dulling the chill that would've otherwise been there. Reese yanked his hood over his head, then took a minute to stretch.

This morning he opted to forgo music. There were some days he needed the motivation, others when he preferred only the sound of his breathing. It allowed him to blank his mind, forcing away all thoughts, all worries. They would be there when he was finished.

"Come on, girl. Let's do this," he said, taking off from the porch, Tesha trotting along beside him.

For now, this was what he needed.

Two hours later, Reese was sitting, laptop and coffee in front of him, at one of the empty desks in the barn, skimming through his emails when the door opened and Brantley strolled in. The tension lines in his face had eased and his eyes were clear.

"Headache gone?"

"Finally." Brantley stopped, pinned Reese with a skeptical glare. "Why exactly are you here? You do know it's Christmas Eve, right?"

"I do know that, yes. But you were sleepin' and I needed somethin' to do. Plus…" Reese nodded his chin in the direction of the second floor.

"I won't bother to ask why she's here," Brantley grumbled.

Reese hadn't either. Last time he'd questioned JJ about why she was at work when she should've been enjoying her personal time, she'd nearly taken his head off.

"Did you get breakfast?" he asked Brantley.

"Bagel." The frown on his face told Reese he wasn't enthused with his morning nourishment.

Usually Reese cooked something for them after their morning run. But since he'd been solo this morning, he'd settled for overnight oats and a bowl of fruit. Not to mention, there were times when strong smells would unsettle Brantley's stomach, and Reese had been wanting to avoid that, too.

"Please tell me there's coffee." Brantley started toward the small kitchenette they used mainly for their daily java.

"It's fresh," he said, his words punctuated by the sound of the dog door slapping closed, followed by, "Tesha!"

Reese looked up, saw JJ snarling from her second-floor loft, her shout still echoing in the wide-open space.

"Dadgum dog!"

If Reese didn't know better, he would think Tesha had it out for JJ.

Now that he thought about it, maybe it was Tesha paying JJ back for her overreaction to Reese's simple questions, like *why are you working on your day off?*

Reese grinned. Tesha was proving to be a loyal dog.

"Where's my shoe?" JJ demanded before hobbling down the stairs.

"Why were your shoes off in the first place?" Brantley asked when he stepped into view, glancing from JJ to Reese, then back again, the look on his face priceless. He clearly could not fathom how JJ could possibly be wandering around without her shoes on.

Then again, their team leader wasn't known for his ability to relax and chill. Being a retired Navy SEAL, Brantley Walker had one main setting: intense. If he was out of bed, he generally had shoes on, along with all of his clothes—which consisted mostly of cargo pants and T-shirts these days. And on occasion, he'd pair some Levi's or Wranglers with those T-shirts. Those rare times Brantley wandered around barefoot usually meant he was either suffering from a headache or urging Tesha to go outside to do her business or he scented bacon and couldn't wait long enough to throw on clothes before he chowed down.

It was in those rare moments when Brantley was caught unawares that Reese found him ridiculously hot. More so than usual.

To his credit, Brantley did run the governor's task force, a group developed for the sole purpose of finding missing persons within the state of Texas, like a well-oiled machine. And unlike many bosses, Brantley wouldn't take full responsibility for the good the team had done. When it came to praise, he insisted it was a joint effort.

On the other hand, Brantley had no qualms taking the heat when they'd done something wrong. Reese figured that was something ingrained in him during his time in the Teams. Brantley was used to being held accountable for his own actions as well as those he led.

As far as Reese was concerned, Brantley was a damn fine leader. He was also a damn fine man in general, which was likely the very reason he'd fallen in love with the man and was now co-habbing with him, sharing the same bed every night.

"Damn it, Tavoularis. Your dog's a menace," JJ declared.

"I don't have a problem with her," Reese replied with a wink. "But you might check the yard."

"If she chewed it, you're buyin' me a new pair," she bit out, limping with one shoe on toward the door.

He heard Brantley say, "Three … two…"

Reese was laughing when JJ came to an abrupt halt, the door opening from the outside. Before she could go after the four-legged shoe thief, the blond detective she'd been avoiding since Thanksgiving appeared. Reese's laughter died off as he watched the encounter as though it was a locomotive barreling down the tracks, seconds away from hitting an oncoming train and resulting in a fiery blaze. One of these days, those two freight trains would collide. It was inevitable.

Sebastian Buchanan lifted a hand, JJ's shoe dangling from one finger. "Missin' somethin'?"

Good news was, the shoe didn't appear damaged.

JJ yanked it off his hand and spun around. Her glare was directed at Reese, but he knew her frustration wasn't for him. Ever since she'd stood Baz up for Thanksgiving dinner with his parents and realized Baz was completely unaffected—her assessment, not Reese's—by her disappearing act, she'd been in a tizzy. Four weeks and counting.

As far as Reese was concerned, Baz was doing a damn fine job *pretending* he wasn't affected. However, Reese saw the way the man watched JJ, so much longing in his eyes. He was most certainly bothered by the current state of their relationship, he just wasn't bothering to say or do anything about it.

Despite the fact he was being stubborn, Reese couldn't help but like the former APD detective, known by his friends as simply Baz. And the reasons had nothing to do with how well he was handling JJ or how forgiving he was being for her freaking out about the fact they had been in a relationship at the time. The guy was good at what he did, and they'd come to depend on him as an integral part of the team.

Baz stepped into the barn, grinned at JJ's back, then made his way over to his desk.

"You payin' Tesha to do that?" Brantley asked when the detective dropped a fast-food bag down beside his keyboard and pulled his chair out.

Baz's eyes lit up. "No, but that's a great idea. Maybe I'll get your trainer to teach her to steal them."

Reese smiled at the thought of his sweet Tesha becoming a shoe thief.

Baz glanced between them, grinned wide, and said, "Mornin'," as though greeting them for the first time since he walked in the door.

"Why're you here?" Brantley said in lieu of a simple hello.

"Nice to see you, too, boss."

"It's Christmas Eve."

"That it is," Baz agreed. "My question to you: why're *you* here?"

"That *is* a question."

Reese laughed. When these two got going, they could banter back and forth like the best of them. *And* they worked well together, a combination that Reese admired in the workplace. He liked that they were laid-back when they could be and nose to the grindstone when it mattered.

Of course, today wasn't a grindstone day, and honestly, he had no idea why any of them were here, aside from the fact it was familiar. Like Brantley said, it was Christmas Eve, and they should've all been at their respective homes, enjoying a day off, time with family or whatnot. Then again, they were family in a sense, so getting together whether for work or for play usually resulted in a good time.

Baz obviously realized Brantley was still waiting for an answer and would continue to wait no matter the banter leading up to it, because rather than sit in his chair, he perched on the edge of his desk.

"Figured I'd spend a coupla hours here, then head over to my mother's."

"Doin' Christmas at her place this time?"

Baz shook his head, sipped from a travel mug he'd brought with him. "Dinner'll be at my dad's, like always. My mother'll be there, too. I spend Christmas Eve with her. It's tradition. She'll make a homemade pizza. We'll watch a movie. Usually *It's a Wonderful Life* but this year I think she's going with *Elf*." He grinned. "Before you ask, I have no clue what that says about her mental state."

"Y'all are close," Reese acknowledged.

"We are, yeah." He took another sip from his mug. "What about y'all? What's the plan for your first Christmas Eve together?"

"Just chillin'," Brantley answered, glancing over at Reese. "Maybe we'll watch a movie."

Reese chuckled. "Yeah? You think you can sit still that long?"

"No one said anything about sittin' or bein' still."

Realizing what kind of movie he was referring to, Reese felt his face heat, the tips of his ears all but catching fire.

Baz laughed, obviously understanding and thankfully changing the subject. "And tomorrow? Y'all've got the fam thing goin'?"

"Yep." Brantley turned his attention back to Baz. "Big breakfast at my folks' place, then we'll head up to Dallas for dinner."

"Sounds like a full day," Baz mused.

That it would be. And oddly enough, Reese found he was looking forward to it. While he had dreaded Thanksgiving, not knowing what to expect at his first meal with Brantley's family, he now knew he had nothing to worry about. Being with Brantley's branch of the family tree was much like the time he spent with Curtis and Lorrie and their wild and rambunctious crew. Seemed with the Walkers, no matter which group, it was about getting together, laughing, joking, and enjoying one another's company.

And while he knew they'd have a good time, he was definitely eager to see his mother, to spend some time with Z and Jensyn. His brother and sister would be joining them for the festivities, as would Z's husband RT. Also in attendance would be Reese's mother's long-term boyfriend, who Reese was no longer leery of but still a bit uncomfortable around due to the fact he didn't really know the guy.

"Full weekend," Reese told him. "We're gonna stay up there for a coupla days. Back here on Monday."

"And y'all are here this mornin' because…?"

"Bored," Reese admitted. "Catchin' up on a few things."

Baz lifted his mug in a mock toast as he stood and walked around behind his desk. "Same."

Reese watched as the man's gaze swung to the second-floor loft. He figured JJ was the real reason Baz was here today. Everyone knew she was spending the holidays alone. Her preference, she had informed them. While Reese knew nothing about JJ's personal life—the woman did not disclose much to anyone—he knew she didn't have a close relationship with her mother or father and rarely saw them.

"Don't worry about her," Brantley said softly, clearly seeing Baz's concern. "We're gonna make her go with us."

Reese grinned, took a sip of his coffee. He knew Brantley wasn't kidding. He'd already stated he had every intention of forcing JJ to go with them to both family meals, even if he had to hogtie her and put her in the truck.

Reese only hoped it didn't come to that.

AFTER SPENDING MOST OF THE DAY FUCKING off, doing not much of anything at all, Brantley was happy to sit down in his living room with Reese, watch the television he'd been convinced he needed to buy to fill up the space. He'd been quite content with the bare minimum in terms of furniture and only one television in the house, but evidently it was customary to furnish the family spaces, as Reese referred to them.

Brantley had conceded to Reese's demand for a couch and a coffee table. At some point, Reese promised they would be adding a table to the dining room, but for the moment it remained empty. Brantley continued to pester Reese for the hell of it, trying to convince him they needed to hang a heavy bag from the ceiling and turn the room into a gym. Who needed more than one table to eat at? The small one Reese had snuck into the breakfast nook was overkill if you asked him. Especially since they sat at the enormous kitchen island for dinner most nights.

However, one new thing Brantley was quite fond of was the Christmas tree they'd put up and decorated. It sat in the corner of the living room in all its artificial and fake-flocked glory, right in front of the big picture window overlooking the backyard.

It had actually been Brantley's idea, and he'd seen the surprise on Reese's face when he suggested they do it. Yeah, yeah, yeah. He was an alpha male who'd spent his life on the battlefield. He'd heard it from everyone, getting harassed by his friends and family. Didn't mean he couldn't enjoy the simple things like colorful flashing lights dangling from a tree and maybe a candle or two on occasion.

Although he hadn't told Reese as much, he looked forward to creating their own traditions as they settled into their life together. It was new for both of them, even if for different reasons. While Reese wasn't a stranger to romantic relationships, Brantley knew being in one with a man was foreign for him. And Brantley hadn't had one for his entire adult life. By design, of course. Until Reese, he'd never met a man he wanted to spend any significant amount of time with. But the day he'd laid eyes on Reese Tavoularis, he'd known there was something different about him.

Brantley glanced over at Reese, saw he was watching him. "What?"

"You're not watchin' the movie."

He smiled sheepishly. "Busted."

"What's on your mind, navy boy?"

His grin quickly morphed into something far more daring. "Definitely not the movie."

"No?"

After placing his beer on the coffee table, Brantley shifted on the couch, moving into Reese's personal space, forcing him to the side and down so that he was lying flat on his back.

Reese's eyes glittered in the twinkling lights from the tree, his grin instantly heating all those places inside Brantley that used to be cold and dark before he came along.

"*You're* on my mind," he whispered, moving over Reese so they were aligned from chest to knee. "You're *always* on my mind."

"What you mean to say is you're thinkin' about sex."

Brantley couldn't help it, he smiled wider. "Busted again." He leaned down, pressed his lips gently to Reese's. "But sex with you happens to be my favorite thing in the entire world, so why wouldn't I think about it twenty-four seven?"

He groaned softly when Reese's hands trailed up his sides, sliding beneath his T-shirt, over his back. He'd never paid much attention to what it felt like when a man touched him. His previous encounters had been about one thing: orgasm. He hadn't spent much time indulging on the way to the goal, but with Reese, he found he thoroughly enjoyed the journey.

Straddling Reese's thighs, he leaned forward, grinding his rigid erection against Reese's, loving the moans he elicited from the man when he did.

When Reese worked Brantley's T-shirt higher, Brantley allowed him to remove it. When it was out of the way, he stared down at the sexiest man who'd ever been beneath him, rocking his hips, enjoying the friction on his dick.

"Push your sweatpants down," he commanded, continuing to watch Reese's face.

Brantley lifted his hips to allow Reese to do as instructed but didn't go far. Once the gray cotton was down far enough to free Reese's enormous cock, Brantley returned to what he was doing.

"You like that?"

Reese nodded, eyes closing as he gently rocked, mimicking Brantley's smooth, unhurried rhythm.

"Now push my sweats down."

Reese's eyes opened, his hands gliding down Brantley's sides again, fingertips dipping into the waistband before pushing them down over his ass, freeing Brantley's cock.

Then they were skin to skin, the heat of their bodies adding an erotic element to their somewhat innocent encounter.

Reese grunted, his fingertips digging ever so lightly into Brantley's back as he held him there, allowed Brantley to continue the bump and grind that provided a unique intensity to their lovemaking.

As much as Brantley enjoyed fucking Reese, sliding deep into his body, he loved this just as much. He loved watching the pleasure contort Reese's handsome features as he accepted Brantley's touch. It was how they'd started out. Slow and easy. Taking their time, introducing Reese to this new realm where a man could bring him pleasure despite what he'd thought he wanted all his life.

"Brantley…"

"Tell me, baby," he whispered, still watching him. "What do you need from me?"

"More."

"More what?"

"Everything."

Brantley leaned in, licked Reese's lips until his mouth opened, allowing him inside. He explored him, loving the way Reese allowed him to remain in control, trusting him to give him the pleasure Brantley knew he needed.

He swallowed Reese's soft moans as he continued to rock his hips, their cocks gently rubbing, friction intensifying.

"You want to feel my mouth?"

"Mmm-hmm."

He nipped Reese's lower lip. "You want me to suck you?"

"Fuck, yes," Reese groaned.

"You want me to tongue-fuck you?"

Reese's hips bucked, his hands firmly gripping Brantley's hips. "God, yes."

"You want to feel my cock deep inside you?"

"Brantley…"

He ground his hips down, increasing the pressure, the friction. "Tell me."

"You're gonna make me come."

"Not yet," he warned. "Not until I've had my fill."

Brantley trailed his lips down the hard line of Reese's jaw, over the corded muscles in his neck, lower. He paused long enough to jerk Reese's shirt up roughly, exposing the smooth, hard wall of his chest. While Reese undulated and squirmed, Brantley tortured and tormented with his lips and tongue and teeth. He laved and nipped Reese's nipples, licked and sucked his hot skin as he ventured lower.

When Reese started to take his shirt off, Brantley told him to leave it on. He liked seeing Reese like this. Mostly dressed but exposed. Sweatpants pushed down to his thighs, shirt up high on his chest. More importantly, he knew Reese enjoyed it, too.

Shifting lower, he kissed his way down Reese's flat, rigid stomach, following the trail of soft hair that led to the treasure reserved only for him.

He teasingly flicked the sensitive head of Reese's cock with his tongue, then licked the velvety smooth length again and again.

"Brantley…" Reese grunted, thrusting his hips up. "Suck me." He growled low in his throat. "Quit teasin'. Put your mouth on me."

He did. Enveloping Reese's throbbing cock in his mouth, sucking him down to the root, holding him there before releasing him. Brantley repeated the action, long, slow draws, listening to the guttural groans that rumbled inside Reese as the pleasure assaulted him.

He fucking loved this man. Every damn thing about him. And he especially loved that he could give him pleasure and that Reese was unabashed when it came to accepting it.

Brantley maneuvered Reese's sweatpants farther down his legs, leaving them around his ankles and using the soft cotton to position Reese how he wanted him, forcing his knees toward his chest, feet in the air, exposing him more.

While Reese groaned, Brantley blew cool air on his balls and anus before leaning in and licking him.

"Oh, fuck … so good. So … good."

He knew how much Reese enjoyed his wicked tongue, so he worked him into a frenzy, tongue-fucking him for long minutes while Reese's hips pitched and plunged in his attempt to get more.

"Brantley! Oh, fuck… Fuck me. Fuck. Me."

He knew a demand when he heard one, and he couldn't resist, his cock so fucking hard it throbbed in time with his heartbeat.

Using his own saliva as lube, Brantley shifted to his knees, guided his cock against the tight ring, and pushed in slow, deep. He watched Reese's face to ensure he wasn't causing undue pain. If he'd been prepared, he would've brought the lube from the bedroom, but he hadn't anticipated this.

"You want me to get lube?" he offered, inching in deeper, going painfully slow, praying Reese said no because he wasn't sure he could pause long enough.

To his shock, Reese's hands curled around his hips, jerking him forward until he bottomed out.

Brantley grunted, the overwhelming pleasure, the exquisite heat of Reese's body threatening to drain him dry before he was ready.

"I'll take that as a no." He shifted, getting into a better position, adding more saliva as he retreated slowly.

After a few strokes, the pre-cum leaking from his cock helped lube the way, allowing him to slide in deeper, faster, the blistering heat of Reese's body making his head spin and his heart race.

"Hard. *Er*," Reese growled roughly. "Now."

He gave him what he needed, slamming home, retreating, slamming in again. Over and over, he fucked Reese, driving them both straight up to the razor-sharp edge until the pleasure overwhelmed. The electricity sparked in his spine, and he knew he was dangerously close as he pounded away, watching Reese, waiting, waiting…

"Oh, fuck, yes!" Reese cried out, his body bucking, cock exploding.

Brantley drove into him one final time and came in a fierce rush that left him breathless and light-headed.

And so fucking content.

Chapter Four

***

THIS YEAR, CHRISTMAS DAY WAS GOING ABOUT the same as every other day. Chaotic and crazy were adjectives Reese would use to describe it.

It had started with breakfast with Brantley's parents, Iris and Frank, as well as Brantley's three sisters, two brothers-in-law, three brothers, the offspring that belonged to them, and last but not least, JJ. Oh, and Tesha. Couldn't forget her. But she'd been on her best behavior, so Reese couldn't really say she'd contributed to the chaos and craziness that had filled that house.

And while it had left him with a bit of a headache, Reese couldn't deny he'd had a great time. The Walkers were an interesting bunch, and he found he enjoyed being around them.

However, he would have to admit, he had also enjoyed the three-hour drive from Coyote Ridge to his mother's house in Plano. During the trip, JJ and Tesha had chilled in the backseat, both of them catching some sleep while Reese had relaxed in the passenger seat. He never even asked to drive, knowing Brantley would've insisted, and since it was Christmas, he figured there was no reason to get into an argument if it could be avoided.

Now, as he sat at his mother's dining room table, he was immersed once again in family, but not so much chaos. Theirs was a much more laid-back kind of get-together.

"So how's work?"

Reese glanced at his brother, saw that Zachariah, better known to anyone he introduced himself to as Z, was directing the question at him.

Fork in hand and halfway to his mouth, Reese answered with, "Good. We're busy."

They had just sat down to dinner—he and Brantley, his mother Cindy and her boyfriend Hugh, Z and RT, his sister Jensyn, and JJ. The eight of them were comfortably scattered around his mother's huge dining room table, feasting on pork roast with potatoes, carrots, and baby onions and his mother's specialty: sweet cornbread while Tesha relaxed at Reese's feet, likely hoping for a scrap or two to make it to her. They'd been told they had to eat the healthy stuff before they could move on to the desserts. The kitchen counters were loaded with more sweets than they'd be able to finish in a week. And that was saying something considering Z's enormous appetite.

"Cold cases?" Ryan Trexler, known simply as RT to his family and friends, asked.

Reese nodded. "For the most part, yeah."

"Any luck?"

"A little," he admitted. "There's a reason these cases are cold."

"Oh, I'm sure. If it were easy to solve missing-persons cases, no one would be missing, huh?"

Reese picked up his iced tea. "Exactly."

"Are these mostly in the Austin area?" Hugh asked.

"Yes, sir." Reese looked his mother's boyfriend in the eyes as he answered, aiming to show him respect being that they'd hardly spoken much to one another.

This wasn't the first time he'd met Hugh Weston, the sixty-six-year-old investment banker born and raised in the suburbs of Dallas, but it was the first time he'd spent a decent amount of time with the man despite the fact his mother had been dating him—exclusively—for quite a number of years.

It wasn't that he had anything against the guy. In fact, he thought Hugh was good for his mother. Since his father had been comatose after his accident, right up until he died, Reese's mother had needed someone to lean on, someone who could be there for her, and Hugh had filled the void. He seemed to make her happy, and for Reese, that was all that really mattered. He simply didn't know much about Hugh, and he couldn't deny the ingrained desire to unearth as much information as he could in an effort to appease his own curiosity.

Not that he would. That would be a violation of privacy, and being that his brother seemed content with Hugh, Reese figured there weren't any skeletons in the guy's closet. After all, Z did work for Sniper 1 Security, had access to information Reese probably couldn't even get his hands on. He could only assume that meant Z had done his homework at some point and deemed the man worthy of their mother's love and attention.

"For the most part, we stay in and around central Texas," Reese elaborated. "We do have cold cases across the state that we've been assigned, but until we expand the task force, we're havin' to focus on local ones."

"When will you be expanding?" RT asked.

Reese glanced at Brantley for the answer to that.

Brantley looked his way, finished chewing, then answered with, "Beginnin' of the year."

When he didn't elaborate, Reese finished for him. "We've got six additional positions approved by the governor's office. It's just a matter of interviewin' candidates."

Again there was an expression on Brantley's face that Reese couldn't quite identify.

"Fun stuff," Z joked. "I know that's how I'd wanna spend my day, closed up in a room with a stranger, askin' all kinds of stupid questions."

"The eternal optimist," RT said with a grin. "One of the many things I love about you."

That earned a laugh from everyone.

"What about y'all? How're things with Sniper 1?" Brantley prompted.

RT wiped his mouth with a napkin then smiled. "We're actually lookin' to expand as well."

Being that Sniper 1 Security was a family-owned business, started by Bryce Trexler, RT's father, and Casper Kogan, it was in the process of being passed down. RT had taken the helm years ago, and recently Casper's son Hunter had stepped up to the plate. From what Reese had heard, they were taking it in a new direction, expanding not just in employees but also in the work that they did.

"Openin' a new location?" Brantley inquired.

"We're lookin' at some property in Austin and some in Houston. Tryin' to decide which'll be more beneficial."

"Not out of state, huh?" Reese asked.

"Not for operations, no. We've got operatives who live in different states, which gives us the coverage we need, but I'd like to keep the general functions close to home."

"Overseas?" Brantley asked.

"We're venturing into it more," RT replied. "Right now, we're assignin' our most tenured agents to those positions."

"What's it like in the private sector?"

Reese was a little surprised by Brantley's question. Anytime they'd discussed private-sector workforces, Brantley tended to tune out. Reese figured that had a lot to do with the fact Brantley'd spent most of his life working for the government. And everyone knew Brantley wasn't fond of major change.

"I'm not sure I could do it any other way," RT answered. "Then again, it's the only way I've ever known. My father and Casper were both in the military, which has helped, I think. They've maintained some connections that way."

"You get much pushback from government agencies?"

"No. As a rule, we don't impede."

"But we have been known to sidestep when necessary," Z added with a grin.

"Yes, we have been known to do that." RT took a sip of his iced tea. "But we keep that on the DL. No sense upsettin' the local LEOs if at all possible."

"LEOs?" JJ asked, leaning forward, fully engaged in the conversation.

"Law enforcement officers," Z supplied.

"Ah." She grinned wide. "Got it."

"I know a couple of guys who might be interested in any overseas positions you've got comin' up," Brantley said, setting his fork down. "Former SEAL teammates. One recently got out, the other's got three months then he'll be stateside again."

Reese glanced at Brantley. "You keep in touch with them?"

"Of course."

Interesting.

Although Reese wasn't sure why he found it interesting. It made sense that Brantley would keep in touch with the guys he used to work with. Just because he left the military didn't mean he no longer existed. They were friends, some he probably even considered family. Of course, he knew Brantley would still be leading his SEAL team if it weren't for the fact he'd been forced into early retirement thanks to the medical discharge.

Then again, Reese hadn't kept in touch—or vice versa—with the guys from his squadron. After he'd been assumed KIA and left for dead, he'd been pretty much on his own. After the torture he'd endured, he hadn't been left with much loyalty for those he'd been abandoned by.

"Anyone up for dessert?" Reese's mother asked when the conversation lulled and plates were pushed aside.

"Let's give the food time to settle first, Mom," Z told her with a smile. "Then we'll be all up in the pie."

"You okay?" Brantley asked, leaning in close, voice low.

Reese jerked his attention over. "Of course. Why?"

Brantley's response was a simple eyebrow twitch, which meant Reese had been internalizing his thoughts and ignoring those around him.

He forced away the memories of that long-ago time. At some point, he would have to deal with the lingering anger he harbored along with the fear that seemed to be surfacing when he was asleep, coming in the form of nightmares that were becoming more frequent. But he certainly had no desire to ruin Christmas by getting lost in his own head by revisiting those hellish months when he'd all but prayed for death.

"Why don't we move this party to the living room," Hugh suggested. "I know there are at least a dozen presents under that tree."

Presents.

Fun.

Several hours later, everyone went their separate ways, retiring for the evening.

RT and Z had left, going back to their house. Jensyn was staying the night, insisting she wanted to hang with JJ and spend more time with their mother, the girls likely gossiping about the rest of them.

Reese and Brantley had been given the larger of the two guest rooms despite their insistence they didn't need more than a sleeping bag and a patch of hardwood. When Brantley had told Reese's mother as much, Reese had laughed at the horror in her expression. Like Cindy Tavoularis would ever let a guest sleep on the floor.

But it'd been when Brantley offered to take the couch that Reese had spoken up, insisting they would be sharing a room. After all, they lived together. It wasn't like he could pretend he wasn't in a relationship with the man. And oddly enough, he found he didn't want to. Not with his family, at least. Once he'd gotten over the initial concern that his brother would pass judgment on him for his recent realization that he wasn't as straight as he'd originally thought, Reese had been getting a better grip on his new reality.

Not that he was ready to flaunt it to the world.

Well, mentally he was. When he sat back and thought about it, he had no concerns whatsoever with people knowing he was in love with Brantley. However, the same could not be said when push came to shove and he found himself in a position that required him to reveal that detail. He still clammed up, got overly anxious, and couldn't bring himself to admit it aloud. But with Brantley's help, he knew one day he would figure it all out.

Like Brantley always told him: it would take time.

Now as he lay in the darkened room beneath a thick, floral-patterned comforter, head resting on pillows that were just a little too soft, his shoulder and thigh brushed Brantley's, and Reese found he wanted to be closer to the man. Maybe it had something to do with the fact he'd realized Brantley was keeping in touch with his former SEAL team and he hadn't bothered to share that fact with him. Or maybe he simply wanted to be close because he craved him like he craved that Jack Daniel's pecan pie his brother had introduced him to.

Whatever the reason, he knew he couldn't wait until they were back home tomorrow night before he satisfied this urge by indulging in the most exquisite dessert in the house.

Without saying a word, Reese rolled to his side, shifted so that he was pressed against Brantley, and let his hand wander beneath the blanket, sliding over the smooth, hot skin he'd become intimately acquainted with lately.

"Mmm," Brantley mumbled softly.

Reese pressed his lips to Brantley's shoulder, smiled. "Shh."

"I'll do my best," he whispered.

Leaning forward, he placed his mouth near Brantley's ear. "As long as you're quiet, I'll continue."

Brantley's response was a nod, which made Reese smile more as he shifted, pushing the blankets down, uncovering them both.

He took his time, caressing, massaging Brantley with his hands and his mouth. The only sounds Brantley made were soft gasps, which spurred Reese to continue, pausing only long enough to get rid of the few clothes in the way and retrieve the lubricant from the overnight bag he'd left on the floor by the bed.

When he urged Brantley to roll onto his stomach, the man did so without question, without hesitation. Reese didn't waste time, didn't linger on the foreplay; instead, he slicked his cock, then slid deep inside Brantley.

Once he'd filled him completely, Reese laid out over him, covering his back, his hands snaking underneath to curl his fingers over Brantley's shoulders. It took effort not to make the bedsprings squeak, but he managed, rocking his hips, fucking Brantley with long, deep strokes that had them both panting even as they kept the noise to a minimum.

"You ready to come?" he whispered in Brantley's ear.

Brantley's response came as he turned his head, nodded, then found Reese's mouth with his own.

Making love to Brantley, tongues dueling, hearts pounding, Reese brought them both to climax.

The best Christmas present yet.

BRANTLEY WOULDN'T LIE, HE'D BEEN EYEBALLING RT and Z the entire drive from Cindy's house to the Sniper 1 Security building.

"I might just hafta get me one of those," he told Reese when they pulled into the parking garage behind Z's Yamaha YZF-R1 supersport bike and RT's Kawasaki Ninja H2R.

"A motorcycle?" Reese snorted. "You'd kill yourself first chance you got."

"I was a SEAL, you know."

"Which translates to king of the adrenaline rush."

"I can hold my own, thank you very much."

Reese laughed. "I have no doubt, but it's more about you pushin' the limit that worries me."

Oh, how he would push the limit if he had one of those. As far as he could. And then some.

"They've been ridin' those things since they were kids," Reese explained. "RT's whole family's got 'em."

Considering how sleek and sexy they were—the bikes, not the men … although they weren't half-bad, just not nearly as sexy as Reese—Brantley understood. Growing up in a small town, the middle child out of seven, there hadn't been room for many vices. Brantley sometimes wondered if that was the reason he'd gone into the military. He'd already been familiar with the routine, and it gave him the freedom he wouldn't get otherwise.

"Come on," Reese said as he opened the truck door. "You're the one who asked for a tour of the offices."

Well, technically, Z had been the one to expand on their topic from dinner last night. Brantley had merely tossed the idea in there. He was curious, sure. Considering Sniper 1 Security was one of the largest and most successful private security firms in the country, he wanted to know what made it tick.

And yes, fine, he was curious about the infrastructure of a privately funded corporation of this nature. Considering he had no intention of letting the task force die, even if the governor opted to shut them down, Brantley figured the more knowledge he had, the better off they'd be.

But more accurately, he'd heard they had some super-secret spy stuff going on, and he was hoping for some firsthand access.

RT and Z were waiting at the elevators when they approached. He considered asking more questions about the motorcycles but decided to leave it alone. As much as he wanted to know, that wasn't always a good thing. If he knew, he'd only want one, and Reese was right, pushing the envelope was his specialty. At this point in his life, Brantley probably didn't need to take any more risks than he already did.

"You own the entire building?"

"We do," RT answered. "Circumstance gave us a chance to redesign some of the space. We converted the ground floor to allow for customer-facing businesses like food services and retail, most on short-term leases. We have quite a few long-term leases with tenants on the lower floors. Sniper 1 now resides on the four highest floors."

"Donuts and coffee every day," Z joked.

"I'm bettin' that's a nice residual income," Brantley mused. "The retail fronts, I mean. Not the donuts."

"Don't knock the donuts," Z muttered with a chuckle.

After they all piled in, RT pressed the button for the seventh floor. "It helps, that's for sure."

"Do you get a lot of walk-in traffic?"

RT shook his head. "None, actually. One hundred percent of our business comes from word of mouth. Granted, it took us years to build a reputation, but now when we greet new clients, it's because they heard about us from someone else."

Brantley nodded, tossing around that information. He figured they would have to work toward that as well if the governor gave them the heave-ho.

For the next half hour, they went on a tour of the various floors that housed Sniper 1's finance, operations, and marketing teams, their IT department, technology division, bullpens for field agents, client-facing meeting areas, as well as the main offices of their executives, including RT and Z.

While Brantley admired all they'd built, he could never see himself sitting at a desk in some fancy high-rise building. He wanted to be where the action was.

"So where's the testing floor?" Brantley inquired when they'd stopped in one of the many oversized conference rooms.

"Testing?" RT asked, glancing over at Z, who in turn looked at Reese.

"That's his polite way of sayin' he wants to see your secret spy toys."

Z's eyes lit up with amusement.

"Don't bother tellin' me that's a myth," Brantley told RT. "Your husband's notorious for sharin' his toys with us."

RT glanced over at Z, clearly not in the loop on the sharing.

"What?" Z shrugged his enormous shoulders. "They needed stuff. We've got stuff."

RT sighed.

"Why don't you be a bit more specific on what you're lookin' for," Reese suggested, nudging Brantley with his arm.

"I want to find Juliet Prince," he stated, all humor gone.

"She's the woman who kidnapped your cousin's daughter, right?"

Brantley nodded. "JJ's runnin' software to track her, but so far we've got nothin'. The couple of leads it's generated were bogus, so I'm not exactly confident we're goin' about it the right way."

RT seemed to consider that before he spoke. "While we've taken on a few high-profile cases in the past, we don't usually search for people. I wish I could tell you we had somethin' that'll give you her exact location at this very moment, but we're not that good."

"No one's that good," Z added.

RT shared a look with Z, then sighed again when Z nodded.

"Fine," RT huffed softly, then peered over at Brantley. "We have been playin' with some new software and algorithms related to facial recognition that might get you closer to findin' her."

"Facial recognition software's not a new development," Reese stated.

"Correct." RT looked between them. "However, we've got teams workin' to develop and refine a variety of options out there. While most facial recognition software already identifies matches based on a number of markers, such as distance between the eyes, height of the ears, compared to what's in a database, we're lookin' to implement it against live feeds."

"Big brother," Reese noted.

"To a degree, yes." It was obvious RT wasn't too happy admitting that. "But it's only as good as the data we can compare it to, so the more live feeds we have, the better off we are."

"Which means we're in bed with the government," Z added quickly.

"In a sense," RT said, shaking his head at Z's outburst. "We're also workin' with various companies, like those who design the doorbells and personal security systems, to partner. If we can have access to their feeds, we'll be able to get eyes everywhere. But the software is proprietary, and we intend to keep it that way."

Brantley understood. However, he also understood the need for more information. Information the government and some businesses already compiled and maintained. When it came to looking for a missing child, Brantley would pull out all the stops. He didn't give a shit what avenue they had to pursue as long as it brought that child back safely to their parents.

The same could be said for catching a crazed woman who had no qualms kidnapping a child in order to dole out punishment for a perceived slight.

"I'll take whatever you've got," Brantley told RT. "Every time we think we've got a bead on her, she's not there."

"Doesn't mean she wasn't," Reese said. "We're just not fast enough."

Brantley wasn't so optimistic in his thinking. There was nothing they'd uncovered that proved to him they'd been close to finding Juliet Prince since she abandoned Kate in a run-down house in Mississippi back in September, just two days after she abducted her. The leads they'd gotten had come from across the country, and while Juliet seemed quite adept at lying low, he didn't believe she was blazing a path across the US. If she was, she wasn't flying, because they had managed to pull some strings and get her on the TSA's no-fly list.

It wasn't much, but it was something.

Chapter Five

Wednesday, December 30, 2020

ALTHOUGH EVERYONE WAS ON OFFICIAL HOLIDAY THROUGH the first of the year, Brantley wasn't surprised that Governor Greenwood had summoned him to his office at the capitol building.

Nor was he surprised the governor had requested he come alone.

And he seriously doubted he would be surprised by the topic of the conversation they were going to have once he got there.

As it was, he'd been putting the governor off for days. Not because he'd been overloaded, more so because he was dragging his feet. He'd started by insisting Monday wasn't good for him. The governor then requested Tuesday, which Brantley also shot down. However, when Governor Greenwood's assistant had simply continued to the next day, offering every hour on the hour from morning to evening, Brantley knew the meeting was inevitable.

The very reason he was walking through the mostly empty capitol building on this chilly Wednesday afternoon.

Unlike normal business hours, there was no one to greet him when he stepped into the ostentatious outer office with its wine-red carpet and dark wood everything. Rhonda, the governor's persistent assistant, was usually perched behind that little desk, headset on, a smile on her face. Today her spot was empty, and if she was lucky, she was spending some quality time with her family.

Exactly where the governor should be, Brantley thought when he stopped at the partially closed door to the governor's inner sanctum.

Before he could lift his hand to knock, he was called inside by a grumbling voice.

"Governor," he greeted when he pushed open the door.

Brantley wouldn't go so far as to call Governor Gerard Greenwood an imposing figure. He wasn't a big man, nor did he have one of those bulldog faces that prevented people from wanting to argue with him. His hair was still thick, although the once inky black had taken on quite a bit of gray over the years, and with his high cheekbones, perfectly straight nose, and well-groomed eyebrows, Gerard was what some considered classically handsome. He stood less than six feet tall, which meant Brantley had a good five or six inches on him, but that didn't seem to faze the man in the least.

"Thank you for coming, Brantley." Governor Greenwood motioned toward the leather armchair across from his desk. "Have a seat, please."

Brantley would've preferred to stand, but he knew when to pick his battles, so he eased into the chair.

"Relax," the governor said. "You look like you're gearing up for a firing squad."

"I thought that was the reason I was here," he answered snidely.

Gerard cocked an eyebrow. "Don't make me the bad guy here."

"If the shoe fits…"

Some would likely say he was pushing it with his rude comments directed at the man who was the chief executive of Texas and the commander-in-chief of the state's military, not to mention his boss, but Brantley didn't give a shit.

He had a bone to pick with the man, and to him it felt personal. Governor Greenwood had been the one to approach *him* back in September, offering to fund a task force dedicated to finding missing people. And now the governor wanted to eliminate their team, as though they hadn't accomplished a damn thing during the three months they'd been working their asses off. Hell, they had found a woman who'd gone missing as a teenager and been held captive for a solid decade. In the process, they'd rescued the governor's daughter when she'd been kidnapped in an effort to hide that crime. After that, they had single-handedly unearthed a serial killer who'd been wearing a detective's shield. A feat not even the FBI had been able to do up to that point.

As far as Brantley was concerned, they deserved a little bit of credit for what they'd done. They damn sure didn't deserve to get the axe.

"Brantley, I know you're upset, and I can't say I blame you. The team's been doing good work. You should be proud of that. Unfortunately, it's the same work that a number of agencies are currently involved in."

So he'd heard … in that email.

"What I don't understand is why you're not fightin' this, Governor," Brantley countered. "We have proof of our value, not just supposition or projection. We've made a difference with the cases we've solved in just a short time. One in particular that had been sittin' in cold storage for a decade."

"You *have* made a difference," Governor Greenwood agreed. "That's not up for debate. The pushback comes from the financial impact."

"They believe the money should be allocated to the law enforcement agencies," Brantley said, repeating what Greenwood had told him in the email. "Question is, if you'd given them the additional funding in the past three months, would they have solved the cases we did?"

"I don't think that's something that can be determined in hindsight."

"Actually, it can. Take the Dallas case. There were a number of cold-case victims attached to that one. We didn't just find the one you called us in to find. You had a serial killer in your ranks."

Governor Greenwood's expression remained solemn. "The fact that it involved serial murders made it the FBI's jurisdiction. We weren't sitting on those cases. They weren't ours to handle any longer."

Brantley stared at him, hating that the man could be so level-headed about this. Brantley was itching for a fight, yet it was clear the governor was not going to give him one.

"Why'd you call me here?" Brantley demanded, sitting up and putting his elbows on the arms of the chair. It took everything in him not to shoot to his feet and march out the door.

"I thought I owed you the respect of telling you face-to-face that, as of January fourth, the task force will no longer exist in the eyes of the state."

"The fourth. Monday. Jesus Christ. You told me there'd be a discussion around it."

Governor Greenwood was watching him, his eyes intent when he said, "It's come to my attention that it's no longer necessary. I'm not in a position to win the vote."

Brantley wanted to slam his badge down on the man's desk, to tell him to shove it up his ass, but he refrained. He immediately thought about Reese, about JJ and Baz, Trey and Charlie. He had a team to consider before he burned bridges he couldn't afford to burn.

He stood, inhaling deeply and nodding at the governor before turning toward the door.

"Brantley, I assure you, this wasn't my plan."

"I'm sure it wasn't," he grumbled on his way out.

An hour later, after taking the scenic route back from Austin, Brantley pulled into the driveway of his cousin's house. Because he hadn't wanted to burden Reese with the news—not yet, anyway—he had called Travis.

"Hey, man," Gage greeted as he was walking up to the front door.

Travis's husband was sitting on the porch swing, one-and-a-half-year-old Maddox—the youngest of their five kids—perched on his lap.

"They relegate you to the yard or what?" Brantley joked.

"Mad likes it out here," Gage said, gripping the little boy firmly when he tried to squirm to the ground.

Maddox didn't appreciate the gesture, throwing his arms out in Brantley's direction, clearly looking for a change of scenery.

Brantley grinned, reached for the kid, and hefted him into his arms. "What's up, little man? You keepin' your daddy busy this mornin'?'

Maddox offered a shy smile, his eyes darting back to Gage as though he wasn't quite as content with his decision to relocate anymore.

Laughing, Brantley passed the baby back. "Travis inside?"

Gage's expression shuttered when he answered with, "In his office."

Brantley considered explaining himself, assuring Gage that he wasn't here to discuss Juliet Prince or the task force's attempts to find her, but he didn't have the breath to do it. He was running on caffeine fumes and mounting frustration as it was. No sense getting into an argument over something that wasn't even on the agenda.

He stepped inside the old, historic Victorian that had belonged to Gage's grandmother, if Brantley remembered correctly. Kylie, their wife, had restored to its original splendor, the hardwood floors and wainscoting gleaming with a thick varnish.

The house smelled like lemon cleaner and fresh bread, a combination that made him think about his childhood home. It had always been welcoming like this.

From somewhere in front of him, he heard the television. Every so often, he heard a couple of kids arguing over what they were going to watch. Even that made him smile.

Turning to the right, he rapped his knuckles on the closed French doors.

"Come in," Travis called out, his gruff, deep voice booming.

Brantley stepped inside, closed the door to block out the noise.

"Hey, man. What's up?" Travis asked, motioning toward the couch that acted as a separator between the desk and the doors. "You didn't give me any details on the phone."

No, he hadn't because he hadn't been sure how to phrase it at that point.

He propped himself on the couch arm rather than sitting down. "Just had a conversation with the governor."

Travis leaned back in his chair, rested his elbows on the armrests, steepled his fingers. "And it wasn't good news, I take it?"

"He's disbandin' the task force."

"What?" All casualness disappeared from Travis's expression as he shot up straight. "Why the fuck would he do that?"

"Somethin' about financial allocation or some shit."

"Well, fuck me," Travis breathed out, sounding sincerely shocked and more than a little pissed.

Everyone knew the task force was currently investigating Juliet Prince's whereabouts. While technically the FBI was involved because of the kidnapping, the task force had made it their main priority.

Not to mention, Travis was a silent partner with the team, providing financial backing when necessary. Probably would've been wise to clue him in when the governor initially warned him this might happen.

"So what're you gonna do now? You got another job lined up?"

"I do not. Nor will I be lookin' for one."

Travis frowned, obviously waiting for more.

"I'm gonna keep the task force," he said, as though it was as simple as that.

A deeper line formed between Travis's eyebrows. "Meanin' you'll run it without the backing of the state?"

"I damn sure can't give up now," he argued, although he knew Travis wasn't pushing him to quit; he was merely curious.

"I'd prefer you didn't." Travis relaxed again. "I'm not sure what I would've done without you and Reese. Seriously. I know y'all haven't worked a lot of cases, but you've accomplished quite a bit in a short time. I think it's smart to take it private."

Brantley stared at his cousin, then asked the one question he couldn't hold back. "I'll probably need some financial backing to start. You still in?"

Travis's spine straightened, his countenance shifting.

Brantley figured this was the businessman he was now having a chat with, not his cousin.

"I don't have a business plan yet," Brantley added quickly. "But I will. I promise you that. I've been talkin' with Reese's brother. Thought I'd seek their help, too. Financially, that is."

"Sniper 1 Security. Smart move on your part."

"Yeah. Not gonna get my hopes up until I have an official conversation with them. What I need to know is whether or not I can depend on you in the same manner you've assisted thus far."

"That I can do," Travis stated firmly. "As for an investment, get me a business plan. I'd like to go over it with Gage."

Brantley nodded. "I'll get it worked up." He stood. "Anyway, I needed to vent before I head back to HQ. Last thing I want is for Reese and the team to think they're out of a job."

"I know the feelin'." Travis stood. "Just remember, you can lean on them, too."

Brantley grinned, starting toward the door when Travis joined him. "Wow, that's downright psychological of you, Dr. Phil."

"Fuck off," Travis grumbled, grinning as he opened the door.

The friendly banter helped to lift some of the weight off his shoulders.

It was enough motivation that Brantley decided he would tuck away the news until after the first of the year. He wanted to enjoy some time with Reese, and that wouldn't be possible if he told the team they were out of a job come Monday.

"Why'd Brantley drop by earlier?"

Travis glanced over at his husband, saw the concern in Gage's eyes.

They'd just sat down for the evening, having spent the past half hour doing the dishes while Kylie got the kids started on their baths and showers. Maddox had gone first, then was passed off to Travis to dry and dress. The little boy was now at Travis's feet, staring up at the television, where an animated snowman was keeping him transfixed.

"Governor Greenwood's disbandin' the task force," Travis told him, watching the stairs for the next kid to come down.

Kate was currently doing the independent things, showering in their bathroom, while Kylie helped Kade and Haden, who were taking a bath together. Last would be Avery, who was gathering up the Barbies she wanted to take swimming in the tub with her.

"Really?" Gage sounded perplexed by the idea. "But I thought…"

"Who knows. He's claimin' it's budget cuts and says he doesn't have support to maintain the team."

"He? As in the governor?"

Travis nodded.

"You talked to him?"

"I did." Travis glanced at the television, down to Maddox, then back to Gage. "Called him this afternoon to see what's up. He sounds bothered by the notion but swears there's nothin' he can do about it."

"Seems a bit abrupt, don't you think? The team's only been in place since September."

"I know."

Travis did not need to be reminded what had been the prompting factor for the task force dedicated to locating missing persons. He'd lived that nightmare and had no desire to rehash it any more than he already did.

"And yes," he continued, "it does seem abrupt. Which is why I called him. He's standin' behind the decision." Travis smiled at Maddox when the little boy looked back at him, pointing at the television. "I know, little guy. Cool, huh?"

Maddox grinned wide then turned back to the TV.

"Brantley's thinkin' about takin' the task force private," Travis continued, glancing over to catch Gage's reaction.

"I think that's smart. They're good at what they do. No sense lettin' their talent go to waste."

"He's chattin' with RT and Z, gettin' the scoop on the private gig."

"They'd have the answers," Gage said.

Travis stared at his husband, realizing Gage had been supportive of every single thing Travis had said since they sat down. Too supportive, in fact.

"Spit it out, Gage," Travis bit out, keeping his voice low, tone as even as he could. "Why does it sound like you're placatin' me?"

"I just wanna make sure you're not goin' down that rabbit hole again."

Travis took a long, deep breath, willed his temper to cool, because this was getting old fast.

Although Travis had apologized and sought Gage's help in keeping his violent need to find the woman who had kidnapped their daughter in check, it was clear Gage still didn't trust him. Two weeks ago, Travis had broken down, and he'd thought they'd moved on from that.

Clearly he was the only one who had, because ever since then, he saw the way Gage watched his every move. As though he expected Travis to snap at any second.

"I'm not doin' this with you," Travis hissed, getting to his feet. "If you don't trust me, just say so. Otherwise, stop treatin' me like a child."

Realizing his outburst had drawn Maddox's attention, Travis forced a smile at the baby. "Sorry, little man. Keep watchin' *Frozen*. It's all good. The daddies are just talkin'."

Or they had been, because once Maddox turned back to the television, Travis left the room.

A second later, he left the house altogether.

He needed a beer.

GAGE HEARD THE FRONT DOOR SLAM SHUT, the sound making him flinch.

He'd done it again. He'd gone and pissed Travis off.

Seemed to be par for the course these days. Almost as though Travis was looking for a reason to get angry.

Gage actually understood that part. He had a feeling he was looking for a reason, too. If he could maintain his anger and frustration, continue to worry about Travis, he didn't have to dwell on the thoughts that plagued him. Ironically, they were the same thoughts he gave Travis shit about.

"Did Daddy-O leave?"

Turning his head, Gage saw Kate standing in the doorway, wet hair tangled, her eyes filled with concern as she watched him.

"He had to go out for a bit." Gage patted his thighs, spreading his feet apart. "Come sit down so I can brush your hair, then you can grab a blanket. We're watchin' *Frozen*."

"You know we've watched this like fifteen times this week," Kate said haughtily, a new thing she'd started recently.

"Yet it's still your favorite," he reminded her.

Kate grabbed a throw blanket and dragged it behind her as she headed over, dropping to her knees in front of him, her eyes already glued to the television screen. He took his time combing her hair, detangling it without making her mad, a skill he'd acquired long ago. When he was finished, she curled up on the couch with her blanket, head on a pillow, her feet poking into Gage's thigh.

This had become their nightly routine as of late. After baths, the kids would congregate in the living room for a bit. Then one by one, they would take them to their rooms. Only in the past few days had Kate started exerting more independence, coming out of her shell after her horrible ordeal. She was still having nightmares of the days she'd spent with Juliet Prince, the woman who had kidnapped her during a field trip to the state capitol, but he had to believe they were making progress.

Although the therapist they were seeing said it was normal for her to continue to have these feelings, Gage wondered. Then again, he wasn't trained to know what was right or wrong in this situation—or whether anyone really was—so he had to take the woman's word for it.

And perhaps that was the reason he continued to keep an eye on Travis. Gage didn't have to hide his feelings there. He didn't have to pretend he wasn't worried about Travis the way he had to pretend with Kate. Kylie continued to remind him their only goal with Kate was to show her support and love, to make sure she knew she was safe.

So that was what Gage did. And when he wasn't plastering on a fake smile, he was projecting all his emotions on Travis.

While the kids watched the movie, Gage continued to watch the door, expecting Travis to return at any moment. Every so often, another kid would join him until all five were scattered around the living room. Kate was still on the couch, Kade had taken up his position in Travis's recliner. Avery was lying on the floor, head on her hands as she intently focused on her absolute all-time favorite movie. Haden had been the last to join, his thumb in his mouth while he sat on the floor between Gage's feet. And Maddox was still where he'd started, only he was now lying down, his eyelids getting heavy.

When he heard footsteps on the stairs, Gage glanced over, saw Kylie coming down.

"Where'd Travis go?" she asked, her voice low so as to not disturb the kids.

"He needed some air."

He immediately saw the concern in his wife's eyes, knew she worried about Travis the same way he did. And while they'd seen a significant change in Travis these past couple of weeks, it appeared that it wasn't all that easy to simply shut off that worry.

It wasn't that he wanted the search for Juliet Prince to stop. No, Gage merely wanted Travis to let it go, to allow the authorities to do their job. There was nothing they could do about it. The woman was long gone, and he didn't see her ever coming back. She'd gotten her revenge by making them suffer for those couple of days Kate was missing. If he had to guess, Juliet had already moved on.

"He's fine," Gage assured Kylie, realizing she was waiting for more.

Kylie's eyes cooled, her expression hardening. "You might try repeatin' that *after* you start believin' it yourself."

Before he could reach for her hand, she spun around and stomped off.

And just like that, Gage had managed to piss off both his husband and his wife.

He was on a fucking roll today.

Chapter Six

Thursday, December 31, 2020

"YOU CAN ONLY HIDE FOR SO LONG," JJ muttered at the image on her computer screen. "I *will* find you, I promise you that. And when I do…"

Oh, there were so many ways to finish that sentence.

JJ had settled into her loft office in the converted barn the Off the Books Task Force utilized as their headquarters about an hour ago, and she had everything she needed to make it a great night. Two cans of Orange Crush, a bowl of Orville Redenbacher's air-popped goodness, and a keyboard. While everyone else was out partying, ringing in the new year together, she had every intention of taking in some caffeine and popcorn while doing some discreet digging—her polite term for hacking—into the whereabouts of the woman who was at the very top of the OTB Task Force's Most Wanted list.

It had been one hundred and eight days since Juliet Prince kidnapped Kate Walker.

It had been one hundred and six days since Juliet Prince went on the run.

And it'd been nine days since JJ had received a notification on any sort of sightings of the woman who had kidnapped one of her boss's many cousins. Or, in this case, JJ figured Kate was actually a second cousin to Brantley Walker, the man JJ called best friend and boss. Not that it mattered whether she was second, third, or tenth, Kate was family and anyone who lived in Coyote Ridge, Texas, knew how close the Walker family was.

Nine freaking days of crickets and it was killing her.

While JJ wasn't a part of the Walker family, or even close to them despite her proximity, she had a vested interest in this case. She'd been a part of the investigation when Kate originally went missing, called in to help by Brantley himself. And she refused to give up until they'd located Juliet Prince and put that crazy beeyotch in a cage where she belonged.

"Why are you here?"

JJ shrieked, jumping back in her chair and damn near toppling over.

Clutching her chest where her heart thumped a little too hard, JJ glared over at the man who appeared at the top of the stairs.

"You scared me half to death, Reese Tavoularis," she chided.

His response: a smirk.

The butthole.

Worse, he smirked, and it had that dimple in his cheek winking, which was oddly endearing and made it nearly impossible to be angry with the man.

"I'm workin'," she told him, doing a double take when her brain processed the eyeful of sexy cowboy.

Reese looked smoking hot in his black button-down, ass-hugging Wranglers, lightly scuffed boots, and a black felt Stetson sitting atop his handsome head.

Somewhere close to six and a half feet tall, not too skinny, not too muscular, with a striking jawline and pretty brown eyes, Reese Tavoularis was a ridiculously attractive man.

Such a shame the guy recently realized he was gay, falling fast and hard for Brantley.

"Why're *you* here?" she asked, not voicing the *lookin' like that* part.

"To find out why *you're* here."

"Did Brantley send you?" she asked, smiling as she turned her attention back to her computer.

"Maybe."

"Well, you can tell him I'm fine. I don't need a babysitter on New Year's." JJ toggled to another screen. "I thought y'all were goin' out."

"We are."

"Well, you better get goin'," she drawled. "I mean, it's good to be fashionably late, but not so late that you miss the party."

"Doubt we'll miss it," he said drolly. "Still a few hours till midnight."

JJ relaxed in her chair, spun it to face him. "Why don't you sound happy about that?"

"I can think of better ways to pass the time."

She popped her eyebrows. "Naked, right? With Brantley? I can—"

"Don't even," he warned, fighting a smile.

"Fine." She wouldn't go there. Aloud, anyway. "Brantley talked you into it, huh?"

"Doesn't he always?" Reese hooked his thumbs in his pockets. "Come with us."

"What?" Before he could answer, she was shaking her head, turning back to her computer. "Nope. No way. I've already imposed on enough holidays this year. I've met my quota."

Reese sighed. "You know he's not gonna accept that."

"He'll be fine," she assured him, casting a sideways glance. "Distract him. Based on the way he gives you googly eyes half the time, I figure you're pretty good at that."

"Googly eyes?" Reese's forehead creased with confusion. "What the hell are googly eyes?"

"Watch him when he's watchin' you sometime. You'll see 'em." JJ chuckled, batted her eyelashes. "But the answer's still the same. I'm not goin' out tonight. Me and Tesha are gonna hang right here."

Another sigh. "Fine. I'm not gonna twist your arm. You wanna spend the last few hours of the year sittin' at your desk, who am I to argue?"

JJ smiled. "I appreciate your generosity."

She turned her attention back to her computer, but when Reese didn't leave, she found she couldn't focus. And when he *still* didn't leave, she knew she was in trouble. There was only one reason Reese would linger.

Sure enough, the door opened below, then there were footsteps on the stairs. While she listened to each thud bringing him inevitably closer, JJ considered jumping out of the single window in her office. It wasn't *that* far to the ground.

Brantley cleared his throat when he appeared at the top of the stairs.

Crap on a cracker.

Hold your ground, sista. You've got this.

Her best friend/boss looked just as strikingly handsome as his partner.

Six foot four and layered with a bit more muscle than Reese, Brantley Walker had it going on. And those eyes—a steely-blue that made any hetero woman's blood heat instantly—*swoon*. She remembered being completely infatuated with the man when she was a teenager. Granted, he'd had no interest in her, rather dating her brother, but that hadn't stopped JJ from having a few hormone-fueled fantasies.

She scanned them both from head to toe, held her chin, and tapped her finger on her lip. "Yep. I think it should be illegal for the two of you to go out like that."

"Like what?" Brantley asked.

JJ nodded her head in their direction. "Like that. All cowboy'd up."

They were both glowering at her.

"Let's just say one of you is more than enough sexy." She waved a hand in their direction. "That much hotness should not be multiplied."

Brantley glanced at Reese, shook his head. "She just doesn't quit, does she?"

"Nope."

Their attention shifted back to her.

"Come on," Brantley said in that commanding tone that left no room for argument.

"Not goin'," she countered.

When he took a step toward her, JJ grabbed the arms of her chair and gripped them tightly, prepared to kick and scream if she had to.

"Brantley Walker, don't you dare."

"You're not workin' tonight," he insisted. "You're goin' out with us."

She shook her head, gripped the arms tighter. "I don't want to."

"Yes, you do."

"No, I don't."

"Do, too."

"Oh. My. God!" JJ exclaimed. "It's like arguin' with a two-year-old."

"Tell me about it," Brantley bit out, reaching for her.

When he did, JJ hopped up from her seat, sidestepping him and putting the chair between them.

"I'm not goin'," she hissed, circling to keep him on the other side of the chair. "And you can't make me."

Aw, crap. Why did she go and say that? Like it was a dare or something. Brantley would never back down from a dare.

He cocked his head to the side, studied her momentarily. She could practically see the hamster wheel spinning in his head. No doubt he was devising a plan to get her down those stairs with the least amount of damage done to her, the building, and himself.

"Let it go, B," she warned, hoping to disrupt his thought process. The man was a former Navy SEAL; it wouldn't take much for him to come up with a plan and implement it before she even knew what happened.

His eyes narrowed.

For a second, she thought he was going to let it go. She should've known better.

Before she could think about which direction to go, the chair slipped out of her grip, rolled across the room, and then Brantley was spinning her, his big, muscular arms wrapping tightly around her from behind. When he lifted her so her feet came off the ground, JJ did the only thing she could…

She rammed her heels into his shins.

"Son of a bitch," he ground out, setting her back on her feet, instantly reaching down to rub his shin. "Are your feet made of steel? That fuckin' hurt."

He was lucky she'd taken her shoes off.

"I'm serious," JJ said, keeping her voice low and without an ounce of mirth so he would know she really was serious. "I can't go out tonight. And even if I could, I wouldn't go to Moonshiners."

No way would she risk running into Baz. She couldn't.

When Brantley looked her in the eye, JJ held his gaze, ensuring he saw her sincerity. He of all people knew how difficult the past month had been on her. It didn't matter that she was at fault, that she'd brought her little world crashing down all on her own. It still had been hard to walk away from Baz.

"Fine," he said through clenched teeth. "We'll go out and you can stay here. I'll spend the night worried about you. If that's what you want…"

"You are *not* gonna guilt-trip me, Walker. No way, no how."

"Then I guess you'll have to go with us."

JJ shook her head. "Can't."

"Can."

"Brantley." She dragged out his name in warning.

Surely he understood. He'd been there for her this past month. He and Reese both. Ever since she stood Baz up on Thanksgiving, she'd been in a bad place, and they hadn't given her shit about it. It had been doubly hard on her considering she worked with the sexy blond detective she was doing her best to avoid.

Plus the holidays, being alone for them. Or rather, the third wheel since Brantley was determined to drag her around with them so she wasn't completely alone.

Needless to say, JJ didn't want to relive the month of December.

Brantley clearly got the message, because he held up his hands in a sign of surrender. "Fine. You win."

JJ exhaled, a little surprised but overwhelmingly grateful he was giving up.

"But you have to call me when you leave here," Brantley insisted. "And when you get home. That way I know you made it safe."

"I will." JJ looked past him at Reese. "You want me to take Tesha to my house tonight?"

Reese was immediately shaking his head. "No. I'd like her home with us. We'll be back around midnight."

"No problem. I'll make sure she's safe and sound in the house before I go."

"Thanks."

JJ nodded, looked back at Brantley. "I'll be fine. I promise."

"I know."

When he reached for her, she gave in to the hug but stepped back before he could pull another stunt like throwing her over his shoulder and going all caveman.

"Now go. Get. Y'all need to go out, get your drunk on. Have fun. And be sure to kiss at midnight. It's good luck, you know."

Brantley frowned, clearly not believing her. Not that she believed it either, but the goal was to send him on his way before he could sweet-talk her into joining him. If he tried hard enough, they both knew she would eventually give in.

"Fine. But don't say I didn't warn you," he said cryptically as he turned and headed for the stairs.

"What does that mean?" she asked, watching as they both headed down. "Brantley! What does that mean?"

"Happy New Year, JJ," Brantley called out, not looking back as they walked out the door.

She stood there, staring down for the longest time, trying to process what he'd said. What was he warning her about?

Exhaling heavily, JJ turned back to her desk. She had things to do. Important things.

She took a deep breath, pushed her chair back to her desk, and eased into it. After flexing and wiggling her fingers, she settled them on the keyboard, eager to get back to it. One of these days, she was going to find Juliet Prince. It *would* happen, but only if she was diligent. Meaning she didn't have time to go out anyway.

"Even if I wanted to," she muttered.

Not that she did.

Nope.

As long as she kept telling herself that, it would be true.

A few minutes later, her phone dinged. She didn't bother pulling up the camera. JJ knew it was a notification that Brantley and Reese had triggered the motion detector as they were leaving.

"Just you and me, girl," JJ said to Tesha, who was curled up on the dog bed in the corner. "Exactly as it should be."

Sebastian Buchanan knew what he was about to do could quite possibly be the worst idea in the history of all ideas.

Worse than the Snuggie for dogs or Smell-o-Vision, or—for God's sake, why change a good thing?—New Coke.

Unfortunately, Baz didn't know another way.

For the past month, he'd waited patiently for JJ to talk to him, to explain why she'd stood him up rather than go to his father's house for Thanksgiving dinner as she'd agreed to do. It was the least he deserved, although he already knew why. He merely wanted to hear it from her.

Baz remembered that day clearly. He'd been waiting for her that morning, expecting her to arrive at his apartment, only to get a text from Brantley to let him know she had cold feet, and rather than letting her spend the day working, Brantley was talking her into going to his parents with him and Reese.

What was Baz supposed to say to that? *No, sorry, she already promised me?*

It didn't work that way, so he'd conceded after attempting to contact JJ only for his texts to go unanswered. Knowing he would drive her further away if he pushed too hard, Baz had gone to his father's without her. And despite the fact he would've preferred she be there, he'd had a good time with his family.

However, leaving it to JJ to explain why she'd ghosted him or maybe just apologize was like waiting for hell to ice over. In other words, it wasn't going to happen. Hell, the woman had a way of avoiding him even when they were in the same room. She was good at it, too.

And yes, he'd considered making the same offer at Christmas but feared it would be a repeat of their previous ordeal, so he'd resisted the urge only to see on social media how she'd enjoyed her time with Brantley's and Reese's families. It was then he decided it was time they addressed this issue once and for all, only that was thwarted when Trey had uncovered a hot lead on a very cold case. The task force had spent the past three days and nights vigorously searching for the needle in the haystack, only they'd come up empty.

In an effort to reset, they were taking a break for one night. One single night.

So here he was, in Brantley and Reese's driveway, climbing out of his truck, mentally gearing up for one of the most important conversations of his life, all the while praying he could maintain his composure and not launch into the many reasons JJ should just give him a chance. He had a list, after all, and was fully prepared to plead his case if she needed him to. His only concern was that he was going to look like a whining, pathetic idiot and she was going to hate him for a different reason.

As he closed the truck door, inhaling the cool night air, he heard footsteps on the front porch, turned to see Brantley and Reese strolling toward him.

Oh, right. They were headed out to Moonshiners. They'd invited him, but Baz had politely declined, fully intending to wallow in his own pity by his lonesome.

Yet here he was.

"Thought you were gonna stay home," Brantley said as they approached him in the driveway.

"I was," he admitted, then nodded in the direction of the barn. "Figured I'd…"

There was sympathy in Brantley's gaze when he said, "She's in her office. Perfect timing, too."

Baz glanced between his two bosses as he tried to decrypt Brantley's comment. He hadn't told anyone he was coming, so how was his timing perfect?

"He's assumin' you were goin' for stealth," Reese explained, patting him on the shoulder.

Baz cocked an eyebrow, still not understanding.

Reese motioned toward the eave of the house. "Camera. Motion detector? She'll just think the alert's from us leavin'."

Ah. Yeah, he could see how that could be construed as perfect timing. Since the grounds were monitored, streaming live video that JJ kept running on the big screen downstairs, the only chance he had of getting by undetected was if she was upstairs in the loft working. Considering JJ was definitely a flight risk, if she saw him on the cameras, he might just find the barn empty.

"If you crash and burn here, head over to Moonshiners," Brantley said. "The first one's on me."

"Thanks." Baz had a feeling he was going to need a beer or three after this conversation.

"Happy New Year." Brantley smacked him on the back. "And good luck."

He would most definitely need it, Baz thought as he rounded the house and headed for the barn. There was a good chance JJ was scaling down from the second-floor window at that very moment.

Chapter Seven

WHEN BAZ DISAPPEARED AROUND THE SIDE OF the house, Reese got settled in the passenger seat of Brantley's truck, buckled his seat belt with a resigned sigh.

Although it was usually the first thought he had when there was a destination in mind, Reese knew better than to insist he be the one to drive because it would get them nowhere. Brantley wasn't keen on being a passenger, hence the reason they were always in Brantley's truck rather than Reese's. Not that Reese was all that fond of riding shotgun, but he figured someone had to compromise. And since there were plenty more compromises to be made in their relationship, Reese had conceded this one. Mostly.

"Prediction?" Brantley asked as he steered the truck toward town.

He turned his attention to the man behind the wheel, admiring Brantley's profile. "On?"

"Baz and JJ."

Reese thought about the conversation that was about to take place between the detective and the hacker extraordinaire. Considering how emotionally charged the air was when those two were in the same room, *anything* could happen.

"I'm not even gonna pretend to know what's goin' on with them. Why? What do you know?"

"Nothin'." Brantley smirked, cutting his gaze over briefly. "Swear. She's keepin' that close to the vest."

Yeah, Reese figured. JJ was a lot of things—fun, witty, smart, irritating, even—but she was not one to let many people get too close. And when it came to her feelings for Sebastian Buchanan, she treated them like they were a national secret.

Granted, Reese had witnessed the train wreck that was Baz and JJ for the past month, had seen how she mooned over the man although she pretended not to notice he was alive. She was delusional if she believed she was fooling anyone. Anyone except for Baz, anyway. For whatever reason, the detective wasn't picking up on the clues that she was still hung up on him. Which, now that Reese thought about it, probably had something to do with all the moping Baz had been doing since they broke up.

Reese wouldn't have had a problem with it except there were only six of them on the task force at the moment, which meant there were very few exchanges taking place when two of those six were going out of their way not to talk to one another. Reese knew Charlie and Trey were feeling the tension because they were the ones forced to share an office. At least Reese and Brantley could get away from them for most of the day since they spent the majority of their time out in the field. And when they didn't, their offices were now in the house.

"You didn't seem surprised Baz stopped by tonight," Reese told Brantley.

"No. Not surprised." Brantley kept his eyes on the road. "I knew he'd break sooner or later."

"They've gotta figure this shit out," Reese said on a heavy exhale. "Preferably sooner rather than later."

"They will. Eventually. But probably not tonight." Brantley was shaking his head. "She's too stubborn. It'll have to be on her time, when she's ready." There was a hint of a smile. "But I figure Baz knows that. He's just doin' his part, puttin' in the effort to prove he's not like the jackasses she usually goes out with."

"You think he's in love with her?"

"Oh, yeah. No doubt about it."

Reese wanted to say that was fast, but he held his tongue. He certainly wasn't in a place to pass judgment. Considering how quickly and how hard he'd fallen for Brantley, he'd be a hypocrite to do so.

"We're stayin' till midnight, right?" Brantley asked as he pulled into the packed parking lot of Coyote Ridge's one and only bar.

"Yeah." Reese glanced at him, raised a brow in question. "Why?"

"Just wonderin'."

Finding the parking lot completely full, Brantley got creative, making his own parking space in the adjacent field. Two more vehicles were pulling in behind them, doing the same thing.

Once the truck stopped, Reese reached for the door handle but came up short when Brantley grabbed his arm, pulled him back.

He fought his natural instinct to look out the window to ensure no one was watching. It was something that made him feel incredibly guilty—kissing someone you loved in public shouldn't require forethought—but Reese still did it. Or had the urge to do it.

Somehow he managed to keep his eyes on Brantley, but it wasn't easy.

"I'll suffer through for you," Brantley whispered, leaning in, his breath fanning Reese's lips.

"Will you?"

"Yep. I'll keep my hands and my lips to myself, even. But you'll make it up to me when we get home."

In a daring move, Reese licked Brantley's lower lip but pulled back quickly. "Deal."

Smiling at Brantley's guttural groan, Reese climbed out of the truck, walked around to meet him. After a trek, they were finally walking into Moonshiners, a place frequented by the residents of the small town, revered by pretty much everyone.

As far as Reese was concerned, this was a home away from home, a place he felt welcome, one he didn't mind kicking back and relaxing in. He figured that had more to do with the people than the décor, because God knows the inside could use a fresh coat of … everything.

He wasn't sure whether Michael "Mack" Schwartz, the proprietor, had updated the interior since the walls were originally erected, whenever that was. The wood paneling was worn smooth and grayed, the floor the same. Tables and chairs—all mismatched at this point—had seen plenty over the years, but they still remained intact, kept in decent condition.

Now the bar, on the other hand … that was kept pristine, waxed and shined, with old stools discarded and new ones added whenever they were needed. Since it was the heart of the place, Reese figured Mack probably had an attachment to it.

Behind the bar tonight, Rafe Sharpe was manning things, a rare smile on his boyishly handsome face.

"Where's Mack?" Brantley asked, squeezing into a vacant spot to order a couple of beers to start them off.

Rafe never stopped moving. "Took the night off."

"The sheriff takin' the night off, too?" Brantley asked, referring to Mack's husband, Jeff Endsley.

"Think so."

"Seriously? Busiest night of the year?" Reese chuckled. "I guess there's a first time for everything."

"Tellin' me." Rafe's grin widened. "So tip big tonight, will ya?"

"You know we will," Reese replied.

It was strange to see Rafe smiling, much less stringing together more than a couple of words. Since the day Rafe returned to Coyote Ridge, shortly after his brother Rex started major renovations on their family's home, turning the infamous old farmhouse on Main Street into a bed-and-breakfast, Rafe had been slowly weaving himself into the fabric of the town once again. Not that anyone really knew much about the man who'd disappeared back when he was just a kid. Reese only knew the stories he'd heard, and from what he understood, Rafe, only ten years old at the time, had shot and killed his own father in order to save his brother's life. It was a fucked-up story, one that had left Reese grateful to have had loving parents growing up.

"Would you look at this." The words were spoken in a slow drawl chock full of wonder, surprise, and a hint of amusement.

Reese turned, finding himself nearly face-to-face with none other than Cyrus Jernigan, Brantley's ex-fuck-buddy and the bane of Reese's existence.

Just like every other time he'd seen Cyrus, his first instinct was to punch the guy in the mouth.

He refrained.

Barely.

"I didn't know I'd be seein' you boys tonight," the man with the goofy grin said, his dark brown eyes pinned on Brantley in that way that pissed Reese off.

He knew he had no right to be jealous of the fact Brantley and Cyrus used to be friends with benefits. That was all it was according to Brantley, and Reese believed him. However, he knew Cyrus liked to pretend they were still carrying on, mainly to get Reese riled up. As much as he wanted to ignore those intruding stares and the come-hither glances Cyrus projected at Brantley, he couldn't.

"Hey, Cy," Brantley greeted as he passed Reese a beer. "Thought you were in California."

"Am. Was." Cyrus grinned. "*Will be*. I'm just in town for a couple days."

Reese took a swig of his beer, silently willed Cyrus to vanish into the ether, with no luck.

"You know if Trey's comin' tonight?" Cyrus asked, his full attention on Brantley.

"He mentioned he might," Brantley told him. "But if I were you, I'd keep your distance."

"Why's that?" Cyrus smirked. "You jealous I've been intimate with your brother?"

Brantley snorted. "Not even a little."

"Then why're you warnin' me off him?"

Brantley's response was a wide, knowing grin as he nudged Reese with his shoulder. "See ya 'round, Cy."

"Maybe we can catch up," Cyrus called out when they were walking away.

"Maybe not," Reese muttered and heard Brantley chuckle softly.

Brantley's tone was meant to reassure when he said, "Nothin' to worry about there."

Reese knew that. He did. But that didn't mean Cyrus didn't get on his very last nerve.

"Did you know Magnus was gonna be here?" Brantley asked from behind him.

Magnus was sitting at a table, chatting it up with a couple of ladies who were blushing and giggling like he was the most interesting man in the universe.

"No," he told Brantley. "Had no idea."

As he weaved his way through the room, he found he was still watching the man with the quick smile and the glint in his eyes.

While some probably considered Magnus attractive, Reese didn't think that was his most appealing feature. It had more to do with his personality, that easy charm that drew people to him, along with the mixture of vulnerability and determination Reese could see in his eyes.

Brantley motioned toward an empty table. "Care if he joins us?"

Reese answered with a nod of his chin, encouraging Brantley to invite him over.

Brantley cleared his throat, the sound loud enough to have Magnus glancing over. Magnus shot them a surprised but exuberant smile, and he was instantly on his feet, saying his goodbyes to the ladies, who didn't appear pleased with his abrupt departure.

"I didn't know y'all'd be here," Magnus said in a gravel-laced drawl.

"Have a seat." Brantley nodded toward one of the empty chairs. "We could say the same to you. Since when do you hang out in our neck of the woods?"

"Got a wild hair up my ass. Needed to get outta the house tonight, go someplace exotic." Magnus gestured toward the bar, grinning, his wide hazel eyes glinting with amusement. "Seemed to fit the bill."

"Exotic." Reese huffed a laugh, took a swallow of his beer. "Never thought I'd hear *anyone* call Moonshiners that."

"Really?" Magnus took a swallow of beer, looked around. "Seems fitting."

"Clearly we're thinkin' of two different words. By which definition is this"—he waved a hand—"exotic?" Reese challenged, still laughing.

Magnus's eyebrows rose as he considered. "All of 'em, I figure. I mean, that picture over there"—Magnus motioned to a palm tree painting in a cheap frame—"kinda gives it that tropical feel. Add in some piña coladas…"

Reese laughed. "Is that all you need? Palm trees and piña coladas and you've got exotic?"

Magnus shot him a lopsided grin. "Of course."

"This comin' from a guy who thinks a strip club's exotic," Brantley commented with a chuckle.

"Hey," Magnus laughed, "*exotic* dancers, right? They're a real thing. I've seen 'em with my own two eyes."

Reese barked a laugh.

Brantley glanced his way, grinned, but Reese was fairly certain he was laughing at Reese's reaction, not Magnus's play on words. And damned if he didn't love when Brantley looked at him like that.

"Good to see I'm not the only one with extravagant tastes." Magnus mock toasted with his Bud Light, glancing around the room. "Speaking of … Trey with you?"

Reese glanced at Brantley, raised an eyebrow. Seemed Trey was the man of the hour.

That wasn't the first time Magnus had inquired about Brantley's older brother since the two of them had been introduced a few weeks ago. In fact, Reese had gotten the impression Magnus was interested. Especially after their last encounter when Magnus was over to work with Tesha and Trey stopped by.

"He'll be here," Brantley said easily, winking at Reese.

"How's that work, anyway?" Reese found himself asking Magnus, slightly embarrassed that he'd said it aloud.

"What's that?" Magnus lifted his beer to his mouth.

"You know. You and, uh … your … dating life."

Magnus's lopsided grin was back. "I thought you had your lesson in the birds and the bees, Tavoularis."

Brantley laughed. Reese felt himself blush.

Magnus leaned forward, elbows on the table. "Oh, you mean because I'm bisexual, and Trey's clearly not?"

Brantley sobered, still smiling. "Now that you mention it, how *does* that work?"

"It's not like I'm askin' the guy to marry me," Magnus answered. "And who knows, maybe Trey'd be interested in—"

"I'm gonna cut you off right there," Brantley inserted with a choked laugh. "One, because Trey's my brother and I've got no interest in his sex life."

"And two?" Magnus probed.

"Two, I know my brother. He's not interested in the ladies. Never has been, never will be."

Magnus tilted his beer to his lips. "Good to know."

As Reese took another pull on his beer, he watched Magnus. Might just be an interesting night after all.

STANDING OUTSIDE THE BARN, MENTALLY PREPARING HIMSELF for the conversation ahead, Baz took a deep breath and keyed in the code to unlock the door. When the lock disengaged, he could hardly hear it over the pounding of his heart and the overabundance of *maybes* and *probablys* running through his head at the moment.

This was the worst idea he'd ever had. *Maybe.*

He was going to get shot down. *Probably.*

Oh, hell. What was he doing?

He shook off the negative thought. Backing out was *not* an option.

When he woke up this morning, Baz had decided today would be the day he confronted JJ. He'd given her a reprieve for the past few weeks because he could tell she felt bad about standing him up. However, he had fully expected her to approach him. Since she hadn't and likely wouldn't, he knew he had to make the first move—bad idea or not.

Which meant he had to do this.

More negative thoughts snuck in.

He would be spending the rest of the night alone. *More than likely.*

He could very well be spending the entire next year alone.

Okay, so that was doubtful, but, hey, it still intruded when it wasn't necessary.

Of course, Baz wouldn't know any of those for certain unless he tried, right?

That right there was a *definite.* What was the saying? You didn't know unless you tried?

On the other hand, it wasn't like it could be any worse than the guy who said, *Hey, Coca-Cola's a great product, but why don't we try something new?*

Here goes nothin'.

He opened the door, stepped inside.

"I told you, Brantley, I'm not goin'," JJ shouted from upstairs. "Might as well give up."

Baz let the door close behind him as he headed for the stairs. His stomach twisted, something it had been doing for the past month. Although he was pulling it off, pretending he wasn't affected by JJ shunning him, there was no denying it hurt. Especially since he'd thought they were making strides in their relationship.

Of course, if you asked JJ, she'd say they hadn't been in a relationship at all.

"Hey," he greeted when he stepped onto the second floor, stopping with his hand on the rail.

JJ's head snapped over, her light green eyes wide. She opened her mouth, closed it, then opened it again. Nothing came out, but Baz continued to wait, content to just stare. She was by far the most beautiful woman he'd ever laid eyes on. And no, he wasn't usually one to wax poetic, but there was something about JJ.

She looked good tonight, as usual, dressed down, casual, with her shoulder-length dark hair piled haphazardly on top of her head, held in place with a big plastic clip. A few strands had come loose, brushing her cheeks, more hanging at the back of her slender neck. The gray University of Texas sweatshirt she wore was at least two sizes too big, covering all those glorious curves. But the jeans... Heaven help him, they were the dark pair, the ones with the rips in the knees, and they molded to her in a way that should be a crime. Her feet were bare, her toenails painted a bright glittery green, and beside her desk was her favorite pair of slippers, the brown suede Uggs with the fuzzy stuff inside.

"Why're you here?" she asked, her voice coming out in a harsh whisper as she got to her feet, clearly surprised to see him.

"Same reason you are."

Her eyes narrowed, searching his face as though she was translating his words into a language she understood.

"Because you'd rather work on New Year's?" she scoffed. "Doubtful."

Baz remained where he was, blocking her only escape path should she decide to run. Knowing JJ, that was certainly something she was considering.

"You shouldn't be here," she stated. "You should be out"—she waved her hand toward the wall—"celebrating with everyone else."

"While you're working? Doesn't seem fair," he replied.

They were at an impasse, staring at one another as though waiting for the other to make a move.

Finally, JJ spun on her heel, started to pace away. Baz prepared to follow despite the fact there was nowhere to go, but realized it wasn't necessary when she turned around suddenly and marched back toward him. Her hands went to her hips, and there was a frown on her beautiful face.

"Why're you really here?" She took another step forward. "And don't lie to me."

Baz found it interesting that she always tacked that on, although he hadn't lied to her once.

"Figured I'd be shitty company if I went out," he explained. "Since I didn't want to drag anyone down, thought maybe you'd like some help."

JJ glanced over at her laptop, back to him. "I'm not workin' on anything important."

A lie, no doubt. Everything JJ worked on was important. And he knew she spent the majority of her spare time searching for Juliet Prince.

"Nothing important?" he challenged.

"No." Her forehead creased with her frown, her hands still on her hips, only her fingers had started to flex and tap. It was a nervous tic, one he wasn't sure she knew she had.

Tesha must've sensed the tension building, because the dog lifted her head, cast a sideways glance their way. Clearly believing it was safe, she curled up tighter and went back to sleep.

When Baz looked back at JJ, he noticed her eyes had glassed over, unshed tears filling them. His heart clenched in his chest.

How they'd managed to make it a full month without having this conversation, he didn't know. But now that he was here, now that she was paying attention to him, Baz knew they had to clear the air between them.

Before he could begin, JJ blurted, "You might as well just say it."

"Say *what*?"

"Don't play dumb with me, Detective."

And there it was. JJ had gone back to referring to him as Detective rather than by name. He'd learned early on that was her way of keeping him at arm's length.

"You know exactly what I'm talkin' about."

Baz leaned his shoulder against the wall, feigned a casualness he didn't feel. "Actually, I don't. Enlighten me, JJ."

"If this is your way of punishin' me, you suck."

Punishing her? What the fuck was she talking about?

He stood tall, frowned. "I'm not punishing you. Why would I?"

JJ held her ground, facing off with him, hands still on her hips. "Because I stood you up on Thanksgiving."

"That was weeks ago." And he'd been biding his time, trying to determine the best approach to ensure they got back to the way things were before.

"Yes," she agreed. "It was. And ... and because of..." She waved her hand.

"Because of *what?*"

"Because I've avoided you all this time."

Baz held her gaze. "Since I'd been expectin' it, perhaps I wasn't all that bothered by it."

Okay, fine. That *was* a lie. Baz *had* been bothered by the fact JJ had ghosted him on Thanksgiving after agreeing to go with him to his father's house for his family's traditional holiday dinner. He'd been looking forward to spending some time with her, time outside of work, outside of her regular routine. And yes, he'd been looking forward to introducing her to his family.

However, he wasn't lying when he said he had expected it. JJ was a complicated woman who'd successfully erected many walls around her heart in an effort to keep everyone out. So, yes, the one thing Baz knew she would do when given the opportunity was run. And hide.

Fortunately, he was a patient man. He'd already told her they would take this at her pace, and the last thing he expected was for this to be easy. The important things in life never were.

"So you're not pissed?" she asked, her eyes sliding over his face as though she was attempting to read his answer by his expression.

He could see the wariness, the concern. And yes, he could see that she had feelings for him even if she would be the first to deny it.

"Pissed, no," he admitted. "Disappointed, yes."

She swallowed hard. "Well, I'm good at that. Disappointin' people. It's what I do, Detective."

Baz closed the distance between them before she had a chance to bolt. He cupped her jaw with one hand, sliding his fingers along the warm, smooth skin of her neck.

"*You* didn't disappoint me, JJ," he whispered. "I want to spend time with you. That's all. But I told you, I'll wait for you."

"I don't want you to wait for me, Baz," she said, her voice quivering slightly.

Now *she* was lying.

He'd gotten rather adept at pinpointing untruths because that was his job. And while JJ wasn't necessarily easy to read, he'd caught on to a few of her tells. When she lied, she pressed her front teeth against her bottom lip. It was subtle, but he'd been looking for it.

"Tough shit," he said, brushing her cheek with his thumb.

Oh, how he wanted to kiss her, to touch her, to make love to her. Before he'd ruined things by pushing her too hard, they'd gotten close. Shared some dinners together, talked endlessly although mostly about work. And yes, they'd ended up in bed together, which had been fucking fantastic. Phenomenal, in fact. And for a few moments, he'd even believed some of those walls were coming down and JJ was letting him in.

He should've known better, but he'd been blinded by his feelings for her. What he felt for her … well, it had taken him completely by surprise. He'd never fallen for a woman so hard, never wanted to spend every waking moment with anyone.

"Baz."

Pulling himself out of his thoughts, he stared into her eyes. "I'll wait for you, JJ," he repeated.

JJ shook her head, took a step back.

Baz had no choice but to drop his hands, to stare at her and wait for her to decimate him one more time because that was what she did to him when she continued to push him away.

"We can't do this," she said softly. "We can't. It just doesn't make sense, you and me."

He could feel his heart shredding in his chest, but he didn't move, didn't speak.

"I'm not in a place where a relationship makes sense. It just doesn't. Not right now." She lifted a finger, pointed at his chest. "And you can't put your life on hold for me. I'm not worth it."

That was more painful than anything. The fact that this woman honestly believed she wasn't worth anyone's time. Someone had broken her heart. The question was who? He doubted it was a romantic interest who'd broken her down. JJ wouldn't let a man do that. But someone had.

"JJ—"

"Please don't," she rasped, her eyes glassy with tears.

That was the only reason he backed off, didn't push the issue. He wasn't sure he'd survive seeing her cry.

"Okay," he finally said. "Okay, JJ. You win."

As he was walking out of the barn, he heard her sob, and it was like a two-by-four upside the head.

Chapter Eight

TREY STEPPED INTO MOONSHINERS NOT KNOWING WHAT to expect for the night.

He'd never been a big fan of New Year's. To him it was celebrating just another day, so he didn't quite understand the rationale behind it. He figured some people needed a reason to party, and this was just another in a long list.

He was not one of those people.

Not to mention, aside from the occasional beer, Trey didn't drink all that much. Had something to do with how he'd overindulged a few years ago, right after his split from his ex-husband. He'd teetered damn close to becoming an alcoholic and it worried him, so these days he shied away from booze.

Granted, he wasn't usually one to pass up a night out, some time to hang with both family and friends, having some laughs, enjoying conversation. Unfortunately, he wasn't feeling it tonight, but he wasn't quite sure why that was. Something just felt off.

However, he wasn't going to give his brothers or his cousins a reason to give him shit, so when they invited him to Moonshiners to ring in the new year right, he had graciously accepted.

And here he was.

"Hey, Trey!"

At the sound of his name, he peered over, saw one of his many cousins waving him over. Holding up a finger in the universal sign for *give me a minute*, Trey went to the bar, waited until the bartender glanced his way.

Tonight, the bar was being manned by Rafe Sharpe rather than by Moonshiners' owner, Mack. That had been the case a lot lately, almost as though Mack was handing over the reins. Whether or not that was true, or if it was simply because Mack was now happily married and spending a large portion of time with his husband, Trey didn't know, nor would he ask, because it wasn't any of his damn business.

Maybe he should pick up the superstitious ritual of making New Year's resolutions. If he did, that would be his main one for next year: mind his own damn business. Starting right now.

"Beer?" Rafe asked.

Trey nodded, figuring he couldn't be heard over the din of conversation anyway.

He waited patiently while Rafe retrieved a bottle, flipped the top off, passed it over.

"Put it on my tab."

Trey's head swiveled around, triggered by the familiar voice, but he quickly turned back to Rafe. "No. My own tab, thanks."

"It's good to see you," Cyrus said kindly.

Yeah, well, Trey wished he could say the same. But it wasn't good to see him. Probably wouldn't be for a while. Not until Trey got over the fact Cyrus had up and moved to California, letting him know by way of text message. Not even an attempt to speak directly to him.

Trey immediately sidestepped Cyrus, taking a long pull on his beer and pretending not to notice the man.

"Come on, Trey." Cyrus's normally monotone voice held a hint of a whine that made Trey cringe. "I'm in town for a couple days. Can't we just be civil?"

To Cyrus, *be civil* actually meant *fuck*.

Trey felt his blood begin to heat, but not from lust or desire. No, this was anger. Hot and potent and directed at the man who'd pretty much dumped him after revealing he now lived fourteen hundred miles away.

Rather than engage in conversation and risk punching the guy he used to fuck, Trey headed for the cluster of Walkers he'd seen on his way in. Noticing the cousin who'd waved him over was now grinning and making googly eyes with some chick, Trey detoured, heading over to where Brantley and Reese were sitting at a table with that dog trainer Reese had recently hired to help him with Tesha. Magnus something or other.

When a firm hand landed on his arm, Trey stopped, turned slowly. He glanced down at where Cyrus was holding, then met the man's dark brown eyes.

"What's your problem?" Cyrus asked, his voice lower than before, his grip tightening ever so slightly.

Before he could launch into all the reasons he wanted Cyrus to take a hike, he heard, "Get your ass over here, Trey," the command coming from behind him, barked by none other than his brother, Brantley.

"I'd love to," he said, glaring at Cyrus before shrugging off his hand.

"You're not seriously pissed off at me, are you?" Cyrus asked, his eyes probing his face as though looking for the answer.

"I'm not pissed, Cy. I don't give a damn one way or the other."

"I took a job," Cyrus complained. "I'm not sure what you wanted me to do."

Giving him a heads-up would've been a good start, but Trey didn't tell him that. Truth was, he didn't care that Cyrus had taken a job in fucking California. Or that he'd moved and didn't bother to tell Trey until he had a new permanent address. Trey was merely dealing with some wounded pride, that was all. And until he could get over being ghosted by a man he'd thought he had a connection with, Trey didn't care to chat it up with him.

Because nothing good would come from this conversation, Trey turned and walked away. He took the vacant seat beside the dog trainer, doing his level best not to look at the guy.

Not an easy thing to do, he would admit. Magnus Storme was one of those guys who caused people to do a double take. Could've been his hazel eyes—heavy on the blue side tonight thanks to the navy-blue Henley he was wearing—or those chiseled features, the purposely stubbled jaw, or even those perfect lips. Or it could simply be the combination. Magnus was put together in a way that most men weren't, and although some would've probably called him pretty if it weren't for the previously broken nose, Trey would have to say Magnus was devastatingly handsome.

And if that wasn't enough, the guy had a body meant to undress slowly. He figured buying T-shirts off the rack wasn't an easy thing to do with arms that size. His chest was impressive, too. As was the fact it tapered to a trim waist, then down nicely to what was a world-class ass.

Not that Trey was looking at Magnus's ass. The guy was sitting down, after all. But he'd gotten a glimpse the day they met and a few times since. And yeah, he'd given the man a once-over.

Okay, twice.

Three times, max.

For Christ's sake, he wasn't interested. He was merely acknowledging a good-looking man. That wasn't a crime.

"Nice to see you again," Magnus said, those hazel eyes glittering with the same charm that oozed from the guy.

Trey jerked his chin in response, tipped his beer to his lips, took another swallow, and glanced up at the bar. He was going to need another. Maybe two. Or shit, he'd just go with the whiskey. That would likely do the trick even if it would send him spiraling down a hole he didn't want to end up in.

When he peered over at Magnus again, he saw the man was still watching him.

Just fucking great. The last thing Trey needed was this ridiculous temptation he'd been ignoring for the past few weeks, ever since he'd been introduced to Magnus.

"Mind if I sit?" Cyrus asked, pulling over a chair and not waiting for a response.

Oh, good. A distraction.

Trey peered over at his brother and Reese, saw that Reese was all but shooting daggers out of his eyes and they were aimed right at Cyrus. Good to know Trey wasn't the only one irritated with him tonight. Although he knew Reese's irritation was permanent and for different reasons.

"Hey, new guy. How's it hangin'?" Cyrus asked Magnus.

"It's hangin'," Magnus drawled, his voice raspier than Trey remembered.

A quick glance at Magnus and Trey saw the man briefly glance over at Cyrus before turning his attention back to Trey, a smirk on his lips.

"Low and to the right, maybe?" Cyrus chuckled, clearly mistaking the response as an invitation. "Name's Cyrus. And you would be?"

He didn't want to do it, but Trey met Magnus's gaze, held it for a second before Magnus politely looked over at Cyrus again.

"Magnus," he answered. "Magnus Storme."

"And how do we know you, Magnus Storme?" Cyrus crooned.

"He owns Camp K-9," Brantley answered. "We hired him to train Tesha."

"Ah." Cyrus looked far too interested in the information. "Tesha's the dog, right?"

No one answered as they were all beginning to look around, as though trying to figure out how to slip out of this uncomfortable situation unnoticed.

Even if Cyrus was a nice guy, even if no one usually had a problem with him—aside from Reese—Cyrus had always been the kind who couldn't take a hint. He was evidently bound and determined to insert himself into this evening, and if that happened, Trey was going to go home early. He didn't care about counting down to the new year anyway.

"Tell me about yourself," Cyrus suggested to Magnus. "I'd like to get to know you better."

"Oh, for fuck's sake." Trey couldn't hide his exasperation. "Is there anyone you won't fuck?"

Several things happened at once. Magnus's gaze, filled with both amusement and heat, shot to him, Brantley snorted a laugh, Reese coughed, and Cyrus … well, Cyrus continued to undress Magnus with his eyes.

Realizing he sounded like an ass but not willing to apologize for it, Trey excused himself, heading for the bar.

As he walked away, he forced himself to focus on the floor in front of him rather than look back to ensure Cyrus wasn't cozying up to Magnus. It wasn't easy, but for the life of him, he couldn't say why that was. There was just something about Magnus Storme that fogged his brain.

Funny, considering just a couple of months ago, Cyrus had been the one fogging his brain.

And that technically made him an idiot, didn't it?

By the time he made it across the crowded room, the urge to look back had caused a buzzing in his head, but still he fought it off, making it up to the bar, waiting his turn. And okay, fine, maybe he did glance back as Rafe was getting him another beer but not on purpose.

Liar.

"You're an idiot," Trey mumbled to himself, turning away from the temptation he hadn't expected to be waiting for him when he arrived.

Trey had absolutely no business wanting that man. None.

Not that he did. Want Magnus. Nope. Not him.

Focusing on the task at hand, Trey waited for Rafe to get his beer.

Even with his back to the room, Trey could see Magnus in his mind's eye. Rock fucking solid. Most notably his biceps and his chest. Trey could only imagine what the guy looked like without his shirt on.

Wait.

No.

He was *not* going to imagine Magnus without a shirt. Hell, he wasn't going to imagine Magnus at all.

"Fuck."

Thankfully, Rafe didn't dawdle, passing over his beer and scurrying off to help someone else.

In an effort to shake off the weirdness that had overcome him the moment he laid eyes on Magnus, Trey headed toward the pool tables in the back.

He considered joining a game, decided against it. It would be in his best interest to go home early, to avoid waking up tomorrow with another naked man in his bed and a boatload of regret to go along with it.

"You can't hide in a place this small, you know that, right?"

Trey briefly peered over at Brantley, who for some dumb-ass reason had come to join him, then returned his attention to one of the games being played.

"So the kid's hangin' out with y'all now?" he asked his brother.

"What kid?"

Trey nodded his head in the direction of the table where the others were still sitting. "I've already forgotten his name," he lied.

"Magnus. Tesha's trainer," Brantley clarified.

"Sure. That one."

Brantley lifted his beer bottle to his lips, grinned. "He's not a kid."

"Looks it. He's what? All of twenty?"

"Twenty-four."

"A baby then."

"That *kid* has been through more than you and me both."

Which was saying something considering Brantley had spent the majority of his adult years in the navy, many of them as a SEAL. And now Trey was even more intrigued.

Damn it.

"That so?" He hoped it sounded nonchalant and not at all probing.

Brantley rolled his head on his shoulders, as though working out the kinks. "Don't give him shit, Trey. He's a good guy."

Good-looking, yes. Trey would give him that. He'd been a bit taken aback by the man the very first time he'd met him. Oh, yeah, the guy tripped his trigger. But even he would admit it was a hair trigger, not exactly a great feat.

Luckily, he'd managed to avoid Magnus for the most part since then. But now … here? Who did they think he was? A fucking saint?

He downed half his beer, not tasting it.

"If you're thinkin' about bonin' him, don't. He's got a girlfriend."

Did he? That was a bit of a surprise considering the way Magnus had been eyeballing him a short time ago.

Hmm. Perhaps he shouldn't write him off just yet.

Wait. Hold up.

Nope.

Nuh-uh.

He was *not* going to see Magnus as a challenge. He didn't need any more fucking challenges in his life, thank you very much. He had more than his fair share, and the men he chose to fuck needed to be willing, eager, and easily cast off. That was a definite. Screwing a guy who worked for his brother would go against every single one of his rules. First being never screw a guy who worked for your brother.

They were new rules. So what.

He took another chug of his beer, briefly wondered where the hell the rest of it had gone.

"Cyrus better keep his damn hands off him," Trey muttered to himself when he peered over to find Cyrus grinning like a loon, all up in Magnus's personal space.

"Trey."

He heard the warning in his brother's tone, chose to ignore it.

"I gotta take a leak," he said, setting his empty bottle on a nearby table with a little more force than he intended.

This was stupid.

He should not be here tonight. Not here, not thinking about Magnus, not worried about Cyrus. What he needed to do was walk right out the front door, hop in his truck, and head home. Alone.

But he didn't go to the front door. Nope, his ass detoured down the narrow hallway—squeezing past a couple who appeared to be engaged in a rather intimate conversation—that led to the bathroom.

Sighing, he opened the door, grateful when he found it was empty.

Once inside, he did his business then washed his hands, focusing on inhaling and exhaling. There was no reason he needed to get in a pissing match with Cyrus tonight. The guy had just as much right to be here as Trey did. And since Trey had no designs on Magnus, they could get as acquainted as they wanted. He didn't give a shit.

As he dried his hands with the scratchy paper towels, Trey stared at his reflection in the mirror, mentally repeated that last part, and nodded his head, as though in agreement.

Feeling somewhat better, he exited the bathroom only to come face-to-face with Cyrus, who appeared to be waiting for him in the hallway.

"What do you want?" Trey barked, figuring they had to hash this out or his night would definitely be in the shitter.

He ignored the eyes that shifted his way, the couple now interested in this tête-à-tête.

"To talk," Cyrus said, his voice lower, lacking that easygoing charm he'd laid on thick earlier.

"Nothin' to talk about, Cy. It's done. It's over. You made it clear what was more important."

When he tried to sidestep Cyrus, he came up short, the other man blocking his path.

"Don't do this," Trey warned.

"Do what? Force you to talk to me?"

"I'm not in the mood."

"No?" Cyrus stepped forward, chuckled softly. "You're always in the mood."

Trey's gaze caught on movement behind Cyrus. That was when he noticed Magnus stepping into the hall, heading in their direction.

"Let it go, Cy," Trey said, this time trying to dodge the other way.

Cyrus blocked him again.

"Why don't we just go back to your place," Cyrus suggested. "We can—"

"Hey," Magnus interrupted, a frown on his face, as though he wasn't pleased by what they were doing. "What's goin' on here?"

To Trey's surprise, Cyrus stepped back, gave Trey room to breathe. If he'd had time to be grateful, he would've been.

"Now it gets interesting," Cyrus said with a mischievous smirk. "The more the merrier. That's my motto."

"Yeah, *no*," Trey said quickly. "You two are welcome to party without me."

Trey wasn't sure what he'd expected to happen next, but it certainly wasn't for Magnus to insert himself where Cyrus had been, toe-to-toe with Trey. Nor was it for Magnus to reach up, slide his hand behind Trey's neck, and pull him down for a kiss.

A kiss he willingly indulged. Why he did, he would never know, and he feared it would be something he wondered for quite some time.

Christ. The man could kiss. Bold and daring, yet there was a vulnerability and easy charm he could sense beneath it. Enough that Trey knew Magnus would surrender control if he so much as whispered the command.

The hand at the back of his neck tightened, Magnus's thumb brushing along his jaw. It was a move he didn't anticipate, one that had his heart kicking into overdrive.

He could feel Cyrus staring, knew he was likely wondering the same thing Trey was: what the fuck?

"It's like that, huh?" Cyrus asked, his tone having lost the happy-go-lucky vibe once more.

"Yeah," Magnus answered softly, staring at Trey. "It's like that."

Trey had no idea what came over him in that moment. Perhaps it was because he knew Magnus was fucking with him or maybe because Cyrus had been the last one to fuck him over. Whatever the motivation, Trey leaned forward, gripped Magnus by the shirt and jerked him closer, fusing their mouths together.

Fuck the whole chaste brushing of lips. This was a buffet, and Trey took advantage of it, sliding his tongue right into Magnus's mouth as he backed the man against the wall, pinning him between the wood paneling and his body.

When Magnus moaned, Trey thought he might lose it.

And when Magnus's hand tightened around the back of his neck again, his tongue joining in on the action, Trey got light-headed.

The only thought that went through his head?

What.

The.

Fuck.

Only this time, it was on repeat.

MAGNUS KNEW HE WAS IN OVER HIS head before he'd intervened, before he'd gotten close enough to get a whiff of that spicy cologne Trey wore, to see the gray striations in his blue eyes, to feel the heat of his breath on his lips.

He'd expected the kiss. Hell, he'd even suspected it might rock his world, but this…

Ho-oly-fu-uck.

He never would've expected to be damn near knocked off his feet, to be manhandled so expertly that his cock fucking hurt from how hard it was. Yeah, he liked being shoved up against the wall, his mouth plundered by this dominating man. So much so, he didn't give a shit that they were in a public place or that this could go sideways at any given moment.

His hand curled firmly on the back of Trey's neck, holding him there as their lips and teeth clanged and clashed. This kiss made the first seem like a prelude. They'd gone from zero to sixty in under three seconds, and Magnus saw no signs of slowing down, didn't matter that there was a proverbial brick wall in the distance.

He moaned, unable to help himself as he bore Trey's weight, content to be pinned to the wall beneath his muscular body. He wanted to strip him bare and get intimately acquainted with every fucking inch, to—

"He's gone," someone said. "You can stop now."

Magnus wanted to punch the fucker who spoke, because it caused Trey to pull away. The only saving grace was that Trey was sucking in air the same way Magnus was, those steel-blue eyes looked as rocked as he felt. He briefly considered explaining what had happened, why he'd inserted himself between him and Cyrus, but wasn't sure it would do any good.

In his defense, his actions were altruistic. He'd done it to get the other guy to back off, because clearly Trey had been attempting to get away from him, and the man didn't seem to be getting the hint.

What were friends for, right?

His good deed had backfired big-time because now that he'd been lip-locked with Trey, he wanted to explore it further, to see just what was behind that sexy, brooding exterior.

Someone cleared their throat and Magnus remembered where he was. It took effort, but he let his hand fall from Trey's neck, pulling back so he could fill his oxygen-starved lungs.

"I need some air," Trey finally said, stepping back.

"Trey. Wait."

He didn't, and Magnus wasn't sure he should go after him. He managed to refrain, heading back to the table, back to where Brantley and Reese were talking.

Brantley glanced around him, frowned. "Where's Trey?"

"Said he needed some air." Magnus picked up his beer and downed what was left of it.

"Not that it's *any* of my business, but if you wanna"—Reese fluttered his hand—"whatever's goin' on with you and … you might wanna go after him."

"I'll give him a minute."

"You won't *get* a minute. If I know my brother, and I do, he's debatin' on whether to come back in or head out. He'll do that for a minute, maybe two, then he's leavin'," Brantley said, stressing the last word.

Magnus frowned.

"Seriously," Brantley added.

Reese's mirroring expression confirmed it.

Magnus glanced over at the door as though he could see out into the night, to where Trey had disappeared to.

Fuck.

"Happy New Year," Brantley called out with a gruff laugh as Magnus walked away.

Heading for the door, Magnus tossed his empty beer bottle in one of the recycle barrels. He wasn't exactly sure why he was going after Trey, other than to apologize for overstepping. The words would only be to placate Trey, of course, or maybe just an excuse to talk to him, because Magnus wasn't the least bit sorry. He would do it again in a heartbeat given the opportunity.

He ventured outside, let the cold air fill his lungs as he glanced left and right before stepping off the wooden porch and into the gravel parking lot.

It was cold out tonight, but not so cold he needed a coat. Especially not since his blood was still flowing thick and hot through his veins thanks to that mind-blowing kiss he'd engaged in.

Magnus scanned the rows of vehicles he could see. The small bar was packed tonight, something he was told happened quite frequently. Probably had something to do with Moonshiners being the only bar in town and a favorite amongst locals. Magnus wasn't exactly a local, having grown up in the small town just east of Coyote Ridge. Close enough to venture through, but rarely ever to stop, until recently when he'd acquired two new clients who lived here.

Not knowing where Trey had parked, Magnus took a chance, heading for the right side of the building.

It appeared to be his lucky night, because there was Trey, leaning against the wall, head tilted back, eyes closed. Debating, apparently.

Magnus cleared his throat to signal his approach.

"Go back inside," Trey instructed without bothering to look his way.

Never good with authority, Magnus moved in closer rather than away.

"Go. Back. Inside."

He continued until he was no more than a foot away. "No."

"Trust me, kid, I'm not a man you wanna fuck with."

"Kid?" Magnus snorted. "Did you really just call me a kid?"

"You're what? Barely old enough to drink?" Trey's head came down to level, eyes opening, his disdain apparent.

Magnus didn't back down. Wouldn't. "Twenty-four," he said, content to know Trey'd had the mind to find out how old he was.

"Like I said. Kid."

"Maybe you're just an old man," he taunted. "You're what? Forty?"

"Pretty damn close," Trey said with a sigh.

He'd pegged Trey for late thirties because he knew Trey was older than Brantley and Brantley was thirty-five, but he'd never really given much thought to an actual number. He didn't give a damn about age. It meant nothing. Certainly not to a man who'd lost his entire family when he was sixteen and had been taking care of himself since. Some didn't have the luxury of being a kid for long, and Magnus fell in that category.

"What happened in there?" Magnus asked, not willing to let this be over simply because Trey willed it to be.

"Not a damn thing."

"Felt like somethin' to me."

Trey's eyes locked with his, and for a moment, neither of them spoke. Magnus relived those too-brief moments when Trey's tongue had been dueling with his own. It had been hotter than anything he'd experienced as of late.

"You're out of your depths here, Magnus," Trey stated firmly.

"Am I?"

Trey's head cocked to the left, eyebrows lowering. "What happened to the girlfriend?"

Magnus frowned, not understanding.

"Brantley told me." Trey sighed. "Warned me offa you right quick."

"No girlfriend," Magnus informed him. "Boyfriend, either."

Trey's gaze skimmed his face. "You're bisexual?"

"I am." No sense denying it. "You got a problem with that?"

Trey continued to stare, but when he spoke, it wasn't to answer Magnus's question. "Like I said, you're outta your depths."

"Why? Because you've got a problem with the walk of shame? Fine. We'll go to your place. I'll be the one shamefully walkin' come mornin'."

"Thanks, but no thanks." Trey stood tall.

When he turned to walk away, Magnus reached out, grabbed his arm.

Not a good idea, he realized when Trey spun around and had him pinned up against the wood-sided wall before his brain could process the move. Did it make him a masochist that he was enjoying that sort of treatment?

"I'm so fuckin' tired of people manhandlin' me tonight," Trey ground out.

Magnus probably should've apologized, maybe given up and walked away.

He did neither of those things.

"Yeah, well, that makes one of us," he rasped as he leaned forward and crushed his mouth to Trey's by palming the back of his head and holding him there.

Like their earlier kiss, it was mind-numbing. His entire body lit up from the inside out. His cock swelled as all the blood in his veins headed south.

For a brief second, Trey kissed him back, and it was fucking amazing. Unfortunately, it ended with Trey shoving away, breaking the kiss.

"I'll shred you," Trey bit out, his voice so deep, so dark, it sent chills down Magnus's spine.

"I'd like to see you try."

"You're outta your depths, Magnus. I suggest you back off."

"And if I choose not to?"

Standing there in the shadows, Trey's big body looming over him, Magnus had never wanted anyone more. There was something about being at this man's mercy that did it for him. He'd never had that before. Yes, he usually preferred women to men, but he had indulged in both being that he was openly bisexual. But he tended to favor the path of least resistance when it came to his sexual encounters.

Until now.

"Because if I have a choice," he continued when Trey did nothing more than stare, "then I choose not to."

TREY HATED THAT HE WAS SO FUCKING weak.

This man…

Practically a fucking *kid*…

He was tempting Trey in a way he had no business tempting him.

"You really want me to back off, you're gonna have to make me," Magnus declared, so much confidence in his tone.

So.

Fucking.

Weak.

Trey hated himself for wanting Magnus despite the fact the man was too stupid to know when to run. Or maybe because of it.

"You know there's only one thing I want from you," Trey told him, moving in close, keeping his voice low.

"Then you should take it."

He was so fucking cocky, so sure of himself, and damn it if that didn't turn Trey on.

"I will shred you," Trey promised. "It's inevitable."

"Maybe. Or maybe I'll shred you."

Unfortunately, Trey knew that was the logical outcome, because he tended to get in over his head, but he was doing his best to warn Magnus off. It would save them both a hell of a lot of time and save Trey another round of heartache.

"Only one thing, Magnus," he repeated

"I'm not expectin' roses and wine here, cowboy." Magnus leaned in, voice low and gruff. "I'm expectin' you to *fuck. Me.*"

Oh, he certainly wanted to.

But he had to be on his turf. That was the only way. He didn't want to know anything about Magnus, not where he lived, not what color his sheets were, not whether or not he kept a clean house. Knowing shit like that made it possible for Trey to want more and he couldn't. Wouldn't. He didn't want more. He wanted one night of passionate, sinful, dirty sex. That was all.

"Follow me."

Magnus peered up at him, his confusion evident.

"To my place."

"You sure that's wise? I'll know where you live, might get the wrong idea."

"How else did you think we'd get there?"

Magnus's smirk was wicked. "I was thinkin' black hood over my head, trussed up in the trunk of a car."

"I drive a truck."

"That works, too. As long as you tie me down."

Trey grinned. Yeah, he could like this one.

Simply because he could, Trey gripped Magnus's jaw, leaned in, and kissed him. This time, he didn't amp it up; instead, he leisurely explored his mouth, lightly licking his tongue, his teeth, letting his other hand glide down Magnus's side, then dipping his fingers into the waistband of his jeans, jerking him closer.

"I will shred you," Trey whispered. "That's a promise."

"Do your worst, cowboy."

Trey pulled back, stared into his eyes. "I plan to."

Chapter Nine

***

"TESHA, WAS THAT THE RIGHT THING TO do?" JJ asked the sleeping dog a short time after Baz walked out the door.

Watching him leave had been more difficult than she'd thought it would be. For whatever reason, she'd thought he would fight for her. For them. Instead, he did the same thing everyone else in her life did: walked away.

And fine, perhaps she was having a mini pity party in the here and now, because yes, he'd left at her request, merely doing what she wanted, so it wasn't his fault. It was just that, deep in her heart, she'd hoped he would ignore her pleas for space and distance. Just once she wished someone would push back, demand that she listen to reason rather than walk away.

"It's the right thing. Makin' him leave … it's the right thing to do," she whispered, more to assure herself than to continue the conversation with Tesha.

JJ glanced at her computer screen one more time, sighed. No way would it benefit her to sit here another minute. As it was, her thoughts were elsewhere, her focus for shit, and every attempt she'd made to find Juliet Prince today had failed.

Maybe she should go to Moonshiners, have a couple of beers with Brantley and Reese. It would be the only way to avoid ringing in the new year alone.

Or perhaps she'd just go home, have some wine, and go to bed early. What did celebrating the new year get her, anyway?

JJ glanced at the full bowl of popcorn and the opened can of Orange Crush. She suddenly wasn't in the mood for those either.

"All right, girl," she finally said, pushing to her feet. "Let's get you in the house."

It only took a couple of minutes to gather her things, another few to let Tesha do her business then get her into the house and settled.

It wasn't until she'd locked the front door and was off the porch that she realized Baz's truck was still in the driveway, the detective sitting in the driver's seat.

Son of a—

Her heart skipped a beat, but she ignored it. This *was* for the best. She had absolutely no business bringing Baz down, which she would do if she let him hang around any longer. It was inevitable. She brought everyone down with her mood swings and her self-loathing. Her father said it was her superpower.

As she clicked the key fob to unlock her little SUV, she wondered whether her father actually believed that made her feel any better about herself. Then again, she seriously doubted Joshua James cared. He did hate her. Both of her parents did. For whatever reason, they blamed her for her brother's death. For years, they'd accused her of letting Jeremy down, not bothering to help him in his time of need, and because of that, according to them, he'd had no other way out, so he had taken his own life.

They couldn't have been more wrong. About all of it.

Without looking at Baz's truck, she reached for the door handle, fully intending to jump in and speed off. No sense making this night worse than it already was.

His window lowered. "JJ."

She sighed, fingers curled under the door handle. So close.

"I don't want to leave things like this," he said, opening the truck door and getting out.

There should've been no reason her body responded to such a simple statement, but it did. Every time. No matter how hard she tried to convince herself she didn't want this man, that they didn't belong together, her body still craved his touch.

"JJ, please."

She doubted it was his words, more so his voice that had goose bumps forming on her arms. She'd always liked Baz's voice. Hell, she liked everything about the sexy detective, had since she'd first laid eyes on him. And that was the problem, wasn't it? There wasn't anything about him she didn't like, which scared the shit out of her. JJ was all too aware of what falling in love could do. Which was the very reason she had no desire to bring about heartache if it was at all possible. After all, that was why she had continued that ruse of a relationship she'd had with Dante for so many years. It damn sure hadn't been because she thought the guy would ever change.

Baz's boots crunched on gravel as he approached. She took a deep breath, let it out slowly. She could do this. She would be strong.

"Why don't we go grab some coffee," he suggested. "Talk this out."

"Baz…"

When she turned around, she found he was closer than she'd anticipated. Close enough she was forced to look up at him. Close enough she could feel the warmth of his body against her front, smell the delicious scent of his cologne. She had no idea which fragrance it was because he was obsessed with so many different ones, but it went right to her head.

And the fact that she found him absolutely irresistible only made it more difficult to stick to her guns.

"Where?" she heard herself ask.

"Your choice. I'm sure there're plenty of places open late tonight," he said, that sexy voice rumbling. "Or, if you prefer, we can go back to your house."

She was already shaking her head, but JJ wasn't sure which of those options she was rejecting. It irked her that Baz had the ability to leave her tongue-tied and confused. It'd been that way since the day she met him.

"The diner's still open," she said, wondering just what she was doing. This was not supposed to be happening.

"I'll follow you."

He did, and all the way to town, JJ berated herself. Not because she had agreed to coffee but because what she'd wanted was to invite him back to her place. To pick up where they'd left off before he'd invited her to have Thanksgiving with his family. Why had he gone and complicated things? She didn't understand it. They'd been doing fine, hadn't they? The sex was off the charts, plus they had enjoyed one another's company. Why did men think women were eager to move things to the next level? JJ was content to stay in the getting-to-know-you phase for … well, forever.

And of course, she would go and find a guy who wasn't looking for a one-nighter or short term or even temporary. Worse, he was open and honest about it, taking things at her pace. He'd been patient with her since the beginning, never rushing, never pushing. Every step they'd taken had been her move.

Right up until that holiday-dinner invitation. He was responsible for that one.

However, agreeing to go *was* on her.

JJ pulled into the diner's parking lot. It was still pretty busy, which she figured would only continue through the morning hours when those celebrating the new year would venture out for a late-night/early-morning meal before spending the first day of the year sleeping it off.

Before she'd even turned off the ignition, Baz was outside her door, opening it for her just like he always did. He was a gentleman of the highest order. Something else she found incredibly hot about him.

Once inside, a waitress approached, and Baz asked for a table for two, preferably in the back. With a glowing smile, Rachel Talbott, the daughter of the diner's owners, led the way to a booth.

"Two coffees, please," he told her before she could disappear.

"Comin' right up."

"I figured you'd be out with Brantley and Reese," JJ said, attempting to make small talk when the silence got too heavy.

He didn't respond, merely stared, those brilliant blue eyes skimming her face and heating her up from the inside out.

God, he was … hot. That strategically disheveled sandy-blond hair, the teal-blue eyes, those sharp cheekbones, and the angular jaw. It all came together to make a remarkable-looking man. Don't even get her started on his body.

To keep the conversational ball rolling, she continued, "They were headin' to Moonshiners. You can probably still—"

"I don't want to talk about Brantley and Reese." His eyes skimmed her face, his expression serious, tone equally so.

Yeah, this was a big mistake. Then again, she'd known it would be.

JJ huffed. "Fine. What *would* you like to talk about?"

"Us."

She refrained from saying, *There is no us.* It was her go-to phrase, the one that had gotten her through all the rotten relationships in her past, of which there'd been many. Okay, maybe not many, but enough.

"I'll take that as a good sign," Baz said softly.

"What's that?"

"That you're not in denial."

JJ couldn't help it, she chuckled. He knew her so well, despite the fact they hadn't known one another for all that long. It hadn't been until they'd encountered him while working on their first official case that Baz had become part of their world. Since then, JJ had relied on him so many times. Not only at work but also … also to make her smile, because that was what Baz did. He made her smile even when she didn't want to.

He held her gaze, those ridiculously blue eyes scorching her down to her soul.

"Baz…"

She could see the question in his eyes. He wanted her to speak her mind.

Like that could ever happen. JJ wasn't one to open up about her feelings, never had been, and she had no desire to start now. It was easier to pretend she didn't give a damn about anything, to take on that carefree air that got her through each and every day.

Before she could shift topics to something more comfortable, her cell phone rang. Since the only person who ever called her was Brantley, and only when a text wasn't suitable for the situation, she snatched it from the table, hit the talk button without bothering to look at the screen.

Holding Baz's gaze, she answered with, "Hey, why are—"

"JJ, I need to talk to you." The words were rushed, dripping with what sounded like panic.

Frowning, she tried to place the voice. Definitely not Brantley.

"JJ? Are you there?"

Pulling the phone away from her ear, she peered at the screen. The number wasn't familiar, nor was it in her contact list, because there was no name.

"I wouldn't call you if it wasn't urgent."

She was about to ask the caller to identify himself when it clicked, the metaphorical lightbulb shining brightly in her head.

"Dante?" She listened for a response, heard only breathing, so she added, "Where are you?"

JJ saw Baz's expression shutter, his eyes darkening, clearly with disapproval.

Dante's tone bordered on hysterical when he answered with, "I didn't know who else to call. I need to talk to you. It's urgent."

"About what?"

"I can't say over the phone," he said in a rush. "It's … life-or-death."

It wasn't the theatrics that got her, because JJ was used to Dante's dramatic flair. It was that he sounded so unlike himself that she agreed. "Fine. Where?"

He was huffing, his words high-pitched. Definitely panicked. "Your house. Ten minutes. Alone. Please, JJ."

Swallowing hard, she nodded as though Dante could see her. "Okay."

The call disconnected abruptly, and she looked up to see Baz was watching her closely.

"Dante's callin' you?" he asked, sounding not at all pleased but at the same time curious.

JJ glanced at her phone. "Evidently." She met his gaze again. "I have to go meet him."

Admittedly, she was using Dante as an excuse to get a pass on this conversation. Despite her feelings for Baz, or maybe because of them, she wasn't ready for them to put the brakes on completely. And if she stayed, she knew that would be the outcome, because aside from being a world-class hacker, JJ's other talent was pushing people away.

"Why?" Baz asked.

"He didn't say." She scooted out of the booth. "I'm sorry."

She didn't give him a chance to speak before she was hurrying toward the door. Any other time, she would've told Dante to go to hell, but right now, she was honestly concerned. She'd known Dante Greenwood for most of her life, and even though he'd fucked her over on too many occasions to count, JJ couldn't leave him in the lurch. Never once in all that time had Dante asked anything of her.

Not like this.

It took less than ten minutes to get to her small house just a few blocks from Main Street. She slowed down on the approach, scanning the street and the houses. There were no other vehicles in her driveway or parked at the curb, which she took to mean she'd beaten him there.

It wasn't until she was unlocking her front door that her heart was jolted by a man stepping out from beside her house.

"Holy shit, Dante," she gasped, clutching her chest. "You damn near gave me a heart attack."

His eyes were wild, his usually perfectly styled hair sticking up everywhere. He certainly didn't look like the well-put-together man she'd known for so long.

Dante scanned the street, the yard, behind him, keeping to the shadows as he approached the front porch.

"We need to go in," he urged, his voice low and still ringing with hysteria.

Figuring she might get answers if he felt safe, JJ opened the door, stepped inside, and was practically mowed down by Dante.

"Lock the door," he insisted, moving toward the kitchen, peeking around the wall.

JJ locked the door and turned to watch as he hurried to check all the rooms, as though he expected her to have company.

"No one's here," she assured him.

"You don't know that."

JJ frowned. "I'd like to think I do. This *is* my house."

"Where's your gun?" he asked.

Now she was really getting concerned. "Dante—"

"Where is it, JJ? Are you armed?"

"It's not on my person, no," she snapped back. "It's locked up. Why?"

"You need to get it." His gaze swung to the windows, the door, then back to her. "You need to have it on you."

JJ was beginning to wonder if he was high. Dante had never been the paranoid type, but he was clearly on edge right now.

"Now, JJ!"

She shrieked at the bark in his voice, instinctively flinching.

"Get it now," he demanded.

"Fine," she huffed, stomping to her bedroom, then into the closet. She placed her finger on the biometric sensor, retrieved the gun, checked the chamber and the safety, then carried it with her back to the living room, where she found Dante peeking out the blinds on her front window.

He shot a look back over his shoulder, so she held it up, showed him she had it.

"Good. Keep it with you."

When he went back to looking out the window, JJ knew she needed some answers, but before she could get them, she was hoping to calm him down some.

"Can I get you somethin' to drink? Water? Tea? Coffee?" she offered.

"I'm good," he said on a rush of air before moving back to the couch and sitting on the very edge of a cushion. It was like he thought the thing would swallow him if he dared lean back and get comfortable.

"Are you sure?"

Dante waved her off, his gaze fixed on the front door again.

Since she'd already talked herself into coffee at the diner, JJ decided she could make a cup. What could it hurt? At the very least, she would be up at midnight, ringing in the new year with all the happy people.

"Give me a minute, then," she said, moving toward the kitchen. "I'm gonna make some coffee."

After setting her gun on the counter, she popped a K-cup into her Keurig then set her mug beneath it. When it started the process of heating water, she stood there, watching it as though that would make it hurry along.

While she waited, she figured maybe she could get Dante started on explaining why he was so freaked out and why he felt she needed to be armed. And more importantly, how he thought she could help.

"So, what's so urgent that you had to come over on New Year's?" she called out, eyes focused on the coffee now dripping much too slowly into the cup.

He didn't respond, but she was used to that. When they had dated, Dante rarely paid much attention to her.

"I can't help if I don't have some details, so you might as well cough 'em up now."

JJ never did get a response.

Then again, the bolt of pain that pierced her skull and had her crumbling to the floor took her mind off the answers.

In fact, it took her mind off everything as the world went black.

Chapter Ten

BAZ HAD HOPED HE WOULDN'T FIND HIMSELF here tonight, but he'd known it was a possibility. After all, convincing JJ to talk to him had been a long shot.

What made it worse was the fact that she had agreed and then she'd hurried off to meet her douche of an ex-boyfriend rather than try to work things out with him.

If that wasn't telling, Baz didn't know what was.

Now as he walked into Moonshiners, he let the sounds block out all the emotional turmoil he'd experienced in the past hour. He wanted to believe her meeting with Dante didn't mean anything, but Baz wasn't one to make assumptions. Not usually and certainly not when it came to JJ. Then again, she hadn't hesitated to rush to Dante's rescue, so what was he supposed to think?

One look at the crowd surrounding the bar told him if he went that route he'd probably still be waiting by the time the clock struck twelve, so Baz bypassed it, hoping one of the waitresses might get to him faster.

He scanned the room, saw Brantley, Reese, and Cyrus chatting at one of the tables. He headed over, smiling and nodding at a few familiar faces. He purposely kept going, not in the mood to chat it up with those who would want to know how he was doing, what he was up to. Right now, the only thing he was interested in was numbing himself with booze.

"I was hopin' you *wouldn't* make it tonight," Brantley said when Baz approached the table.

Baz could see the concern in his boss's eyes, knew Brantley had been hoping for the same thing he was: for him and JJ to work things out. Unfortunately, neither of them got their wish tonight.

"You and me both." He nodded at Reese, then Cyrus. "But here I am."

"Grab a seat."

Baz glanced around, noticed there weren't any to be had. His gaze snagged on a couple of ladies looking his way, a pretty blue-eyed blonde wearing a dark purple sweater, smiling brightly. Baz managed a smile back, thinking that she was the polar opposite of JJ, and he wasn't sure that was a bad thing right now. Considering the woman he was in love with had left him high and dry so she could go traipsing after her ex-boyfriend, maybe it was time he found someone who could take his mind off Jessica James. Even if for only one night.

"Here, take mine," Cyrus offered, standing. "I've gotta make the rounds."

Dragging his attention away from the woman whose flirty smile had turned coy, Baz nodded, said, "Thanks, man."

When he took a seat, Baz noticed Brantley glancing at his phone.

Reese obviously noticed, too, because he leaned in, resting his forearms on the table, staring over at the man. "You've been watchin' your phone for half an hour now. There a problem?"

Baz watched the crease form in Brantley's forehead as he stared at the screen. "JJ was supposed to text me when she left HQ."

"That's my fault," Baz told him. "I waited for her. We stopped at the diner for coffee."

There was a hint of relief on the man's face mixed with an inkling of confusion. "And yet you're now here."

One of the waitresses—a pretty redhead named Lydia—hurried by, tapping him on the shoulder as she did. "Usual?"

"Yes, ma'am."

She shot him a quick, playful wink. "Comin' right up."

There was something to be said about frequenting a bar in a small town, something he'd never done until he came to work for the task force. He'd always been a big-city guy. Nightclubs, one right after the other, keeping him entertained for hours on end.

"Didn't go well with JJ?" Brantley prompted when Baz turned back to them.

Hell, he'd thought it was going in the right direction, right up until… "Dante called," he announced, "interrupted our conversation."

He saw the shift in Brantley as the man sat taller, eyes going hard. "What did he want?"

To profess his undying love? To convince her they belonged together forever and ever? To see if she'd feed his fish while he was out of town? Or walk his dog? It could've been any number of things, but Baz was already assuming the worst.

However, he wasn't going to admit that aloud. "She didn't say, just hightailed it outta there. Said she had to go meet him."

"Where?"

Baz shrugged. He hadn't gotten the details, and he wasn't sure he would've wanted them had he thought to ask.

"What the fuck does Dante want?" Brantley grumbled.

Since it sounded rhetorical, Baz didn't bother to answer.

"Son of a bitch," Brantley muttered.

"Are you texting her?" Reese asked when Brantley began keying something into his phone.

"Yeah. She told me she'd text me when she got home, too. She owes me that much."

"I'm sure she's fine," Reese stated. "She's a big girl. Knowin' her, she's already hip deep in an argument. That seems to be how the two of them communicate."

Baz knew very little about JJ's relationship with Dante, past or present.

"She hasn't talked to him in a couple of months," Reese tacked on. "Dante, I mean. I know that much."

Baz nodded, glanced around for the waitress. It really wasn't his business. He had no claim on JJ. She'd made it very clear that wasn't what she wanted from him, and despite how much he loved her—and he did, there was no doubt—Baz had no desire to beat his head against a brick wall over and over again.

Thankfully the waitress swung by, quickly passing him his beer.

"Thanks."

"I'll be back to check on you in a bit," she said in a seductive whisper, her hand gently curling over his shoulder.

Baz glanced at her hand, up to her face, saw the invitation there.

Tilting the beer to his lips, he watched her sashay away, admired the way those jeans hugged her cute little ass.

His gaze snagged on the blonde at the next table. She was watching him, her lashes fluttering, another shy smile on her mouth. He tried to imagine what she'd look like with her perfectly coifed hair mussed from rolling around beneath him.

The sad part was, he couldn't picture it no matter how much he wanted to.

And yes, he fucking wanted to. More than he cared to admit. Baz was not the sort of man who wanted to be slogging after some woman like a lovesick puppy, and that seemed to be all he'd done since the day he met JJ. Where had it gotten him, huh? Here on New Year's. Alone while JJ was off with Dante doing God only knows what.

When Baz turned back, he swore he saw sympathy on Brantley's face. It bothered him, but he managed to keep his mouth shut.

"Let's make a toast," Reese prompted, lifting his beer. "To starting fresh in the new year."

Baz considered it, then lifted his beer. "To starting fresh," he echoed.

And as he clinked his bottle against Reese's and Brantley's, Baz tried to tell himself it was a good plan. Start fresh in the new year.

He glanced at the blonde once more.

Perhaps it was time for a change.

As the minutes ticked by, Brantley remained seated at the table with Reese. He watched Cyrus flirt with men, both gay and straight, getting shot down at every turn. Knowing Cyrus, the man would still manage to go home with someone before the night was through.

Brantley observed Baz pretending not to make eyes with the little blonde at the table next to theirs, saw the redheaded waitress keeping her eye on Baz as though she was calling dibs. It both surprised him and didn't that Baz would consider someone other than JJ. There was no way Baz could deny how he felt about her. On the other hand, JJ had stuck to her guns thus far. Evidently, she really didn't want a relationship, and a man could only take so much rejection before he needed some sort of validation.

While he actively observed what was going on around him, Brantley continued to glance at the door, wondering whether or not Trey and Magnus would return. *That* was certainly a match he hadn't seen coming.

When an hour went by, he knew his brother was no longer pondering decisions in the parking lot. He was gone, and since Magnus hadn't returned, he could only assume he'd gone with him.

"I think there's somethin' in the water," Brantley said, still processing all that he was seeing.

"Your brother's a big boy," Reese stated. "He can handle himself."

Brantley glanced at him. "Who said I was talkin' about Trey?"

Reese grinned. "You weren't?"

"Well, yeah. But still. You're not allowed to be a mind reader."

"No?"

"No. It'll make all the dirty thoughts I have of you awkward." He grinned, took a sip from his beer. "For you."

Reese laughed, a blush creeping up his neck.

Yeah, he fucking loved that about Reese.

"But seriously," he continued. "Magnus and Trey? Did you see that one comin'?"

If Cyrus's earlier reaction was anything to go by, Brantley wasn't the only one surprised. The man had come marching out of the hallway with rage burning in his gaze. Truth was, Brantley'd never seen Cyrus pissed before. Hell, he hadn't figured the man was even capable.

"I did not, no," Reese said as they both now stared at the door where Trey and Magnus had escaped a short time ago.

"They're not comin' back," he told Reese.

"Nope." Reese tipped his beer back, and after draining the bottle, he looked over. "Why're we still here?"

"Because I like to wine and dine you."

"Do you now?" Reese smirked.

"Although I'd prefer you naked when I do," he admitted, grinning back.

More color came into Reese's face, and it made him smile wider. God, he loved this man. Every damn thing about him.

The doors opened, and Brantley's gaze shot over because he'd been watching it for so long. Nope, still not Trey or Magnus. He didn't recognize the newcomer.

Reese leaned in closer, motioned toward Baz with his beer bottle. "What do you think about this?"

"I think it's unfortunate but probably necessary. He's gotta move on sometime."

Reese stared back at him as though he couldn't believe the response.

"What?"

"You said they'd figure it out. He and JJ."

Brantley nodded. "Yeah. I was hopin' they would."

Unfortunately, since Baz was vigorously flirting with the blonde now, he didn't think that was going to happen.

"Are you second-guessin' yourself now?"

Was he?

Reese chuckled. "You know it's okay if you're wrong."

Brantley tossed back the rest of his beer. "I'm not wrong."

"Sure you are."

"Tell me one time I've been wrong."

"Today?"

Brantley frowned. "When was I wrong today?"

Reese nodded toward the door. "You said Trey wasn't over Cyrus yet. I suspect you were wrong about that."

He had said that, huh? Just that morning over breakfast. Hmm.

Brantley exhaled, leaned back in his chair. He did his best not to look at his watch, although he'd been wishing for the past hour that it was midnight. They still had a couple hours to go.

He peered over at Reese. "Remember what JJ said? About kissin' someone at midnight bein' good luck?"

"I remember."

"You think it's true?"

"Never heard it before."

Neither had Brantley.

"But I have heard that who you kiss at midnight's gonna be who you're with for the year," Reese noted.

Brantley considered that for a minute. "Is that so?"

Reese shrugged. "Don't know if there's any proof it's valid, but yeah, I've heard it."

Brantley leaned closer to Reese, lowered his voice. "Usin' that logic, what's it mean if you're also fuckin' the one you're kissin' at midnight?"

He probably should've, at the very least, let Reese take his drink before he asked the question. Because he hadn't, Reese choked on his beer.

And then in a move that surprised the shit out of Brantley, Reese leaned over, put his mouth right to his ear and said, "Not sure. But maybe we should go home and find out." Reese paused. "You know, *after* midnight."

It took everything in him not to rip Reese right out of his chair and drag him out the door.

Chapter Eleven

BRANTLEY WASN'T SURE HOW HE MANAGED TO make it to the countdown.

For the past few hours—no, scratch that—ever since he saw Reese sporting the hat and boots, the only thing he'd wanted to do was find a horizontal surface and ... hell, he didn't have an agenda after that. As long as they were naked, it didn't much matter what they engaged in. It was always sinfully hot and intensely satisfying.

And now that they'd toasted the new year like friends—he had no desire to put Reese on edge by expecting anything more in public—Brantley was ready to take their party back to the house and start the naked part of the evening.

"Please tell me you're ready," he said to Reese, leaning in close to his ear since the bar was still loud.

"I am, yeah."

Brantley pulled back, sighed his relief.

"You think we should convince Baz to jet, too?" Reese asked.

He glanced over, saw Baz downright cozy with the blonde. Looked as though he'd finally made a decision, considering he'd been flirting with both the redheaded waitress and the blonde all night long.

As much as he hated to see it, to know that Baz was moving on, Brantley couldn't blame the guy. After all, this was what JJ had been pushing him toward for the past month. Right into the arms of some woman who would not allow Baz to think about JJ for at least a few hours.

"Nah. He's a big boy," Brantley answered. "But we will take his truck, make sure he doesn't drive in his current condition."

"Good idea."

While Reese convinced Baz to hand over his truck keys, Brantley went to the bar, closed out their tab, covering Baz for the night, too.

Reese approached holding Baz's keys up. "I'll see you back at the house."

After signing the credit card receipt, Brantley hightailed it out of there. He made good time getting home, shaving nearly a solid minute off the time all because he was eager to get his hands on Reese.

When he arrived, he found the house was still dark, but Baz's truck was parked out front, meaning Reese had double-timed it, too.

"Reese?" he called out when he made it inside.

Toenails clicked on hardwood, and he glanced down to see Tesha moving toward him, a little hesitant but no longer cowering at any and every sound.

"Hey, girl," he greeted, scratching her head when he moved close enough. "It's all good. Just me."

Evidently she was happy with that, because she turned and trotted back to her bed in the living room.

Hearing sounds coming from their bedroom, Brantley headed that way, pausing in the doorway.

The bedside lamp was on, and Reese was stripping off his shirt, revealing the deliciously sculpted body Brantley loved to ravish every chance he could.

"Damn," he muttered, leaning his shoulder against the jamb. "I like the show."

"Do you?" Reese taunted, looking up as his fingers moved to the button on his jeans.

"Oh, yeah. Keep goin', cowboy."

The blush that crept up Reese's neck made Brantley's dick hard. There was something so sinful about a shy yet confident man.

He watched as Reese did a slow, slightly uncoordinated strip tease. He'd mistakenly believed he could remain cool and collected through it all, right up until Reese's boxer briefs disappeared and the man stared back at him with a bashful but ridiculously sexy smile on his face.

Brantley took a step forward, setting his hat on the dresser then unbuttoning his shirt. He closed the distance between them, while Reese stood gloriously naked, watching him. Once he tossed his shirt to the floor, he was on Reese, fusing their lips together while his hands roamed over smooth, hot skin.

"Do you know how hard it is to keep my hands off you?" Brantley whispered, sliding his lips down Reese's jaw, his neck. "All fuckin' night, the only thing I could think about was touchin' you." He nipped Reese's neck. "Tastin' you."

He trailed his lips over Reese's collarbone, down. Reese moaned when Brantley licked one taut nipple while tweaking the other as Brantley eased down to his knees.

Taking Reese's cock in his mouth, he stared up at the gorgeous man, enjoying the way Reese's mouth opened as another moan escaped him. He teased and tormented, taking his time, listening to those rough, needy groans coming out of the man he loved.

"Don't make me come," Reese said gruffly, palming Brantley's head. "Not yet."

"You have somethin' else in mind?" he asked, releasing Reese's hot, velvety flesh from between his lips but not his fist.

"Oh, yeah." Reese pumped his hips, fucking Brantley's fist.

"You sure about that?"

"Yes," Reese huffed with a laugh, pulling out of Brantley's grasp before urging Brantley to his feet. "And it requires you to be naked."

"Does it?" Brantley took care of that in a hurry. "Now what's on the agenda?"

Reese's smile was both salacious and mischievous, telling Brantley it was going to be a damn good rest of the night.

They eased down onto the bed, hands continuing to roam, lips and tongues melding as they savored one another. Although there was a tension that was building to an ultimate crescendo, Brantley didn't want it to end, so he maintained a steady pace, backing off when he feared they would get to their destination before he was ready.

"Christ," Reese breathed out. "I need you so fuckin' bad. Let me have you, Brantley," Reese ground out, his tone becoming more demanding.

"You've got me." Brantley nipped Reese's lower lip. "Tonight and always."

"Now," Reese commanded.

It was a side of Reese he'd seen more of in recent weeks. Truthfully, he'd never considered being with an alpha because he was one and ultimately liked being in control. But it worked with Reese somehow. Despite, or maybe because of, that delicate balance.

Without complaint, Brantley conceded control, allowed Reese to take over.

On his back, he was manhandled into place, tormented with Reese's wicked touch until he was panting and pleading. And the moment Reese drove into him, Brantley was ready, accepting him to the hilt.

He banded his arms around Reese, held him firmly while their tongues thrashed and Reese's hips pumped.

"Fuck, yes," Reese mumbled against his lips. "Tight. Hot." Reese pulled back, stared down at him. "Perfect."

Brantley held Reese's gaze. "Don't make me beg."

Reese's grin was wicked, his strokes shifting to slow and shallow.

Brantley grunted, tried to take more of him. "Damn it."

Reese leaned in, his words a dark rasp when he said, "Beg me."

"Fuck. Me." He nipped Reese's bottom lip. "Now."

There was no hesitation. Reese pinned Brantley's hands to the bed, forced his knees up by his chest as he slammed in deep and hard. Brantley relaxed, letting it take him under, allowing the sensation of being filled so brutally to calm his mind and take him to the one place he never wanted to leave. Right here with the man he loved.

"God, yes," Reese grunted, driving into him over and over, faster, deeper.

Lacing his fingers with Reese's, Brantley held on for dear life. "Harder, baby."

Reese hovered over him, drilling his hips down, his cock buried to the hilt with every thrust. Again and again, Brantley was assaulted by a pleasure so intense he wondered how he would survive it.

He held on for as long as he could, content to watch Reese as he chased his own release. By the time they'd both developed a fine sheen of sweat, Brantley was barely hanging on by a thread.

There was no warning when the orgasm ripped through him, shards of electricity racing up his spine.

"Oh, fuck, yes," Reese growled, driving into him one final time as he shouted Brantley's name.

Accepting Reese's weight, Brantley held him as they both came down.

"No doubt about it," Reese rasped, "that was one hell of a way to start the year."

"Damn straight." He banded his arms tightly around Reese. "New Year's resolution: get fucked within an inch of my life every single day."

Reese lifted his head, grinned widely. "Perhaps we should see how many days in a row we can make that happen."

"I'm game if you are."

HE WAS DRUNK.
No, amend that.
He was fucking wasted.

Worst part about it, Baz knew he was, yet he was using it to justify his actions. Hence the reason he was here with this woman he did not know.

"Hence," he muttered. "Hence. Hints. Sss. Hensss-uh. Hen. Sa. Such a stupid fuckin' word. "

Blondie returned from the kitchen with the glass of water he requested, her eyes hooded, a smile on her kiss-swollen mouth. "Did you say something?"

Baz shook his head, forced a smile, and downed the entire contents of the glass. When he was finished, Blondie—she'd told him her name, he knew that, but for the life of him, he couldn't remember it—was at his side again, her thigh up against his, her hand gliding closer and closer to his traitorous cock.

"What should we do now?" she asked, her voice breathless, likely what she considered seductive, but sounded more like innocence and hope.

She answered her own question with, "I can think of a few things."

God. What the fuck was he doing here?

Because he didn't want to talk, Baz pulled her closer so he didn't have to look her in the eye as he indulged in something he didn't necessarily want.

The kissing went on for what felt like an eternity; all the while Baz enjoyed the euphoric feeling that overwhelmed him. It had nothing to do with this woman or her lips but rather the blessed absence of his feelings for JJ. The alcohol was doing its job, suspending him in a lovely state of … nothingness. And the blonde was helping things along by being all soft and sweet and making those little whimpers that told him she was definitely into this.

"I think I'll slip into something more comfortable," Blondie said when she pulled away the next time.

Baz found his own *comfortable* by flopping onto his back and tucking a throw pillow beneath his head as he smiled up at her. At least he hoped it was a smile. He couldn't really feel his lips anymore. The whiskey had taken care of that, too.

"Don't go anywhere," she said sweetly, fluttering her eyelashes, something he'd noticed she did often.

When he tried to reply but no words would come out, Baz settled for shaking his head, not bothering to lift it from the cushion.

Once her footsteps had receded in the next room, he glanced around, took in Blondie's apartment.

Frowning, he turned and lifted his head, noticing for the first time all the twinkly lights on the ceiling and walls. For a minute, he thought his eyes were affected by the whiskey, too, but then he realized those were really little lights she'd used to decorate. Fairy lights, he thought they were called.

How the hell he knew that, Baz wasn't sure. Nor did he want to know. The only thing he knew for a fact was that JJ would laugh her ass off if she came home to find someone had put up little twinkly lights all over her house.

Nope. Nuh-uh. He was not gonna think about JJ anymore.

And clearly Blondie was a big fan of purple, too, since the only other thing he could see besides the twinkling shit was purple shit. Every-fucking-where. Jars and vases filled with purples stones, different shades, different sizes. Trinkets and frames. Rugs. Blankets. Flowers. Pillows. Pillows with flowers. It was like an explosion of … the purple people eater.

Yep, even his thoughts were drunk.

What the fuck was he doing?

Twisting his head, he peered toward the bedroom door as cold washed over him. Baz did not want to be here. He shouldn't be here. He should be home in his bed. Alone.

"I hope you're ready," came a singsong voice from down the hall.

"Oh, hell," he muttered before clamping his eyes shut and sliding down so he was lying on the couch again.

If he was lucky, she would think he was asleep.

"Oh, no, you don't," she teased, the weight of her returning as she straddled his hips.

Instinctively, he reached up, put his hands on her thighs, slid them up to her hips.

And damn it all to hell, she was curvy and soft and so damn feminine. His cock made the connection, decided it liked the fact that she was hot and eager for attention. And his brain … well, his brain was completely on board with the euphoria that came along with the distraction. His heart, on the other hand… That damn organ was clenching tightly in his chest, shouting that this was wrong, that he loved JJ and he was stupid to be here.

But his brain and his cock overruled his heart, telling the damn thing it was stupid. JJ didn't love him back and he was simply wasting time.

When Blondie leaned down, her breasts pressing against his chest, her lips sliding over his neck, Baz kept his eyes closed, allowed the sensations to mingle with the whiskey, numbing him once again. All thoughts of where he was, what he was doing, and whether or not he would have regrets come morning slipped away. As did his clothes, hers.

And a short time later, after she rode him like a wild stallion, Baz lay in the darkened room, let her cover him like a blanket while self-loathing tried to seep through the lingering effects of the whiskey.

Thankfully, it wasn't long before he drifted off.

Or maybe a better way to describe it was passed out.

The next thing he knew, Baz was rolling over, opening his eyes, trying to acclimate to where he was, why he was there.

He exhaled heavily, before closing his eyes with a groan as it all came back to him. The bar, the whiskey, the blonde with the soft, curvy body and all her purple twinkly shit.

"Good morning, sleepyhead."

The cheerful voice had him wrenching open an eye, peering up at her.

Nope. It wasn't a dream. There was the blond woman from the bar, smiling down at him like she was happy to see him.

Oh, hell. Had he…? Had they…?

"Feeling better?" she asked with a giggle.

"I don't know," he admitted truthfully, trying to ignore the unease tightening his gut. "Am I?"

He forced his head to clear so he could recall the rest of the events of last night.

Going to HQ. Talking to JJ. The diner. Moonshiners. Beer.

Definitely didn't explain the blinding pain behind his eyes.

Oh, right. He'd only started off drinking beer last night. That had quickly turned to whiskey. One Jack and Coke, then another. After that, those morphed into half a dozen shots until he'd had enough to make driving impossible. But since he was here with Blondie in what he assumed was her apartment, apparently that hadn't been an issue.

"You passed out on me, you silly boy."

Silly boy? What was she, twelve?

Jesus Christ, please don't let her be under eighteen. She couldn't be. She'd been drinking last night.

He exhaled his relief.

"And to think, I got all dressed up for you and you didn't even take time undressing me again." Another giggle. "You just *whooshed* it all off me like a starving man."

There were flashes of memory, her, him, the couch. Her lying on him, rolling on a condom, riding him like he was a contender in the Kentucky Derby.

God, he'd lasted, what? All of three minutes, maybe? The whiskey had certainly affected his ability to perform.

Not that you'd know it by the enormous smile on her face.

Hating himself, he let his gaze run down her form from head to toe. She wasn't dressed up for him now.

"I got dressed, silly goose," she said, swatting his shoulder and giggling as though he'd told a joke.

Oh, shit. He'd said that last part aloud.

He forced another smile then grimaced because even that hurt.

"Didn't want to tempt you too much," she continued. "I'm meeting some friends this morning for brunch. We're kicking off the new year right. Thought maybe you'd like to go with me."

Baz winced. He wasn't sure if it was from the thought of food or the thought of spending more time with this woman when all he wanted to do was jump in the shower so he could get clean.

"It'll be fun," Blondie added, clearly not picking up on his discomfort. "I can introduce you to everyone. And when we're finished, we can come back here and pick up where we left off. Without the alcohol this time."

Where they left off? They'd had sex. Once. Which was one time more than he'd intended.

His gaze shifted over to Blondie, who was whistling while she tucked things into her purse.

Pathetic. That was what he was. Absolutely fucking pathetic.

Sitting up, he dropped his head in his hands. Surprisingly, the hangover wasn't as bad as he expected. Sure, his head hurt, but it was only a dull throb as long as his eyes were closed.

His gaze snagged on the glass of water and bottle of aspirin sitting on the small glass coffee table, right beside a basket of purple flowers.

He didn't hesitate, snatching the bottle, pouring out a couple of pills, then downing them with the water.

"So? Would you like to go with me?" Blondie crooned happily.

"Sorry," he muttered, setting the glass down and reaching for his phone. "Can't." He forced himself to look up at her. "How did I get here?"

"I drove you." She smiled brightly. "Your friends took your truck."

Right. He remembered Reese prying his keys from him, insisting he not drive. Said he could get his truck at HQ in the morning.

Fucking great.

And now he was stranded... "Where are we?"

This time Blondie frowned, her sky-blue eyes darkening with displeasure. "We're at my place."

"I figured that much," he grumbled, motioning to the purple shit everywhere. "I mean, where? What city?"

"Round Rock."

At least that was good news. Round Rock was just a hop, skip, and a jump from Coyote Ridge. He could get to his truck in minutes. Probably even walk it if he was so inclined.

Which he wasn't.

Pulling up his Uber app, he intended to call for a car, but Blondie interrupted his attempt.

"I'll drive you," she blurted. "I mean, if you want me to."

Although it would certainly be easier, Baz knew it wasn't a good idea. The last thing he wanted was to lead this woman on, to make her think there was any chance of something happening between them. Something *more*.

Without responding, he keyed in his information on the Uber app, submitted it. It appeared luck was on his side, because there was a car only a few minutes out.

"I don't want you to be late for your ... brunch."

"It's only eight o'clock," she said, pouting. "I've still got a couple of hours."

He stared back at her, confused as to why she looked like she was ready to walk out the door. Before he could ask for details, he realized he didn't care. He needed to get out of there before he did something stupid, like fuck her to make her feel better. He never had been all that good with confrontation.

Thankfully, his phone buzzed, signaling his driver was approaching.

"I gotta go," he said, getting to his feet.

He felt for his wallet, tucked his phone in his pocket, then paused and peered over at her. It was then he realized he had no idea what to say to make this situation better. Hell, he didn't even know her fucking name.

So, to avoid making it weirder than it already was, Baz made a beeline for the front door. When he stepped outside, the sun speared his brain through his retinas, but he ignored the pain.

After all, it was the least he deserved.

Chapter Twelve

Friday, January 1, 2021

JJ WOKE TO A THROBBING IN HER skull so sharp it dragged a moan from her.

The instant she tried to open her eyes, it was like a thousand tiny ice picks began hacking away at her brain.

Not doing *that*.

Closing her eyes again, she lay completely still in her bed, attempting to breathe through the pain, trying to remember why she'd decided to tie one on last night. Hadn't she learned her lesson the last time she'd overindulged? She remembered clearly promising to never do it again for this very reason.

Stupid idea.

A deep breath in through her nose, out through her mouth became her sole focus as she fought the wave of nausea that overwhelmed her. She didn't know how long she remained like that, but it was long enough for the feeling to abate somewhat, but not long enough for her to be in the clear, because the instant she tried to get up, she was leaning over the edge of the bed, retching.

As she fought to breathe deeper, she became aware of the smell. She couldn't quite put her finger on it, but it was horrid. And likely the reason—combined with the throbbing pain in her head—why she was trying to expel whatever was in her stomach, which appeared to be nothing at all.

What the fuck had she done last night to make her bedroom smell like that? Good God, it was awful.

JJ clutched the edge of the mattress, dropped her head to the pillow, and forced one eye open to look at the clock.

Eight thirty. In the morning?

She groaned.

What the hell? When was the last time she'd slept that late? Then again, she hadn't gotten obscenely drunk in a really long time either, so it made sense, she was simply dredging up all those bad habits she'd purposely disregarded when she'd decided to be a better person.

She needed to get up, get moving. A shower would likely work wonders to clear the fog. That and some aspirin, some coffee. Oh, God, yes. Coffee. It sounded heavenly right now.

When she went to move, the ice picks started up again, so she squeezed her eyes shut and relaxed.

Okay, maybe not *right* right now. Soon, though.

Wanting to block out the light streaming in through the windows, JJ smacked her hand behind her, attempting to find one of the many extra pillows she kept on her bed so she could cover her head. There were half a dozen, she just needed—

It wasn't a pillow she felt.

Whatever it was was wet.

"Eww. What the hell did I do? Throw up in the bed?" she whispered roughly, thoroughly exasperated with herself.

Because she refused to lie in vomit no matter how bad her head hurt, JJ forced herself to sit up, let the dizziness fade while she breathed through the pain.

"A little better," she finally said, covering her nose to avoid inhaling the stench.

With every jarring movement, her head hurt worse, so she took a minute. Sitting on the edge of the bed, she swiped a hand over her hair only to find a lump. A painful one.

"What the fuck?"

Then, as though that knot was the button to release her memories, it all came back to her.

Coming home.

Dante. Paranoid.

Making coffee.

Pain.

"Oh, shit."

JJ was on her feet, but that lasted all of a second when she turned around to find—

She barely managed to stifle the scream as she covered her mouth again and stared in absolute horror at the scene in her bedroom.

Blood everywhere.

Soaking her bed, her pillows. There were bloody handprints and streaks down her walls. It looked like a room right out of a horror flick, one where the serial killer just finished hacking up his twentieth victim.

Slowly she peered down at herself, cringed when she saw she was also doused in blood. It decorated her sweatshirt, her jeans, but oddly enough, it wasn't on her hands or arms. What had she done? Wash up before she went to bed?

To make sure it wasn't her blood, she dared to pat her stomach, chest, legs, feeling for some sort of pain that might alert her to an injury.

Nope. Not her blood.

Did that make it better or worse?

The overwhelming coppery stench permeated her nose, made her stomach churn.

She could not be sick. Nope. No way. It would only make things worse. This was a crime scene. It had to be, right? Based on the amount of blood, someone was in need of a hospital. Or maybe a morgue.

Her breaths came in harshly, escaping on broken sobs as she stumbled to get out of the horror show. She made it to the doorway, paused to look at the dried blood that had dripped down the jamb. What the hell had happened?

On to the bathroom door in the hall, but she didn't stop. She used the wall to keep her upright, her knees threatening to give out as she moved toward the living room.

JJ made it two more steps...

This time the scream escaped, barreling up her throat and piercing the air.

AFTER THE UBER DROPPED HIM AT BRANTLEY'S, Baz opted to go into HQ for a minute. Not only did he have to take a piss, he figured some coffee would go a long way to clearing the fog from his brain, allowing him to be a bit more coherent when he got behind the wheel of his truck.

That and he was stalling, he figured. What was there to do at his apartment besides sleep the rest of the day away? That or plant his ass on his couch in front of the television and drown in his own self-loathing. Either way, it was a pretty pathetic way to start the new year.

Then again, a one-night stand with a woman he knew he didn't have a single thing in common with was pretty pitiful, too.

As was waking up on some stranger's purple-flowered couch.

Looked like he was *still* on a roll.

Baz had just made it into the small kitchenette to start the coffee brewing when his cell phone rang.

His heart both leapt and fell when he saw JJ's name on the screen.

Without hesitation, he tapped the screen to take the call.

"Hey," he greeted, aiming for chipper despite the overwhelming guilt that swamped him.

"Baz." She was sobbing, her voice bordering on hysterical. "Oh, my God, Baz."

Every cell in his body went ice cold at the fear he heard in her voice.

"JJ? What's wrong?"

He could hardly understand her when she said, "Please. I need… Oh, God, Baz. It's… I don't know what happened. I… God … I don't know what to do. I need you."

"Don't know what to do about what?" he asked, although he wasn't waiting for an answer, already out the door of the barn and making a beeline for his truck. "Are you at home?"

"Yes," she sobbed. "Can you… Can you come over?"

"Of course I can." He reached his truck, searched above the front left tire for the spare key. There it was, still in the little magnetized box he kept there. "Don't move, JJ. I'll be there in five minutes."

The call disconnected, and he considered calling her back to keep her on the line but figured it would be easier for him to focus if he wasn't listening to her breathe. Something was seriously wrong. In all the time he'd known her, never once had he seen or heard JJ cry. He figured for her to do so, she would have to be in a pretty bad place.

He made good time into town then over to JJ's. More than five minutes but less than ten, then he was walking up to JJ's front door.

From the outside, everything looked normal. JJ's SUV was parked in the driveway. There were no other cars. He took that as a good sign that Dante wasn't lurking about. Just the thought of JJ bringing him back to her place made his gut cramp painfully tight—almost as painfully tight as when he thought about how he'd had sex with a stranger.

He took a deep breath, expelled it slowly. He would not think about JJ and Dante. The same way he wouldn't think about Blondie and the clusterfuck that was last night.

Another breath in. Out.

Baz knocked lightly on the door, then stepped back and waited for JJ to answer. When a minute passed and she didn't, he checked the doorknob, saw that it was open.

When he stepped inside, his heart stopped beating.

At least it felt like it, because fear washed over him, more cold seeping into his pores and down into his bones.

He'd seen plenty of crime scenes over the years, but what was laid out before him looked like something right out of a horror flick. It looked like a bomb had gone off in the house. The furniture was overturned, the rug askew, the television smashed.

But it was the blood that made it a freak show.

He steeled his spine, focused, forcing down the fear for JJ.

"JJ, where are you?"

A whimper sounded, and he hurried past the blood on the floor and the overturned furniture. He reached the short hallway that was the crossroads of the house. There on the floor in front of the bathroom was JJ. Her back was against the wall, her head on her knees.

"JJ?"

When she looked up, his breath lodged in his throat.

Instantly he was squatting down in front of her. He was scared to touch her, there was just so much blood, but he couldn't help himself. He needed to know where she was injured.

"We need to call an ambulance," he stated firmly, taking her wrist, pulling her arm away to find the injury.

"It's not mine," she whispered, her voice rough. "The blood. Not mine. I'm not hurt. And I ... I didn't do this."

Baz watched her, trying to process everything she was telling him.

"I... Oh, God, Baz. Is he ... dead?"

Keeping his voice level, Baz stared down at her. "Is *who* dead, JJ?"

She jerked her chin toward the living room. "In there."

Concerned she was hallucinating, he kept his voice calm. "JJ, there's no one in there."

"The..." Her eyes were filled with tears. "The finger," she whispered.

Turning, he scanned the space, found what she was referring to on the short bookshelf that acted as a divider between the living room and dining area.

Sure enough, there was a severed finger—a man's from the looks of it—lying on the open spine of a book, as though tucked there to neatly mark the page.

JJ sobbed. "I didn't do that, Baz. I didn't… I couldn't… I—"

"Breathe," he ordered, turning his attention back to her. "Whose finger is that, JJ?"

She shrugged. "I didn't do it. I—"

"I know," he interrupted, gripping her chin and forcing her to look up at him. "I know you didn't. I need to know what happened."

JJ dropped her head in her hands, sobbing softly. Baz was at a loss as to how to help her. He needed details to figure this out, to decide what the next step should be.

He gave her a minute, keeping his hand on her knee as reassurance. When she finally calmed down and lifted her head, he leaned down so they were eye level. "Tell me what happened."

This time when she met his gaze, he saw her eyes were bloodshot, rimmed in red, and her pupils dilated. That mixed with the tears tracking down her cheeks did little to comfort him.

"I left the diner, came here," she said in a barely there whisper. "When I got here, Dante was here."

"He was here? In the house?"

"No. Outside." JJ shook her head, her voice growing stronger the more she spoke. "I was on the porch about to come in when he came from the side of the house. He told me we had to hurry and get inside." She took a deep breath, her gaze swinging to the living room then back to him. "He was paranoid. When he came in, he went through all the rooms like he thought someone was here. I made him sit down while I went to make coffee."

Baz wanted to touch her, wanted to take her in his arms and console her, but he didn't. Not yet. She was holding it together by a thread, and he didn't want to fray it any more than it already was.

JJ reached up, felt the back of her head. "I remember a sharp pain. Someone must've hit me on the back of the head. It knocked me out."

"Did Dante do this?" he asked, feeling rage begin to boil deep within him.

"I... I honestly don't know." Her gaze swung to the living room. "He wouldn't." When she peered back at him, her eyes were wide. "Would he?"

Since the question was rhetorical—Baz didn't know Dante—he moved forward with his questioning. "What did he say to you?"

She took a deep breath, looked away. "That's the thing. He didn't tell me anything. He was only here for a few minutes. Five, maybe, before someone knocked me out."

"Then what, JJ?"

"Then I woke up. At eight thirty." She motioned toward her bedroom. "I was in my own bed. Covered in blood."

Ignoring that last part, Baz tried to do the math on the timing. "You came here right from the diner?"

"Yes."

Roughly eight thirty last night. It would've only taken her a few minutes to arrive, another few to get Dante into the house, to start coffee. If someone knocked her out, she should've come to sometime during the night, not eleven hours later.

If he had to guess, someone had drugged her after they knocked her out. And he didn't want to think about what they might've done to her while she was unconscious.

"How do you feel? Do you think you were drugged?"

She shrugged. "Besides the headache, physically, I feel okay." Her gaze swung to her bedroom. "It's a bloodbath in there," she whispered. "None of the blood's mine. Not that I can tell, anyway."

Baz stood tall once more, dared a look in her bedroom. She was right, there was blood everywhere. So much, if it all belonged to one person, he seriously doubted they were still alive.

He scanned the space and was about to return to her when something caught his eye. There was a glint of light off something metal on the bed, and that's when he noticed the knife there. Not just any knife, either. It was the one from the butcher block in her kitchen, and if he was right, based on the blood on the blade, it was the one someone had used to hack off that finger.

He felt his stomach twist in a knot.

"I didn't do this, Baz. I swear it."

Turning back to her, Baz schooled his expression. He had no idea what had happened here last night, but the one thing he knew with absolute certainty: JJ was telling the truth. She hadn't cut off someone's finger and played in their blood.

"What do I do?" JJ asked, her green eyes pleading as she stared up at him.

"The first thing *we* do is call Brantley," he told her as he squatted down once more.

"Do you believe me?"

"Yes, darlin'. Of course I do. Now we have to figure out who did this. And what message it is they're trying to send."

But they were going to need help in doing that.

Chapter Thirteen

"I'm makin' pancakes," Reese announced. "Like you requested last night. Unless you want somethin' else."

Brantley forced his eyes open, groaned when he realized he'd been dragged out of one hell of a dream. In it, he was having his wicked way with the man who, rather than hovering on the edge of a fantastic orgasm, had been ... cooking him breakfast? Seriously?

Figured.

"Up and at 'em," Reese commanded. "Breakfast'll be ready in five."

"Son of a bitch."

So not the way he'd wanted to kick off the first day of the new year.

"When did I ask for pancakes?" he grumbled.

"Right as you were fallin' asleep."

Yep. He could see that. Since he'd been sated sexually, his brain had shifted to food. Otherwise, Brantley would've been thinking clearly and asked for sex in the morning.

He rolled to his back and stared up at the ceiling. The room was bright, the day already underway.

"What time is it?"

"Almost oh-nine thirty. You slept late," Reese called out before disappearing down the hall.

But not late enough. He would've preferred to finish that damn dream, thank you very much.

"Why don't you come back in here and join me?" he suggested, his voice not nearly loud enough to carry through the house. "Get naked and let me use that mouth for a bit," he rambled to himself. "Christ Almighty, I don't think I'll make it through the day."

Obviously not hearing him, Reese didn't return so Brantley could sweet-talk him back into the bed, which meant he had only one option: get up.

With a lingering disappointment, he crawled out of bed and headed for the bathroom. He was about to flip on the shower when his cell phone rang. Reversing course, he went back to the bedroom, snatched it off his nightstand.

Baz.

Probably couldn't remember where his truck was or maybe he was merely calling him from Brantley's kitchen, wanting to rub his nose in the fact he was enjoying Reese's pancakes already.

"Hey, man, what's up? I thought you'd be—"

"We've got a major problem," Baz said, his voice low.

The hair on the back of his neck stood up. "What is it?"

"JJ."

His throat went tight and every muscle in his body tensed. "Is she all right?"

"She's alive and unharmed. Physically, anyway."

The exhale was filled with relief as he waited for Baz to continue. Brantley had to be cool, had to remain calm. No sense losing his shit if he didn't know what the problem was.

"I can't do this on the phone," Baz said quietly. "I need you to get to JJ's. See for yourself."

"I'm bringin' Reese."

"Good idea. But leave Tesha at home."

In all the time he'd known Baz, the man had never been overdramatic, so he knew something was seriously wrong.

"Why?"

"You'll see when you get here. I'm serious, Brantley. Leave the dog at home and get here ASAP."

"Give us fifteen," he told Baz.

"Hurry. And bring gloves."

The call disconnected, and Brantley tossed his phone on the dresser while he grabbed clothes, pulled them on.

Footsteps sounded down the hall seconds before Reese appeared, chuckling. "What the hell are you doin'? Tactical pants? Seriously? It's—"

"We have to get to JJ's," he said, cutting off the good-natured ridicule, holstering his weapon on his hip. "Baz called. Said he can't talk about it on the phone. Come on. We gotta go. And he said not to bring Tesha."

He could tell Reese wasn't happy about that, but he nodded, said, "Give me one minute."

It only took three minutes before they were out the door and getting into Brantley's truck. Another three and they were coming into the town proper.

Neither of them spoke, although Brantley knew Reese probably had a dozen questions running through his head. Brantley damn sure did, but until he knew what they were dealing with, it would only be wasted breath.

Because he was one who believed fully in reconnaissance, Brantley drove down JJ's street once to see if he could get eyes on what was going on. He saw JJ's little crossover SUV in her driveway, Baz's truck on the street. Everything else appeared normal. From what he could tell, anyway.

He circled back around, pulled his truck behind Baz's, partially in front of the neighbor's house.

As they got out, he scanned their surroundings, noticed Reese was doing the same thing. Still nothing set off his internal alarms, so he headed for the porch.

Rather than linger at the door, Brantley walked right in.

And immediately stopped.

Reese was at his side, also not moving as they both took it all in.

The only view he had was of blood and chaos. It covered the living room, made the usually tidy space look like it belonged in another house, certainly not in JJ's.

"Baz?"

"In the hallway," he called out. "We haven't moved from this spot since I got here."

Taking that to mean it was safe to move, he stepped past the sofa, past the pool of blood coating the carpet beside the overturned coffee table.

He maneuvered around the furniture, stopped when Reese called out to him, pointed to the bookcase.

There, lying on an open book, was a severed finger.

"Oh, Christ," he said harshly.

"I didn't do this, B," JJ rasped, her words churning with emotion.

He peered over at her, noticed the blood on her clothes.

"I swear to God I didn't do this."

Brantley looked at Baz, saw the man's concern laced with fear.

Baz stood tall, motioned toward the bedroom. "There's blood in there, too. Like I said, we haven't moved from here. Figured we'd let you decide how to handle this."

How to handle this? The question was, what the hell was *this*? They had a severed finger, far too much blood, all in JJ's house, which appeared to have been tossed.

"Who would do this?" JJ inhaled sharply, her words rushed, panicked. "Why? They made it look like I did it. I don't understand."

Brantley wasn't so sure that was the intention, but he could see where she was coming from. On the other hand, it looked more like a temper tantrum had been thrown during the crime.

At least, that was his initial take on it.

"Who's they?" Reese inquired, stepping over to JJ. "Are you sayin' it was more than one person?"

She shrugged, looking so small, so scared. "The only thing I know is that Dante was here last night. He was scared. He called me, said to meet him here. He was hidin' on the side of the house when I got home, practically shoved me inside and ... and I don't remember much after that. I was makin' coffee. Someone hit me. I woke up in bed, covered in blood. Dante's gone and there's..." JJ took a deep breath, her hand waving in the direction of the finger.

"There's a knife in her bed," Baz informed him.

JJ's eyes went wide. "Oh, my God. I didn't... Brantley, you have to believe me."

Stepping over to her, Brantley cupped her face firmly, stared into her eyes. "I know you didn't. But I need you to stay calm so we can figure this out."

He took a deep breath, moved away from her. As much as he wanted to comfort JJ, to give her all the assurances he could, Brantley knew they had to figure out what the hell happened. And most importantly, where Dante Greenwood was.

"I don't wanna go to jail."

Brantley glanced at Baz.

"Honey, you're not gonna go to jail," Baz assured her.

Sighing, Brantley took stock of the house, the scene. As much as he wanted to make the same assurance, he didn't. Right now, it looked bad for JJ. Based on the amount of blood, if it all came from one person, they would be looking for a dead body, not a nine-fingered man wandering around.

"JJ said Dante was actin' paranoid when he came in. Then someone knocked her out. Do you think Dante did this? Lured her here then hit her?" Reese said from beside him.

"Anything's possible," he replied. "But why would he?"

That was what Brantley didn't understand. Dante was a lot of things—many of them not at all admirable—but he wasn't the type to set JJ up for ... for whatever the hell was going on here.

"I'm inclined to think the same thing," Reese agreed. "But that would mean someone else was in the house."

"He called me for help," JJ explained, her words still rushed. "Why would he do that just to hit me and leave me here? That ... that doesn't make sense at all."

"She has a point," Baz said.

Yeah. She did. Brantley didn't understand it either. Dante would have nothing to gain. From what he knew of the man, he got his kicks from leading JJ on, dating her, cheating on her, dumping her, coming back for more only so no one else could have her. Sure, he'd laid hands on her, but JJ had explained the one time that had happened, she'd been the one who had been hitting him. Dante had simply tried to stop her and ended up accidentally hitting JJ in the process.

No, he didn't think Dante would hit JJ. Not with the intention of seriously hurting her.

However, he did believe Dante was capable of setting something like this in motion. The man was a spoiled brat, and he would go to great lengths to get what he wanted. The question would be: what the hell could he possibly want that would warrant all this?

Brantley glanced back down at the opened book, the finger.

Granted, Dante was also a vain idiot. Brantley seriously doubted the guy would hack off his own finger to make a point.

"I have a hunch that belongs to Dante," Baz said quietly.

Yeah. That was what Brantley feared as well. Which meant this was just getting started.

"We need to find Dante," Reese stated. "At this point, he's the only one who can give us answers."

Provided all this blood didn't belong to him, they might have a chance of that.

"Definitely a good place to start," Brantley agreed, but worried that would be where they ended, instead.

"MAYBE YOU SHOULD TRY CALLIN' HIM," BAZ suggested, glancing from Brantley to Reese. "I would but I don't know the guy."

Brantley was still scanning the room as he pulled out his phone, dialed.

Baz waited patiently, hoping Dante Greenwood would answer and they could get some answers. He had no idea what those might be, or how they could possibly make any of this make sense, but what else did they have?

It was a reach, he knew. Baz seriously doubted this would be simple—who the fuck went to these lengths only to answer the phone and cop to the crime?—but some wishful thinking certainly couldn't hurt.

Unfortunately, the ringing that sounded from somewhere in the living room was the next clue that getting answers from Dante wasn't going to pan out.

"Where is it?" Brantley asked, holding his phone away so he could listen for the direction of the ring.

Baz pointed to the couch.

It only took a moment to retrieve the cell phone that was tucked into a small area between the couch arm and the base. It almost looked as though it had been left there on purpose considering how everything else was in disarray. Had Dante managed to slip it there? Leaving it as a clue, maybe? Did he want them to find it?

Brantley picked up the phone using a plastic glove he pulled out of one of his many pockets. "Let's get Charlie to go through this, see—"

"No," JJ snapped. "That's my job."

"Right now, your only job is to get checked out by—"

"I'm fine," she bit out, most of the fear Baz had witnessed earlier erased.

JJ and Brantley faced off from their respective spots, neither of them backing down.

As much as Baz agreed JJ needed to take care of herself and let them worry about the rest, he was happy to see some fire back in her eyes. Even if it did ring with a hint of petulance.

"We need to call the sheriff," Reese stated, interrupting the standoff as he held out his hand for the phone.

Reese was right. They needed to know what happened here last night. Not only because Baz wanted to help JJ move forward but also because he could feel the fiery rage brimming beneath his skin. Whoever did this to her ... hurt her ... put that fear in her eyes ... they would pay for the hell they put her through. That he could promise.

Brantley was slow on the transfer, his eyes brimming with frustration. Finally, he passed the phone to Reese, who slid it into a clear plastic bag, then set it on the table next to the finger.

"We need crime scene techs to comb through it," Reese explained, motioning toward the living room.

"What about JJ?" Baz asked. "She's gonna be the prime suspect in Dante's disappearance."

He could see Reese was aware of that when he said, "If Dante wasn't the governor's son, I'd say we could finagle this to our liking, but we don't know what this is about. It could be a mess Dante's gotten himself into..."

Reese's eyes shifted to Brantley, and Baz saw something pass between them, but he couldn't translate it.

"Or it could be politically driven," Brantley added, almost as an afterthought.

"Political?" Baz looked around. "What the fuck does this get them? This is JJ's house. For all we know, Dante's the one who bashed her over the head."

"Well, we won't know until we investigate."

Baz hated that Brantley was right. This very well could be aimed at the governor and whoever was targeting Greenwood was simply using JJ to relay the message. It seemed a stretch for him, but then again, Baz had seen the criminal element at work. Often there was no rhyme or reason. Logically, at least.

"I need to get her out of here first," Baz told Brantley and Reese, ensuring they heard the concern in his tone. "We all know there's enough evidence to throw suspicion on her, and if we have any hope of finding Dante, we can't have her detained."

"Nor can Dante afford for the cops to be focusin' in the wrong direction," Brantley agreed before glancing over at Reese.

"Whatever we do, this place has to be treated like a crime scene. We can't confirm that's all Dante's blood until we test it," Reese added, as though that should've been an obvious conclusion.

This time Baz heard the underlying meaning. If that was all Dante's blood, the chances of him still being alive ... well, they were very, very slim, and unless he was at a hospital already, they were growing slimmer by the second.

"Good point. JJ, why don't you go change." Brantley nodded at Reese. "You call the sheriff, report the scene."

Baz watched as JJ went into her room. She moved slowly, but he wasn't sure if it was because of the blood or because she had a head injury.

"And you"—Brantley tapped Baz on the shoulder—"call Charlie. Tell her we need her over here ASAP."

"Will do."

"And I'll call Trey," Brantley continued. "Have him bring over a kit. I won't notify the governor until we know for a fact this is Dante's finger. To know that, we'll need to fingerprint it."

Reese pulled out his phone. "I'll step outside to make the call."

No one spoke as Reese ventured out the front door and into the bright morning sunlight.

"Yes, I need to speak to Sheriff Endsley," Reese said, his voice trailing off as he stepped onto the porch.

Baz sighed. "I can't wrap my head around this. I thought Dante was more of a douche than a dirtbag."

"He is," Brantley confirmed. "Which is why I don't think he did this. Or if he did, he didn't do it on his own."

"You don't think he's capable of hurtin' JJ?"

"Physically, no."

Baz wasn't sure why that made him feel moderately better, but it did.

"I don't wanna go to jail," JJ whispered, drawing all eyes to her as she emerged from her bedroom wearing a clean sweatshirt and jeans, a pair of Nikes on her feet.

"You won't," Brantley stated firmly.

"You don't know that," she argued.

As much as Baz wanted to believe Brantley could control this situation, maneuver the outcome in their favor, he had his doubts. Reese was right, this place had to be handled like a crime scene. Unfortunately, JJ was smack dab in the middle of it all with the blood covering her, the knife likely used to cut off Dante's finger in her bed... There was just too much that implicated her, especially as seen by an unbiased spectator.

"She's right," Baz said. "Whoever did this wanted to implicate JJ. There's the knife in the bed, which no doubt will have her prints on it."

"It's *her* knife," Brantley countered. "Of course it will."

"Her *bloody* prints," Baz snapped, feeling the thread of his control beginning to pull tight. "Why would she be holding the knife with bloody hands? Think about it."

"You said she didn't have blood on her hands."

"I didn't," JJ confirmed, holding her hands up.

"She's been unconscious for hours, Brantley. We have no idea what happened here."

Brantley glared, obviously refraining from ripping Baz a new one. He appreciated it.

Regardless of whether the cops found something that might implicate JJ or not, Baz wasn't willing to take that chance.

"She doesn't have an alibi," Baz continued. "She was probably the last person Dante called. Plus this is her house, her knife. She was definitely the last person to *see* Dante besides whoever's behind this."

Brantley was staring at him, that unflappable control firmly in place, looking as though he had the ability to fix everything simply by willing it to be so. But he couldn't. No one was that powerful.

Even if they all wished he was.

"Call Charlie," Brantley breathed out slowly. "Tell her to come over here." He jerked his phone from his pocket. "I'll call Trey. We need to process the scene, then we'll decide how to proceed."

Christ Almighty. He just didn't get it, did he? The more people they brought in, the worse they were going to make it.

"Brant—"

"Call her," Brantley barked, not bothering to look back.

Fuck.

Baz waited until Brantley walked out the front door before turning to JJ. She was staring up at him, her eyes glassy, as though she wasn't quite sure what was going on.

"Let me get you outta here," Baz whispered, putting his arm around her shoulder.

She leaned in, as though it was natural, and the only thing he could think about was keeping her safe, ensuring no one else hurt her. He felt her shudder, knew the shock was setting in since the adrenaline was waning.

Because he only had one option, Baz took her hand and led her out the front door. Reese and Brantley were nowhere in sight, which he took to mean they were walking the perimeter of the house, giving him the perfect opportunity.

Later he would wonder if Brantley had done that on purpose.

"Should we tell them we're leavin'?" JJ asked, her words soft with a slight tremble.

"No."

To his surprise, she didn't argue and he didn't elaborate.

Once in the truck, Baz buckled JJ's seat belt for her, started the engine, and double-timed it out of the neighborhood. He hadn't made it a mile when his cell phone began ringing, Brantley's number on the screen.

He ignored it. Once he got her somewhere safe, somewhere the police wouldn't find her until they solved this, Baz would call him and explain.

"Where are we going?" JJ asked a short time later, once they were on the interstate heading south.

"My father's," he said simply.

"Baz, that's—"

"He's not home," he told her quickly, not wanting her to panic. "They're out of the country. Won't be back for a couple of weeks."

Either she believed him and felt no need to argue or JJ was in shock, because she said nothing.

Every so often, he would look over, noticing that JJ's eyes were closed, her head resting on the window. It made him nervous to think she might be injured more than she would admit.

Knowing it would likely infuriate JJ, Baz decided to make a call. If she wouldn't let him take her to a clinic to get checked out, he would have someone come to her.

It was times like this when he appreciated his father's wealth. Especially since it meant there was a doctor who made house calls.

Chapter Fourteen

"I NEED A FUCKING DOCTOR," DANTE GROANED, using the dollar bill he'd turned into a makeshift straw to sniff the white powder up his nose.

He sighed as the relief was almost instantaneous. Thank God for cocaine; otherwise, losing a finger would've fucked him all to hell.

"You'll live. Quit your whining."

Whining? *He* was whining?

Dante sniffed again, glaring at his partner. "I think I've earned the right."

After all, they had agreed on the plan to go to JJ's, knock her out with a dose of something that would keep her out for a while, then spill blood everywhere. The objective was to make her think Dante had been kidnapped and injured, so that way when the ransom demand came in, his father would be more likely to believe it.

But *nowhere* in any of the scenarios they'd come up with had it said anything about lobbing off his damn finger.

"Who're you texting?" Dante asked, watching Marcus as he paced the room, phone in hand.

"My girl," he said simply, leering as his thumbs tapped the screen.

"You mean *my* girl," Dante countered.

After all, Dante had been talking to Kat first. *He* was the one who'd answered her from his online dating profile. He was still unclear how Marcus started chatting her up, but he found he didn't really care anymore. The woman wasn't all that interesting, anyway.

"What does she want?" he heard himself ask although he honestly didn't care.

Marcus's eyes were shining. He was definitely high. "She said she wanted to be in on the plan, so I was telling her how it went."

Dante's entire body went cold. "What? You asked a complete stranger to be part of this?"

Was the guy a total fucking moron?

"She's not a stranger, and yes. She was excited. Even asked me to do something for her. Her contribution, she said."

This man really was insane, and now Dante was neck deep in a scheme he wasn't sure would play out. What was to stop this Kat chick from turning them in? Maybe she was a cop and this was a setup. Son of a bitch.

Closing his eyes, he thought back to last night, let it play out in his head as he'd done repeatedly since they'd left JJ's. Everything had gone perfectly up to the point Marcus showed up. Dante had called, lured her back to her house, and she'd come without question. Of course, he had to give his acting skills some credit. He was rather believable when he wanted to be.

"What took you so fuckin' long?" Marcus demanded when Dante opened JJ's front door, his voice a harsh whisper. "Where's she at?"

"In the kitchen. Be quiet." Dante's gaze darted behind him to ensure she hadn't returned to the living room.

"What's she doing?"

"Making coffee."

"Good." Marcus's eyes glittered, a hint of insanity brightening them. "You get the drug?"

Marcus held up a hypodermic needle, flipped it between two fingers, then stepped into the house. He strolled right by, leaving Dante to close the front door, doing his best to not make a sound. He turned and watched the small, wiry man in the cheap, dirty clothes move across the room with purpose.

This was the part they were improvising on. Considering they hadn't been certain JJ would even let him in her front door, they had agreed they would let things play out.

On his way, Marcus grabbed something off one of JJ's decorative shelves.

Dante frowned, his brain making a dire effort to figure out what Marcus was planning to—

He'd made it two steps when Marcus disappeared into the kitchen. Another when the first thud sounded. The second thud was louder, the equivalent of a body hitting the floor.

Oh, God. What the hell had he done?

Racing into the kitchen, Dante saw Marcus leaning over—

Oh, Jesus. JJ's motionless form was crumpled on the floor, and Marcus was leering down at her like a lion might an injured deer.

"You did not mention how hot she is," Marcus crooned, cutting a look at Dante. "Damn, but she's hot."

"Did you hit *her?" Dante exclaimed. "What the fuck? I thought you were gonna give her a shot. Knock her out."*

"This was easier," Marcus said, grinning when he looked over at Dante. "Faster, too." He nodded to the syringe sitting on the counter. "But don't worry, I've got it covered."

It was then the horror of the situation had become real for Dante. Up until that point, it had all been a plan to extort money from his father. Using JJ had only come up because Dante had been telling Marcus about the task force his father had created. Together they decided it would be the fastest way to get his dad to agree to a payout.

The only thing Dante had to do was call JJ, get her to meet him at her house. He'd decided to pretend he was panicked, maybe tell her someone was after him, because she was a do-gooder like that. It was likely the only way JJ would help him considering she'd turned her nose up at him this last time.

What Dante hadn't considered was how JJ could get hurt in the process. Just because he was irritated with her did not mean he wanted her hurt.

"You gonna help me or what?" Marcus snapped.

Dante shook off the foreboding feeling, focused on what was in front of him.

Marcus grabbed JJ's wrists and was dragging her toward the dining room, her shoes dragging on the floor. Dante immediately grabbed her ankles so they could lift her up, carry her into the bedroom.

"Get her on the bed," Marcus insisted.

Dante hesitated. He didn't like the idea of putting JJ in that bed. Definitely not with Marcus ogling her the way he was.

"For fuck's sake, Greenwood. Get with the program," Marcus shouted. "I ain't got all fuckin' night."

It pained him to do it, but Dante did what Marcus asked. The two of them managed to get JJ's limp body onto the bed. In the process, her sweatshirt had lifted, revealing her flat belly. When he saw Marcus grin, Dante immediately yanked the shirt down, covering her.

"Take her shoes off."

"Why?"

"Just fuckin' do it."

Dante gritted his teeth in frustration but did as he was told while Marcus slipped out of the room.

Once he was finished removing her shoes, Dante looked down at the woman he'd been in love with at one point in his life. Well, as "in love" as he was capable of, anyway. JJ'd been right to dump him half a dozen times, of that he had no doubt. But the last time… The last time, Dante had intended to do right by her. Unfortunately, the addiction had won out, and he'd fucked it all up again.

Marcus returned. "Catch."

Dante had just enough time to lift his hands to keep the plastic two-liter bottle full of animal blood from hitting him in the face.

"Douse the whole place. Top to bottom."

"I'll do this room," Dante told him, starting immediately. "You get the living room."

Thankfully, Marcus didn't put up a fight.

Half an hour later, they'd completed their task, the walls, the floors, the furniture all bloodied. There were smears on the walls, the linens, even the hardwood.

Dante's mind had cleared the closer they got to the end. The only thing he could think about was his next fix. Marcus had promised him he'd get all he needed once they took care of setting the scene.

He eyed JJ, who was still unconscious in her bed. He hoped she didn't wake up. Not until they were gone. Then he hoped she panicked when she saw the blood and remembered how scared he'd been. If all went well, she would call his dad, tell him she thought he was kidnapped ... although he was a bit confused about that part. Why would JJ think someone had taken him? He hadn't had a chance to set the scene with a story.

Dante was still pondering that dilemma when Marcus returned to the room wielding an enormous chef's knife.

"What's that for?" he demanded, coming to stand to block JJ.

"Don't worry, you big sissy. I ain't gonna cut her." Marcus sidestepped him, then grabbed the syringe. "I'm gonna give her this so she'll sleep till morning. The longer the better."

"Why the knife?"

Marcus glanced at the shiny blade then back to him, smirked. "Just felt like the thing to do. Now get outta the way."

As much as it pained him, Dante kept his eyes on JJ the entire time, watched as Marcus jabbed her in the arm with the needle, right through her sweatshirt, then pushed the plunger and filled her with the drugs. Not once did it cross his mind that she might not wake up from that. Not until after it was done.

"What now?" Dante asked, hating that his stomach was churning. What he needed was another hit, something to get him through the rest of the night.

"Now you leave."

Turning, Dante walked out of JJ's room, into the minuscule hallway. He didn't make it very far when Marcus started laughing.

When he turned, it was to find Marcus standing with his hand on the door, gearing up to close it so Dante was on the wrong side of it.

"Why don't you go wait in the car," Marcus said with a snort. "I'm just gonna be a few minutes."

Instinct took over and Dante slammed his hand on the door, pushing it open. His other hand went to the jamb, allowing leverage to keep Marcus from closing himself in the room with JJ.

"I can't let you do that," Dante growled. "Let's get outta here. Now."

Marcus's eyes were a little wild when he said, "You're not gonna let me?"

"You'll screw up the whole plan," Dante warned, wanting to get back on track. He knew better than to push Marcus. The guy was a lit fuse as it was, but no way was he going to allow Marcus to assault JJ. No way.

"Ain't nobody gonna be the wiser." Marcus glanced over his shoulder to where JJ lay unconscious on the bed. "Certainly not her."

"I said no," Dante demanded. "Not part of the deal."

When Marcus's eyes met his again, that sense of foreboding returned. Only this time, there was good reason.

"Fine. You win." Marcus let the door swing open as he stepped forward.

Relieved, Dante gripped the doorjamb to keep himself upright. "Now can we get outta here? I need another fix."

That was the moment Marcus took advantage, swinging the knife like a heavy hitter, the blade severing Dante's finger clean off before lodging in the doorjamb.

Slouching back on the couch, Dante cradled his arm to his chest, willing the throbbing in his hand to abate. The white bandage he'd fashioned around the missing digit was showing blood again, but surprisingly, it was a lot less than he'd thought. What he needed was a doctor, but Marcus was right when he'd told him their plan would fail if he sought medical treatment, because they would realize he hadn't been kidnapped.

If the fucking idiot hadn't hacked off his finger, they wouldn't be in this predicament.

Dante watched through drug- and pain-hazed eyes as Marcus paced the floor, his eyes continuously sliding from his phone to the clock on the wall and back again.

"Why aren't you calling them? Making demands?" Dante asked.

After all, that was the plan. Stage the abduction, let JJ warn his family, then call with the ransom demand. Maybe not exactly smart, but it sounded foolproof. And as much as Dante hated to do it, he knew there weren't a whole lot of options. Since he was eyeball deep in debt to both his bookie and his dealer, and Marcus had been sent to collect for the failed bets, Dante didn't have much of a choice. He damn sure wasn't waiting for the next collector to appear.

Marcus smiled down at his phone, then tucked it into his pocket. "We've got to be patient," he replied, his hands wringing as he continued to pace. "I figured the drugs've worn off at this point. She's probably awake." Marcus glanced his way. "Such a shame you had to be such a dick. I could've left her something to wake up to."

Dante's stomach lurched, the thought of what Marcus had intended to do to JJ making him nauseous.

"Oh, well. Maybe next time." Marcus started pacing again. "You said the first thing she'd do is call your old man, right?"

Yeah. Dante had said that. That and a whole lot more. "Or her boss," Dante supplied.

"He's the cop guy, right?"

"Task force," Dante corrected. "But yeah. Once he knows what happened, *he'll* call my dad. They'll be expecting a ransom call."

Even as the words came out, Dante couldn't believe he was saying them. He couldn't believe he'd stooped this low.

He blamed it on the drugs. While he was capable of moving through life pretending not to be high as a kite, Dante had long ago given himself over to his addiction. It was an expensive habit, but it allowed him to get through each day, to deal with the shitty hand he'd been dealt. People thought it was easy being the son of a politician, but they were wrong. So many rules, so many expectations. Everyone thought he had it easy because his parents paid for most of what he had—his two-bedroom apartment overlooking Lady Bird Lake, his brand-new Lexus LS.

Dante didn't see it as them providing for him. It was more of a payment. For him to continue to play the dutiful son. After all, his father expected so much, said he had to always be on his best behavior. Whenever he went to a strip club, he'd get read the riot act. God forbid he went to a club and was seen with a hot chick who wasn't some debutante. No one should have to live like that.

"Once they see all that blood, they'll think you're dead," Marcus mused.

They would. And that, Dante knew, could be a problem. The intention had been to make them believe he was seriously injured, to plant the idea that the kidnappers weren't playing around. But the amount of blood they'd left in JJ's house … no way would anyone survive an injury like that.

The majority of the blood—which was supposed to be *all* the blood—that they'd decorated JJ's house with had been that of animals. Dante hadn't been a part of the blood-gathering process, thank God. Marcus had gladly offered to gather what they needed to make the scene believable. As for what they'd do when the task force decided to run a DNA test on the blood and found out it wasn't human, Dante had no idea. But he seemed to be the only one worried about it. According to Marcus, it was handled.

Only a little while longer. Another hour. Two. Then it'd be time to call his father, demand money. Once it was delivered to Marcus—a plan that, in Dante's opinion, was also rather foolproof, too—Dante would be returned safely.

At least that was what Dante was telling himself. He absolutely did not want to think that Marcus could actually be a crazed killer and, in doing this, he'd unleashed the beast.

JULIET PRINCE SAT CROSS-LEGGED ON THE bed in the cheap, run-down motel room, her pawn-shop-purchased laptop open in front of her.

No, her accommodations weren't what she was used to, but she'd been learning how to deal. She had enough clothes to last her three days, enough quarters to wash those clothes when it became necessary again, and free Wi-Fi. What more could a girl ask for?

Everything.

That was what Juliet wanted. She wanted every goddamn thing. And she wanted Travis Walker to give it to her.

Lifting her head, Juliet caught sight of the peeling tan wallpaper just beneath the water stain on the ceiling in the corner.

Yeah, she fucking hated it here. It smelled like cheap booze and piss, and she refused to think what they might actually wash the sheets with. If they washed them at all.

But it was easier staying in the rent-by-the-hour, no-questions-for-cash motels than worrying about identification and whatnot. Since she'd been forced to give up her identity thanks to that bastard Travis Walker, she was honing a new skill: adaptation.

In the interim, of course, because this damn sure wasn't how she intended to live out the rest of her days. Nor did she intend to spend a minute in a cage.

She glanced at the burner phone sitting beside her, saw that Marcus had moved on to the raunchy portion of their conversation. Juliet was happy to ignore it. No way in hell would she touch that man. Not with another woman's vagina, thank you very much. However, he'd become the perfect patsy when she'd hit a roadblock during her attempt to seduce Dante Greenwood.

Juliet wouldn't say it'd been luck that had brought Dante to her attention. No, that was due to an incredible amount of research into the life of Travis Walker. Through myriad connections to various people, Juliet had lucked out in finding the one she thought would be the perfect target. When she had learned that Travis Walker's cousin was the one who had found Kate and forced Juliet to run, she'd looked more into him. It was then she learned that the governor of Texas had created a task force and put Brantley Walker in charge of it.

Meaning there was a connection between Travis Walker and the governor, and *that* was an avenue she found far too intriguing to ignore.

She'd reached out to the governor's son, Dante, via an online dating profile he'd created, which was rather bleak if you asked her. The guy honestly had nothing much going for him except for material things. Not that Juliet cared. She wasn't looking for love or romance, nor had she been when she came across him.

Unfortunately, the man was far too wrapped up in himself to be of much use to her. When she had attempted to get details about his past, he'd shut down real quick, fostering more discussions about sex in order to find out what her various fetishes might be. And since the only reason she'd made the connection was to get dirt on Travis Walker and those he associated with, and Dante wasn't willing to dish, she decided not to waste her time.

Granted, striking up a conversation with the Marcus guy had been pure coincidence. Or luck, either way. She'd been making one last-ditch effort to connect with Dante when she got a response from this guy.

Based on the few text conversations they'd had, she was pretty sure he was batshit crazy, but Juliet figured that could certainly work in her favor. When he mentioned a plan to extort money from the governor of Texas, she'd thought he was delusional. Nope. He wasn't. They had in fact concocted a fake kidnapping scheme that they were hoping would net them a million dollars.

What was amusing was the fact Marcus actually thought a million dollars was enough to incentivize her to screw him.

In that he *was* delusional.

But she couldn't write Marcus off just yet. When he had informed her they were using Dante's ex-girlfriend—Jessica James, also an acquaintance of Travis Walker—in their plan, she knew she'd hit gold.

Well, a little bit of the credit had to go to Samuel Aldering, a man who Juliet had gotten acquainted with a couple of months back. He happened to be a computer genius and quite the hacker to boot. Getting him to assist had required some effort on her part. But who was she if not dedicated?

Fucking the man so she had something to hold over him had been relatively easy. Being that he was married with four kids and didn't wish to have his wife find out he was a lying, cheating bastard, he had gladly given Juliet the access she requested.

Which was how she'd ended up sitting here watching the scene at Jessica James's house play out. It was disappointing that two of the cameras weren't working, so she was restricted to only seeing what was going on in the front yard, but it was getting interesting. She'd just watched one man whisk Jessica away while Brantley Walker, the Navy SEAL who had spoiled her plans in Mississippi, and his partner, whose name she still did not know, did a cursory search around the house.

"Come on. It's time to go back inside," Juliet whispered to the men on screen. "Don't you want to take one more look?"

Juliet peered up at the clock on the screen. She had set a timer to count down based on what Marcus had told her. When it reached the sixty-minute mark, she intended to send a text that would set everything in motion. By the end of today, she would be home free, and her plan to end Travis Walker once and for all would be a success.

"Not long now," she muttered at the screen.

Not long at all.

Chapter Fifteen

"WHAT THE FUCK!" BRANTLEY EXCLAIMED, WATCHING BAZ's truck disappear down the street.

"Somethin' wrong?"

Turning his attention back to the man on the other end of the phone, Brantley answered his brother the only way he knew how. He lied. "Nothin' that wasn't already wrong. I'd appreciate if you could get over here. We've got a crime scene to process."

"What do you mean a crime scene?"

"I don't have time to explain, Trey. Get your ass over to JJ's."

"At least tell me she's all right," Trey demanded.

"Yes. Shit. Sorry. She's fine." Not to mention, gone. "Can you put a rush on it?"

"Give me fifteen."

"Better make it five or the sheriff's likely to get here first," Brantley told his brother before disconnecting the call.

He immediately dialed Baz's number. No surprise, the guy didn't answer.

Reese strolled out from the side of the house. "I didn't see any unusual tracks back there, but— What's wrong?"

"Baz just hauled ass outta here," he said on a huff. "With JJ."

Reese peered down the street, as though that might give him insight, maybe? "Did you try callin' him?"

Rather than answer, Brantley gave him the *do you think I'm an idiot?* stare.

"And did he answer?" Reese drawled, clearly irritated by the look.

"No. You talk to the sheriff?"

"I did. He's on his way. I told him to bring only his most trusted deputy for now. We don't need this to leak before we know what we're dealin' with."

"Good call." Brantley only wished he did know what they were dealing with.

There were simply too many avenues to pursue and not nearly enough evidence. Especially considering Dante was the governor's son, which made him high-profile. His first thought was that this was a kidnap and ransom. It was the most logical conclusion.

On the other hand, the scene inside JJ's was a bit dramatic for that. What was with all the blood? And why tear up JJ's place? It felt personal to him and most K and Rs weren't.

He glanced around the yard, the driveway. "Why'd Dante come here?" he mused aloud. "Why'd he involve JJ? If he was comin' to her for help, I have to assume someone followed him here. Which means, by callin' her, he led them right to her door."

"Good point. Maybe he didn't know they were on to him, and he thought she'd be able to help."

"Yeah. Maybe. But surely he knew he was in danger. JJ said he was panicked. Why the fuck would he involve her?"

That was what pissed Brantley off the most. Fucking Dante. He could've reached out to Brantley for help. The fool did not need to drag JJ into this.

Then again, Dante never was the brightest bulb. He tended to leap before he thought, and this time was obviously no different.

"Come on. Let's go inside and have a look around before the sheriff gets here." He pulled another pair of gloves out of one of his many pockets, passed them to Reese.

Reese fell into step with him as they returned to the house.

"I'd bet Dante called her because she's probably the only one he knows who wouldn't tell him to get fucked," Reese said, closing the front door and blocking out the bright light.

Brantley chuckled. "Yeah, probably. Although she's the first one who should."

It was no secret that Brantley didn't care for Dante. Not even a little. They weren't friends, and Brantley had no qualms making that fact known. However, he had a sworn duty to his position on the task force to uphold the law and to protect the governor's best interest. Although the relationship between father and son was strained, Brantley knew Governor Greenwood wouldn't want any harm to come to his son.

Then again, unbeknownst to everyone, the task force wouldn't exist come Monday, so did he really have any loyalties there?

"Did you get ahold of Charlie?" Brantley asked, careful not to disturb anything more than he had to as he pulled out his phone and began snapping pictures.

"I did, yeah. She's on her way." Reese moved when he did. "The sheriff's gonna want to talk to JJ."

"He's got every right to want to. Doesn't mean it's gonna happen." He glanced over at his partner. "She doesn't know anything."

"Doesn't matter. She was the last to see Dante, and her house is covered in blood."

"Blood that belongs to Dante," he conceded.

"Yes. Although we don't know that for a fact. Could be some of that blood belongs to whoever's got Dante. Maybe there was a fight. We don't know anything at this point."

Brantley stared at Reese, wishing the man wasn't always so rational. At the moment, he was considering praising Baz for getting JJ away from all this shit. Although he'd told her she wouldn't go to jail, he'd been placating her. He knew nothing of the sort. And truthfully, they didn't have time to prove she hadn't had a hand in this. If he was a law enforcement officer stumbling on the scene, the first thing he'd do was arrest JJ. The second would be to search for the body, because with that much blood...

"You believe the finger's Dante's?" he asked Reese.

"No doubt about it. It's their way of provin' they're serious."

Yeah, he figured as much, but he was hoping there was another scenario that worked here. Unfortunately, the way it played, it looked as though Dante Greenwood had been kidnapped, and whoever took him was serious about whatever it was they wanted from him.

"So who took him and why?" he wondered aloud.

"I figure it could be a couple of things."

Curious, Brantley turned his full attention to Reese.

"Could be he's in deep with the mob, and they're lookin' to make a point."

"The mob? Dante?" No, he just didn't see it. "Or?"

"Or someone's lookin' to maneuver the governor to their liking."

That was the angle Brantley was leaning toward. K and R didn't have to have a financial motivation. Could be they were looking to get the governor to swing one way or the other on something. He figured the finger was the key here. They wanted someone to know they had Dante and that they weren't opposed to hurting him to get what they wanted.

However, he still couldn't see how JJ played in all of this. It wasn't working out in his head just yet.

"I JUST DON'T UNDERSTAND WHY STAGE THE scene like this," Reese told Brantley as they moved toward the kitchen. "What does it get them? Why toss the knife in the bed with JJ? Seems sloppy to me."

"Sloppy or emotional," Brantley stated. "Take your pick."

Yeah, Reese could see either.

They were both quiet for a few minutes while they moved through the house, starting in the kitchen. Reese noted the coffee mug sitting on the Keurig. JJ'd said she was making coffee when someone hit her over the head. He walked over, peeked down inside the cup. Sure enough, it was full and the coffee was cold.

"She was in here," he said to himself as he stood in front of the machine. "Dante's in the living room where she left him. She's standin' here, waitin' for the coffee, when someone comes up behind her."

Reese peered over his shoulder. Behind him was the open doorway, which meant whoever hit her could've been anywhere in the house. The house was likely built sometime in the late fifties, early sixties, and like most from that era, it didn't have an open floor plan. There were walls separating each room, blocking visibility from the front of the house to the back. If she wasn't expecting them, they could've easily snuck up on her.

He glanced toward the back door.

"They couldn't come in that way while she's here," he noted. "She would've seen them."

Which meant they would've either had to be in the house already or they came in the front door while JJ was in here. And for *that* to happen, Dante would've had to let them in. Reese didn't really see that one playing out. Probably had something to do with the severed finger.

Reese took a step back, stared down at the floor, imagined JJ crumpled on the tile after being knocked out cold. What had they hit her with? Something heavy? Something hard?

He glanced around the countertops. The only thing he noticed that seemed off was a single slot in the knife block was empty, meaning whoever it was likely did use the knife from JJ's kitchen. Was that opportunity? Or part of the plan?

Turning his attention back to the floor, Reese saw a couple of scuff marks. He snapped a picture.

"They dragged her out of here," he mumbled, imagining the scene as it played out, JJ being dragged, her shoes leaving the marks.

From the other room, he heard Trey's voice. When Brantley responded to him, he kept his focus, figuring they could start gathering samples.

Clicking on his phone's video camera, Reese backed out of the room as he let the scene play out in his head. JJ said she woke up in her bed, which meant whoever knocked her out would've had to take her there. Where was Dante during all of this? Had they knocked him out, too? If so, they would've had to do it quickly, otherwise JJ would've been alerted to their presence.

He continued to walk, through the dining room, down the little hallway, and into the bedroom. JJ was relatively small, so it wouldn't have taken much to drag her, but the same couldn't be said about lifting her up onto the bed. Perhaps it wouldn't have been terribly difficult if she was conscious and willing, offering a little assistance. But she wouldn't have been. She would've been deadweight, which would've made it more difficult. Whoever lifted her would've needed to be strong. Or they would've needed help.

Was there more than one? Someone to overpower Dante? Then JJ? But why wouldn't JJ hear something if someone came in? Surely Dante would've shouted.

Reese looked at the bed, the rumpled blankets, the knife that was conveniently sitting there. When he moved, the light caught on something, and he leaned in, noticed it was JJ's cell phone. With gloved hands, he picked it up. Taking another evidence bag, he sealed it inside, tucked it in his pocket. He doubted it would give him any information, but he wasn't willing to take any chances. There could be fingerprints.

There was only one nightstand, and it was on the far side of the room, which meant JJ slept on the other side. However, the blood was not over there. Oddly, it was in a body-shaped design, as though it had been placed there after JJ was on the bed. What would be the reason for that?

Without moving or touching anything, he gave the room a cursory scan. The bed was unmade, but other than that, not much was out of place, with the exception of the closet door standing open.

He peeked inside, saw clothes had been moved aside and a small wall safe was standing open.

"Where does JJ keep her weapon?" he called out to Brantley, who was in the living room.

"Her safe's in her closet," Brantley shouted back.

Yes, it definitely was.

The biometric safe, which was just big enough to hold her gun and a couple boxes of ammunition, was open and empty. Meaning what? JJ had gotten her gun out? Why? Had she needed it? Or had she simply not locked it up and someone else took it?

He searched the room for the weapon but was distracted by the sound of an engine outside the window. He slipped his finger between the slats in the blinds, peered out.

"Did you call Travis?" he hollered.

"No. Why?"

"Because he's here."

"What the fuck?"

Not wanting Travis to walk in on the horror show, Reese made a beeline for the front door, Brantley and Trey beating him to it. They managed to cut Travis off at the pass, making it halfway across the yard as Travis approached.

"Well, I guess it's a party," Travis said in greeting, glancing between them. "Why're you here?"

Trey greeted Travis with a wave as he headed to his car.

"Where's he off to?" Travis asked, eyes tracking Trey.

"Get a kit from the car," Brantley said. "Why're *you* here?"

Travis's confusion was apparent. "I got a text from JJ. Said she had some information I might be interested in."

Reese felt a cold chill snake down his spine.

"When?" Brantley asked, his tone reflecting his concern.

"I don't know. Half an hour ago, maybe." Travis frowned. "What the hell's goin' on?"

Reese looked at Brantley, a new scenario coming to light.

"Where's Kylie and the kids?" Reese immediately asked.

Travis's expression went stone-cold. "Why?"

"Where are they?" Brantley demanded.

"Someone better start fuckin' talkin'," Travis demanded even as he was pulling out his cell phone.

"JJ's not here," Brantley told him. "Not right now, anyway. She was." He motioned toward the house. "When all this went down. But she was unconscious from what we can tell."

"Unconscious? What the fuck are you talkin' about?" Real fear glittered in Travis's eyes. "Why'd she text me?" he asked, his phone to his ear.

"She didn't. Her phone's right here," Reese said, pulling it out of his pocket for Travis to see.

Reese looked at Brantley again, and he saw the same concern in his partner's eyes.

"Gage? Where's Kylie and the kids?" Travis barked into the phone. "Did they go to my parents' yet?"

Reese stared, unable to hear the other side of the conversation, but the relief he saw on Travis's face said the news was good.

"Okay. Stay with them. Don't let any of 'em outta your sight." Travis disconnected the call, glanced from Reese to Brantley. "This is that bitch, isn't it? Juliet Prince?"

If it wasn't … well, that was one hell of a coincidence. Possibly a deadly one.

"We don't know anything at this point," Brantley said, his tone cooling, as though he was attempting to defuse the situation. "JJ called Baz, Baz called us."

Travis listened intently as Brantley relayed the details of what had evidently happened last night after JJ got a phone call from the governor's son, Dante Greenwood. Came home. Knocked out. Woke up. Lots of blood. Severed finger.

"You said Dante called her?" Travis asked, wanting clarification.

"Yeah. Called and asked her to meet him. She said he was freaked when she got here," Brantley explained. "But she never got any information out of him."

"Was it a setup?"

"Could be, but we're thinkin' more along the lines of he was runnin' from someone," Reese said. "He reached out to JJ for help."

Travis didn't know JJ all that well, only from what little they'd worked together over the past few months in the search for Juliet Prince. He couldn't say whether or not she'd be a go-to for getting out of a jam or not.

Nor did he know Dante Greenwood. He knew *of* him, sure. Had even talked to him a few times because of the small town and the relationship the governor had with Travis's family, but he didn't know the guy. Of course, he'd heard a few rumors. None of them painted him in a great light, but Travis hadn't heard anything that would lead him to believe he could do something like this.

"We don't know how he got involved or who we're dealin' with. We were tryin' to piece it together when you showed up," Reese said. "We're waitin' for the sheriff to arrive."

"Where's JJ and Baz?" Travis asked, peering up at the house.

"Baz took JJ … elsewhere."

Meaning Baz fled a crime scene with the witness. Not that Travis blamed him.

"If you want, you can take a look inside, see for yourself," Brantley said, gesturing toward the house. "At this point, we don't know who or—"

Brantley didn't get to finish that sentence, because the world exploded around them, the force of the blast coming at them knocking them back.

Travis slammed into his SUV, the impact sending him on his ass. His ears were ringing, his shoulder screaming from being jarred. It took a moment for his brain to catch up, to catalog what had happened, to tie it all together and make sense of it.

JJ's house had exploded, the brick, wood, and glass turned into projectiles.

The noise seemed to go on forever, a cacophony that rang in his ears. The roar from the flames, the repetitious blare of a smoke detector, his own harsh breaths, and the shouts coming from people spilling out of their houses.

As he got to his knees, Travis looked around, instinct having him check for anyone injured. He saw Reese crumpled on the ground a few feet away, unmoving. Brantley was on his other side, pushing to his feet but moving slowly, unsteadily.

"You okay?" Trey asked, hurrying to his side.

"Yeah. You?" Travis answered, his own voice sounding muffled in his head.

"I'm fine. Brantley? You good?" Trey called out, turning toward his brother.

Brantley nodded, then moved faster than most men Travis knew the moment he noticed Reese on the ground. The man was on his knees in a second, gently touching Reese, obviously checking for injuries.

Travis became aware of neighbors rushing over to check on them, a couple on the phone, likely calling 911. Some on their phones being assholes and recording the destruction.

"Sir, I'm a nurse," a woman said as she approached. "Are you injured? Do you need medical attention?"

Travis could only shake his head, continuing to watch the way Brantley hovered over Reese. He could see real fear on his cousin's face.

"Help them," Travis told her, his words muffled inside his head like he was speaking underwater.

Time seemed to slow as the woman marched over, knelt beside Brantley. She said something that had Brantley taking a deep breath, sitting up straighter but never taking his eyes off Reese. Travis sat there, observing the chaos. The house had been leveled. Everything around it destroyed. The bushes that lined the front charred, the little SUV in the driveway—JJ's he assumed—smashed by debris raining down on it.

It was a fucking mess.

As he got his bearings, Travis discreetly took stock of the people standing around. Most of them were shoulder to shoulder, muttering to one another, likely gossiping about what had happened. There would be half a dozen rumors spreading through their small town before the day was out.

"I'm good," came a garbled response, drawing Travis's attention.

He glanced over, saw Reese sitting up, a gash on his forehead sending a river of blood trailing down his face.

"She tried to kill us," Travis said, speaking to himself.

This had to be Juliet Prince. Based on what he knew of her, she was crazy enough to blow up a house and anyone in it. Which meant she was the one who had texted him, lured him. Probably had intended for the house to blow up with him inside of it.

Was she doing it? Was she playing them like puppets? Looking at it rationally, it wasn't difficult to put the pieces together. Probably wouldn't take much for her to find out who Travis was associated with. She would likely recognize Brantley and Reese since they'd been on the news after Kate's rescue. The task force had gotten some press lately. She could easily tie the team to the governor.

Had he not given her enough credit? Here he'd thought they were dealing with a vengeful woman, but this… This spoke to something else entirely.

Travis shook his head, managed to get to his feet as the sirens grew nearer, flashing lights already blanketing the houses as an ambulance pulled up.

"Fuck," he groaned, pulling out his phone.

Wouldn't take long for Gage to get wind of what had happened, and he needed to call them to let them know he was all right before they came looking for him.

"Please tell me you're not involved in whatever just happened," Gage said without so much as a hello.

Evidently he already knew.

"I'm fine," he assured him. "Brantley and Reese and Trey are fine. That bitch blew up Jessica James's house."

There was a brief pause, then, "You know for a fact it was her?"

"You've got a better explanation?" he snapped defensively.

"Faulty gas line," Gage growled softly.

"Deadly fuckin' coincidence if that's the case, Gage," he bit out.

"Quit makin' this into—"

Before Gage could rip him a new one, Travis heard rustling on the phone.

"Come home, Trav," Kylie insisted, her tone heated but not as angry as Gage's. "Let Brantley and Reese deal with their stuff. JJ shouldn't be callin' you over there." Her tone cooled, held a wealth of concern. "You promised you'd let them handle this."

He didn't bother to tell his wife that it wasn't JJ who'd texted him. Nor did he tell her the house he was at had blown up, because it didn't sound to him like she knew. More than likely, Gage had gotten one of those automated text updates from the sheriff's department regarding the fire. Later they would see the aftermath on the nightly news. At that point, he would earn a bit of sympathy.

"I'll be home in a minute," he promised.

"Okay. Hurry, please. It'd be nice if we could have lunch together today."

Travis promised again, then disconnected the call. When he turned back, Brantley and Trey were standing beside him.

"Where's Reese?" he asked, scanning the area.

"With the EMTs," Brantley said, his tone level but hard. "Probably needs stitches, but he's refusin' treatment."

Of course he was.

"You all right?" Trey asked, giving him a once-over.

"Fine." Travis massaged his shoulder. "Nothin' some ibuprofen won't fix."

"Was it rigged to blow? Or did someone set it off?" Brantley asked, all three of them peering up at what was left of the house.

Damn good question.

"I'm leanin' toward rigged," Travis replied. "She thought we'd all be inside that house. Otherwise, she would've waited until we were."

"She?" Trey questioned.

"Juliet Prince."

"Right now, there's nothin' to say this was her," Brantley said firmly. "I believe in followin' the evidence, and right now, I don't have anything to say she's involved."

Travis didn't bother telling him he had nothing at all since his crime scene was still burning.

"What would she have to gain by kidnappin' Dante Greenwood?" Trey asked, sounding sincerely perplexed by the notion. "It just doesn't fit."

Travis sighed, hating that the man made sense.

"Charlie just got here," Trey said. "Lemme go fill her in on what's goin' on. I'll check on Reese, too."

Travis noticed the concern in Brantley's gaze as he glanced over at the ambulance on scene.

"He's tough," Travis told him.

Brantley turned back. "I know it."

Yet he still worried. Travis could understand. He was in the same boat. Although he knew Gage could hold his own, he worried about the man the same way he worried about Kylie and the kids. That was what happened when you loved someone.

"Why don't you get outta here," Brantley told him. "If by chance this is her, I'd prefer to keep you off the news."

"I'm happy to talk to the sheriff."

"Not necessary. Get home to your family. Keep an eye on them. We'll deal with this here."

Once more looking at the burning rubble, Travis nodded, then glanced over at Brantley, held his cousin's gaze. "If this *is* her... If she tried to put me in the ground..." He lowered his voice. "I'm gonna need a solid alibi, Brantley, because she won't get away this time."

His cousin had the decency to simply nod.

They both knew there was no talking him off the ledge. Because if Juliet Prince brought the fight to Coyote Ridge, she wouldn't walk away from it this time.

He would make damn sure of that.

Chapter Sixteen

"I DON'T NEED A DOCTOR," JJ INSISTED when Baz pulled up to a quaint two-story house.

"We'll let the doctor determine that," he said, just as he had when she'd asked where they were going after she'd woken to hear him on the phone.

JJ swallowed more arguments, because the truth was, she didn't feel all that well. Now that her adrenaline was waning, the pain had returned full force. Not only was there throbbing behind her eyes, she was nauseous, and if she had to spend much more time in this truck, she was probably going to embarrass herself.

"This is my father's personal physician," Baz explained as he put the truck in park. "You can tell him as much or as little as you'd like. He understands discretion."

JJ was hoping not to tell him anything more than that her head hurt, but she nodded in agreement.

With Baz's help, she got out of the truck and walked up the steps to the porch with its colonial-style columns. The red door opened before they could ring the bell. An older man with a head of white hair and sympathetic brown eyes gave her a thorough assessment before stepping out of the way.

"Thanks for seein' us, Doc." Baz kept his arm around her.

"I'm glad I was home. A few more minutes and I would've been on the golf course. Right this way."

The doctor led the way into a formal living room complete with a settee and matching ornate armchairs.

"Let me get my bag."

When Baz assisted her to the pretentious little couch, JJ glared up at him. "I will be fine, you know."

"I'm sure you will. You're hardheaded and all, but I just want to be sure."

Since it wasn't like she could run out of the house, JJ resigned herself to the checkup, hoping it would be quick and painless, because she really, *really* wanted to lie down.

BAZ WAS GRATEFUL IT WAS ONLY FIFTEEN minutes from the doctor's house to his father's because he wanted to get JJ off her feet and into bed, although he suspected she would fight him tooth and nail on that.

As soon as Dr. Medley gave his official diagnosis, a mild concussion, which explained her headache, nausea, and grogginess, Baz's concern had grown.

But it had been when he'd asked the doctor if she'd been drugged that Baz had seen red. Although he didn't draw blood or have any way to confirm, Dr. Medley believed there was a very good possibility. His best guess—which Baz had to pry out of him because doctors evidently did not like to *guess* at anything—was ketamine or something along those lines had been injected into her left arm, where he'd found what appeared to be a puncture mark.

The prescription: bed rest, a lot of fluids, and Tylenol—for the first twenty-four hours—for pain. After that, ibuprofen was safe.

Baz had left wishing JJ would let him take her to the hospital, but she had refused. Only when she had agreed to let Dr. Medley make a house call tomorrow had Baz decided to take her to his father's house as they'd planned.

"My father and stepmother are out of town," Baz reminded JJ as they entered the house. "But we're stayin' in the guesthouse, so we won't see them even if they come back unexpectedly."

Plus, they would have privacy in the *moderate-sized*—as his father referred to it—house, one of three enormous structures that sat on the twenty-three-acre estate. While Baz appreciated the privacy and the accommodations, he wouldn't go so far as to say it was moderate-sized. For a full-time family of five, maybe, but not for a place for people to temporarily lay their heads when visiting.

At thirty-seven hundred square feet, the contemporary modern structure, with its clean, neat lines, large, picture windows, and sustainable building materials had pretty much everything one would need for an overnight, including four bedrooms, a game room, media room, a gym, a fully stocked kitchen, butler and housekeeper service, and a variety of clothing in various sizes. You know, in the event someone came without their own things.

Baz knew they fell into that category, so he wouldn't bitch too much about it now.

"Let's get you into bed," Baz told JJ, holding her hand and leading the way through the open floor plan and down the hall to what was one of four enormous suites.

"Shower first, please."

"Of course."

They'd made it to his father's house without incident, and while Baz hadn't had quite the night JJ had, he was feeling some of the exhaustion from the waning adrenaline. He wanted nothing more than to shower and fall into bed for a few hours himself, but he knew that wasn't an option. He needed to contact Brantley, explain his actions since he'd spent the past hour and a half avoiding all incoming calls, including one from Brantley, one from Reese, and two from Charlie.

"Come on," he urged, knowing the adrenaline would fade completely once JJ realized she was safe, and she'd be hard-pressed to do much of anything at that point. "You can get cleaned up then into bed."

She peered up at him and nodded. It was pretty much the same response he'd gotten since they'd left her house.

Once in the bathroom, Baz turned on the water, then left her alone so he could grab her a robe for when she was finished. When he returned, she was still standing in the middle of the space, arms wrapped around her middle as though she was holding herself together.

"JJ?"

She turned to face him.

"We'll figure this out," he assured her.

What he wanted to say was that everything would be all right, but since he had no way of knowing that, he figured empty promises wouldn't make either of them feel any better.

The next thing he knew, she was in his arms, her face buried in his chest as she sobbed.

As much as he hated that she was crying, Baz held on to her for dear life. She was alive, and that was all that mattered to him at the moment. The thought of anything happening to her... He didn't want to think along those lines because he might find himself breaking down into tears.

When she pulled herself together, Baz dropped his arms, stood still while she stepped back.

"There're clothes in the closet. On the racks and in the drawers. All new and probably a few things in your size. When you're done, we'll get you settled in bed. But please, take your time. There's no rush."

He left her to clean up, stepping out of the bathroom to give her privacy, but he left the door partially opened so he could hear her if she called for him. He remained outside the door until he heard her moving around, the shower door open, close.

Content she could handle that task, he went into the kitchen, started a pot of coffee, and grabbed the iPad his father kept for guests to use. He would've preferred a computer, but until he could have one brought over from the main house, this would have to do.

Before he could create a guest account to log in, his cell phone rang. This time it was Trey, so he answered, knowing he would have to face the music eventually.

"Have you heard?" the man asked as soon as Baz said hello.

Baz walked over to the coffeepot. "Heard what?"

"JJ's house," Trey said, his voice low. "It blew up."

He nearly dropped his cell phone. "What do you mean it blew up?"

"I'm not sure how else to explain it to you. It just kinda went boom."

"Jesus Christ, Trey. Is anyone hurt?"

"No. God, I wouldn't be jokin' if they were. Brantley, Reese, and I were outside talkin' to Travis—"

"Why was Travis there?"

"Someone texted him, pretendin' to be JJ. Asked him to come by."

Holy shit. That…

"Everyone's wonderin' the same thing," Trey went on, as though he had read Baz's mind. "Is it just a coincidence? Or did Juliet have a hand in all of this?"

"What do you think?"

"I think it's all fucked up, that's what I think." Trey sighed. "But I'm takin' my cues from Brantley. He wants to look at the evidence, not jump to conclusions."

"You mean the evidence that was blown up in the explosion?"

Trey chuckled. "Yes."

"Good luck with that."

"Well, the good news is, Sheriff Endsley's on the scene. Brantley's leadin' the charge here. He wanted me to call, check in."

"He said that?"

"Not in so many words, no, but I got the gist of it."

"Is he pissed?"

"I think he would be if it weren't for the fact it was the smart thing to do," Trey answered. "That and JJ's house blowin' up and all that shit. How is she, by the way?"

"Holdin' it together." He gave Trey a high-level rundown of the doctor visit.

"Well, you keep her off her feet and let us worry about the rest. Cool?"

"For now."

"Good. We'll keep in touch."

Before he could ask more questions, try to dig for details, Trey disconnected.

Baz had come here to keep a low profile until they could figure out what happened at JJ's. Now that the crime scene was destroyed, did they have to stay hidden? Or would they be better off at HQ? Somewhere they had access to the equipment needed to track down Dante and whoever was responsible for this mess.

He considered calling Brantley, asking him, but decided against it. For now they would stay put, see what they could do from this end. JJ needed a quiet place to rest. And once she was feeling better, she would need some time to pull herself together. Not to mention, Baz wasn't keen on spending the day tiptoeing around the office to appease the masses.

When he heard the shower shut off, Baz headed back down the hall to the bedroom. He waited patiently for JJ to emerge from the bathroom. She was wearing a robe, her hair wet and hanging down her back.

"Here," he said, hurriedly pulling back the blankets on the bed. "Rest for a little while."

She didn't argue and he knew that meant she was in pain. Otherwise JJ would've told him to get bent so she could take care of business.

"I'll come back to check on you in an hour."

He left JJ curled up on her side, still wrapped in the robe, blankets pulled up to her neck.

Baz returned to the kitchen, poured himself a cup of coffee, and sat down at the bar with the iPad.

His first goal was to call the local hospitals, see if Dante'd been brought in. If that didn't work, he would retrace Dante's steps for the past few days, find out what had prompted him to contact JJ the way he had, figure out where he'd gone. And yes, that was him holding out hope that Dante wasn't stuck in some dungeon, bleeding out from a missing finger.

He called every hospital and emergency clinic within a fifteen-mile radius of Coyote Ridge. And that was saying something considering with the last economic boom, those freaking twenty-four-hour jobs had popped up on every street corner. Unfortunately, none of them had seen a man missing a finger. At least not in the past day or so.

Refreshing his coffee, Baz considered options for tracking Dante. He figured digitally was a good start, since he was stuck here, and the rest of the team was dealing with JJ's house.

Christ. How the hell was he supposed to tell her about that? That everything she'd had was now gone?

While he pondered how to do that, he ventured back down the hall, peeked in on her. She was exactly as he'd left her.

With her still resting, Baz had time to do something that would lead to him giving JJ some hopeful news when she joined him. It first required him to reach out to Charlie for a bit of information to help with the search. She graciously gave him Dante's phone number and a message from Brantley that basically said they would talk later. Luckily for him, Charlie was much nicer in relaying it than he figured Brantley would've been.

Turned out, finding Dante was next to impossible. His phone was turned off, or—if it was the one they'd found this morning—it had been destroyed if it was still in JJ's house. Regardless, the last cell tower it had pinged happened to be the one closest to JJ's house, which was no surprise. He decided to look at the other towers it had pinged in the past forty-eight hours, but that proved futile. The other few Dante'd been tracked by were close to downtown Austin and the route to Coyote Ridge. Which told him absolutely nothing.

When he heard footsteps in the hall, Baz paused his research and went to start another pot of coffee.

JJ appeared, looking a little better than she had. Her hair was still damp, but she was wearing a pair of light gray sweatpants, a plain black long-sleeve T-shirt that swallowed her up, and on her feet were a pair of thick wool socks.

Baz pulled out one of the barstools for her. "Feel any better? Can I get you anything?"

"Maybe some coffee," she said softly.

"Comin' right up."

He retrieved the pot, pausing the brew long enough to pour her a cup. When he took it to her, he found JJ staring at the iPad screen.

"I was tryin' to retrace Dante's steps," Baz explained. "Seein' if I can figure out where he's been. Thought it might tell me where he is now."

JJ nodded as though she'd expected as much.

He was surprised when she didn't take over his tablet, instead resting her elbows on the island, her hands wrapped firmly around the coffee mug.

"JJ?"

"Hmm?" She looked up at him as though seeing him for the first time.

"Talk to me. What's on your mind?"

She was staring at him, her eyes shifting over his face.

"JJ?"

"Why do you smell like perfume?"

Baz nearly dropped his own coffee, the question catching him completely off guard. "I … uh…"

JJ's expression remained stony. "Were you with someone last night, Baz?"

The question was so direct—likely her intention—that he couldn't skirt it. He would've given anything to take back what had happened last night, but Baz knew he couldn't. Which meant he had to own up to his mistakes even if he knew it would destroy any remaining hope that they could patch things up between them.

"Yes." He glanced down at his coffee mug. "I was."

When she didn't respond, Baz forced his gaze up. She was still watching him, disappointment and what looked a hell of a lot like hurt in her eyes.

"I'm so fuckin' sorry, JJ."

He started to move toward her, but she sat up straight, holding her hand up.

"Don't."

Baz didn't move from there. "JJ, let me explain."

"No." She shook her head, wincing when she did. "I don't want to hear about it. You're entitled to live your life, Baz, and I'm happy for you. But I…" She swallowed, holding his gaze. "I can't handle the details."

He found himself nodding in agreement. Not that he'd intended to give her details, but he did want to tell her why it had happened. It wouldn't change anything, but maybe it would help if she understood.

Then again, anything he said would sound like an excuse.

JJ gripped her mug again. "I keep replayin' last night. Seein' Dante…"

Looked as though they'd moved on.

Her eyes scanned his face. "He was actin' so weird. Anxious. Paranoid."

Although he would've preferred to clear the air between them, Baz knew this was more important. "But he didn't say anything?"

"He was freaked when I got there. Nearly knocked me down when we got inside." She slid her hands over her coffee mug as though the ceramic might warm them. "First thing he asked me was if I had my gun. I told him it was locked in the safe. He insisted I get it." She looked up. "I should've demanded he talk to me. Instead I was stallin', makin' coffee. I wasn't ready to hear more of his crap. If I would've made him tell me what he was scared of, maybe…" She shook her head. "I don't know if I can ever go back there. I don't think I'll ever not see blood everywhere."

Baz moved closer, standing across the island. "JJ, somethin' else happened after we left."

Her eyes were wide with concern when she looked up at him.

"There was an explosion. Your house … it's gone."

"Oh, my God. Brantley and Reese? Are they…?"

"They're fine," he added quickly. "Trey was there, too, but no one was in the house when it happened."

He decided not to tell her how Travis had been lured over. She didn't need to carry the weight of that just yet.

"Brantley's dealin' with things on that end. And we can stay here as long as we need to," he reassured her. "There are plenty of guest rooms. If you'd like to be alone, I can go over to the main house, stay there."

JJ shook her head. "No. I don't … I don't want to be alone."

"Then I'll stay here. But I'll give you space."

She nodded, picking up her coffee mug. "Why would Dante come to me last night? I haven't talked to him in months."

Baz figured that was the million-dollar question. And unfortunately, he didn't have an answer.

BRANTLEY DID HIS BEST TO ANSWER SHERIFF Endsley's questions while he watched Reese get checked out by the paramedic. The only thing he could think about was seeing Reese completely still after the blast, his limbs askew, body lifeless.

Fear had made his blood run cold, the thought of losing Reese… Brantley honestly wasn't sure he'd ever felt anything that terrifying. Including the day he thought he would die beneath the rubble of that building.

The moment he'd realized what had happened, Brantley hadn't given a second thought to himself or any possible injuries Travis or Trey might've sustained. His entire world had shifted into a pinpoint focus on Reese. Even with his brain temporarily scrambled from the blast, he'd known he had to get to Reese, had to help. Thankfully, the damage to them had been minimal. Especially considering what it could've been if they'd been closer to the house. Or worse, inside.

"You said JJ had a visitor last night," Sheriff Endsley prompted, interrupting Brantley's thoughts.

Brantley nodded, adjusted his focus once more. "Yeah."

"Who?"

"I'll tell you, but for right now, this stays between you and me, Sheriff. Understood?"

He could tell the older man wasn't keen on taking orders in his own jurisdiction, but the truth was, because he was on a special task force for the governor of Texas, Brantley's authority won out over any and all. For a few more days, anyway. And since this particular case involved the governor's son, he would be taking it, regardless of any pushback he might receive.

"Fine," Endsley grumbled.

"Dante Greenwood," he said, ensuring he kept his voice low and his mouth obstructed on the off chance someone was recording them. He'd seen half a dozen phone cameras out already, and a news van had arrived a short time ago.

Sheriff Endsley's face tightened, his expression turning hard. "Are you sayin'—"

"Right now, I'm not sayin' anything," he interrupted. "What I need from you and your team is for you to work this crime scene."

The sheriff's gaze swung to what was left of JJ's house. "Not much to work with." He looked back at Brantley. "In case you hadn't noticed."

"Trust me, I noticed," he growled hotly. "Had it not been for Travis showin' up, I wouldn't be here talkin' to you now, Sheriff. I woulda been inside. With Reese *and* my brother."

Sheriff Endsley's eyes flashed with sympathy. "Understood."

"Before the explosion, we hadn't gathered much of anything. We were reviewin' the scene."

"And where was JJ durin' all of this?"

Brantley knew he had to tread lightly here. "She was distraught, so I had one of my team take her somewhere safe."

"Which is where?"

"Right now, she's safer without anyone else knowin'."

That seemed to pique the sheriff's interest. "You think she's the target?"

"I think Dante's the target, but I think whoever's got him is willin' to do whatever they have to. So, can you do that? Can you process the scene? Get a fire investigator out here? See if they can determine what caused the explosion?"

They both knew he'd merely phrased them as questions.

The sheriff's hazel eyes narrowed again. "You're gonna owe me one, Walker."

Considering the sheriff wasn't asking the difficult questions, he already owed him one.

Brantley left Sheriff Endsley to deal with the aftermath of the scene, rounding up his team and sending them back to HQ with what they had. When Travis told him he was going home and would keep his nose out of the investigation, Brantley had some doubt. However, he had no reason not to take him at his word. Travis wasn't one to say things unless he was going to follow through. Nor was he one to excuse himself if he thought he might have something to contribute.

"How're you feelin'?" Brantley asked Reese once they were in the truck heading back to HQ.

"Fine." Reese peered over. "Seriously, Brantley. I'm fine. It's a scratch. Nothin' more."

A scratch that had bled like he'd opened an artery. It had scared the shit out of Brantley when he'd seen all the blood. And since there was currently a butterfly bandage holding it closed, it probably needed a few stitches.

"You sure you don't want to go to the hospital?" he asked, simply because it would make him feel better if Reese got a complete checkup.

Reese huffed. "What would you say if I asked you that question?"

Brantley grinned. Yeah, he understood where Reese was coming from, but that didn't mean he couldn't ask.

"I'm just glad Tesha wasn't with us," Reese said softly.

Brantley saw the concern in the man's eyes, knew he'd grown seriously attached to that dog. If anything happened to her, it would be a rough day for everyone involved.

"I'm not willin' to leave her alone again," Reese added. "Not when we don't know what's goin' on here."

The way he said it had Brantley cutting a quick look over. "What're you thinkin'?"

Reese shrugged one shoulder, continued to stare out the side window. "Without anything to go on, we can't be sure Dante was the target. It makes sense that he was, yes. However…" Reese looked over. "What if JJ was the target and they used Dante to get to her?"

"Good question. The answer is we don't know until we work it. And the first thing we have to do is find Dante. Regardless of the motive, Dante's missin'. Findin' him'll give us the answers. We can take Tesha to JJ if you want. If you think she'll be safer."

"I thought you didn't know where JJ was."

"Technically, I don't."

"Technically?"

"They're holed up at Baz's father's," he told Reese, not wanting to reveal how he knew that. Probably wouldn't go over well if Reese knew Brantley had a way of tracking all of them.

"Might be a good idea to keep her away from all this for a little while."

Brantley agreed, but he said, "Just let me know what you decide. For now, I think our only priority is findin' Dante."

"How do you propose we do that without JJ?"

"I've got a secret weapon," he admitted.

"Lemme guess. You called Luca?"

Brantley couldn't hide his surprise. "You know Luca Switzer?"

"Who *doesn't* know Luca?"

"Let me rephrase that," Brantley stated. "How do *you* know Luca?"

"My sister was friends with Holly. When I came back, I ran into her. We got to talkin'."

"Holly? Luca's little sister?"

"Well, she's all grown up now, but yeah. Why?"

"Small world," Brantley mused.

"More like small town," Reese said with a gruff laugh that didn't quite hide his pain. "How do you know Luca?"

"He used to date my sister."

"Which sister?"

"Bryn. Back in high school." Brantley pulled into the driveway. "I guess it's really true. Everyone knows everyone in Coyote Ridge."

"I was thinkin' more along the lines of half the people in Coyote Ridge have dated the other half."

There was no arguing with that, and still Brantley refrained from asking Reese if he had dated Holly. He honestly didn't want to know.

"Luca agreed to work with us?"

"He heard about the fire on the scanner. Answered on the first ring."

When Brantley pulled the truck to a stop, they both got out, headed into the house.

Tesha was there to greet them, her tail wagging. Brantley had to admit, it was a relief to see her. He'd had a morose thought a short time ago, feared that if they were the target, someone might go after one of them. And a surefire way to hurt Reese was to hurt his dog.

And hurting Reese … well, that was a surefire way to have hell rain down on you.

Brantley wouldn't have to worry about Travis going off half-cocked because he'd take them out without a second thought.

Chapter Seventeen

JULIET STARED AT THE TELEVISION, WATCHING THE breaking news about a house fire in Coyote Ridge, Texas.

Ever since she'd lost access to the live feed from Jessica James's cameras, she'd had to resort to getting the information from the media. If she could've gotten a hold of good old Samuel, maybe she could get access to one of the neighbors' cameras, but the bastard wasn't answering his phone.

So here she was, on the edge of her seat, desperately waiting to hear what the body count was from the explosion that had rocked that stupid little town.

Honestly, she'd thought Dante's kidnapping plan was the most ridiculous thing she'd ever fucking heard. But she considered herself an opportunist, which was why she'd come up with the idea of using Marcus for her own devious scheme. She would even take credit for coming up with the idea to put a bomb in the house, one that would wipe out any trace they'd been there at all. At least that was what she'd told Marcus. Her real plan had been to wipe Travis Walker from the face of the earth.

"Behind me you can see what remains of the house that exploded just a short time ago," the field reporter announced.

Juliet held her breath, her hands wringing in her lap. "Let them all be dead," she whispered harshly.

"Despite the obvious devastation, there is some good news."

"No," Juliet muttered. "No good news, dammit."

"We've been told by the EMTs that no one was in the house when it exploded, and the injuries to those nearby were minimal."

"No!" Juliet screamed, not caring if someone in the neighboring rooms might hear her.

This could *not* be happening. Not again.

"How the fuck does he keep doing this?" she ground out through clenched teeth.

She was sick and fucking tired of making the effort only to have it backfire in her face. And that do-gooder Travis Walker continued to get away with destroying her life.

He had single-handedly brought everything down around her with that stupid resort of his. If her pathetic ex-husband hadn't insisted they go do perverse things with other couples, Juliet would be back in Mississippi, getting her hair and nails done, going shopping whenever she wanted, buying whatever she wanted.

She damn sure wouldn't be in this moldy, roach-infested motel in Grand Rapids, Michigan. She'd been hoping to make it to Canada and slip out of the US unnoticed, but something kept holding her back, so she was stuck here.

All thanks to Travis Walker, who'd taken her entire life away from her by sending Nicholas that stupid invitation to come live out his fantasies at that stupid fetish resort. And because Juliet had felt her relationship with Nicholas beginning to fray at the edges, she'd had no choice but to agree to accompany her husband.

No, maybe she hadn't actually loved Nicholas, but who gave a shit? He hadn't seemed to notice. Or maybe he had and she hadn't cared enough to realize it. So, when he told her he wanted to participate in partner swapping to spice things up between them, she'd figured why not. She would've taken it all back if she'd known the guy she got to screw was only a smite better in bed than Nicholas, which meant she'd been yawning before he ever rammed his dick inside her.

It wasn't long after they'd left Alluring Indulgence Resort that Nicholas started acting funny. He became secretive, going on more business trips than usual, not coming home for days on end. Juliet probably should've given a shit, or pretended to, because if she had, Nicholas wouldn't have blindsided her with his demand for a divorce.

Divorce!

It wasn't like she missed him. Hell, she didn't even like him. But her kid … she did miss Lana most of the time. She definitely missed the money she should've gotten when the courts granted her full custody. Only they hadn't because Nicholas had brought up that stupid incident when Juliet had left Lana in the backseat of the car that one time. One freaking time. It wasn't *her* fault she'd had to get her hair done and the nanny had failed her, claiming she had something else to do at the time. And it wasn't like Lana had died. It hadn't been all that hot or anything. The EMTs had gotten her to the hospital, and they'd hooked Lana up to an IV, but only for fluids. She'd been a little dehydrated, that was all. Juliet still didn't understand why anyone made a big deal out of it.

But Nicholas had used it against her, telling the courts she was unfit. Juliet knew she wasn't unfit, she just didn't want to be bogged down with a child all the time. She hadn't been the one who wanted to have a baby. That was Nicholas's idea, and she'd agreed to it because she knew it would get her more money if he ever did divorce her, which he'd threatened to do on more than one occasion.

In one fell swoop, thanks to that fucking visit to that fucking resort, Juliet had lost every good thing she ever had. No child support, no alimony. The only thing she had left was the measly seven hundred and fifty thousand dollars that she'd drained from the bank accounts before Nicholas cut her off.

All thanks to Travis Walker.

She growled, her fury igniting into rage.

Pacing back and forth between the queen bed and the wall in the tiny room, Juliet attempted to come up with a new plan.

Her thoughts drifted to Dante. More accurately to his extortion plan.

She could do that.

Taking a deep breath, Juliet shoved her hair out of her face, stood up straight.

Yes, dammit. She could do that. But not a kid this time. She didn't have the time or energy to put up with a whiny brat.

Maybe she could take the resort hostage. The whole place. She'd be able to get some money out of Travis Walker that way. He'd probably pass it hand over fist to get his precious hotel back.

Juliet shook her head. No, that wouldn't work. Too much of a risk. Too many variables.

She needed to take the one thing Travis loved the most. From the articles and snippets she'd read about him, he was a family man. He was close to his mother and father, his brothers. He also had a husband and a wife—a true pervert.

One of them would do. Maybe his mom. She was old. Juliet shouldn't have any problem overpowering her, holding her hostage until Travis forked over some money.

"But what if she's fragile?" she wondered aloud.

What if she kidnapped the mom and she died from a heart attack or something? Juliet would be right back at square one. Not where she wanted to be.

She would have to think on it a little more. But it was definitely time she got her hands dirty again. More chance of success that way.

Yes. She would go down the road and buy that sexy little blue Mustang she'd had her eye on and drive to Coyote Ridge and take care of this problem once and for all. And the time it would take to get there would give her an opportunity to come up with the perfect plan.

The one that would take Travis Walker down once and for all.

REESE FOLLOWED BRANTLEY OVER TO THE BARN, keeping an eye on Tesha as they went.

From the moment JJ's house had exploded and he'd seen that Brantley was all right, his only thought had been for the safety of his dog. He would probably go so far as to say he worried more about her than himself, so knowing she was safe and sound was reassuring, enough that he could actually breathe easier.

"I think it's in our best interest to inform Governor Greenwood," Reese told Brantley when they stepped into the barn.

"We don't have any proof that was Dante's finger."

"No, we don't. But we're inclined to believe it is. And if this is a K and R, he should be receivin' a ransom call. We need to be there if and when that happens."

"And if it doesn't happen?"

Reese sighed because he knew Brantley was playing devil's advocate.

"Okay, say we wait. What's the governor gonna say when he realizes we knew about this and didn't tell him? Hell, he'll likely hear about the explosion from someone. Then he'll be callin'. Wouldn't you rather we reach out first?"

Brantley's eyes were narrowed. "I'd prefer you don't make so much damn sense."

Reese smiled, couldn't help it. "You didn't fall in love with a dumb ass. What can I say?"

"No, I certainly did not," Brantley muttered. "I just hate to give them anything more to worry about. Not until we're positive somethin's happened to Dante." Brantley peered over at him. "They went through so much with Corinne."

Reese understood Brantley's reasoning. After what the Greenwoods had gone through when their daughter had been abducted a few months back, he didn't like the idea of making them worry again, either.

"We have to tell them," Reese stated. "You know it's the only way to do this."

Brantley stared back at him for a few long seconds before he blew out a lengthy breath. "Fine. But we go to him. I can't do this over the phone."

The chime from the alarm sounded, signaling someone had arrived.

Reese peered over at the monitor on the wall, saw Trey's truck and another parking in the driveway.

"That's Luca," Brantley informed him. "He brought Holly. Said they'd do whatever we need them to do."

"You know JJ's gonna go apeshit when she realizes you've replaced her," Reese told him.

"No one's bein' replaced," Brantley grumbled. "He's fillin' in temporarily."

"Temporarily, my ass," Reese countered. "I know how your brain works. This is an unofficial job interview."

He could see the truth on Brantley's face. "Okay, maybe you don't tell JJ that part."

Oh, he wouldn't. Reese knew there was more than enough work for them to bring on another with JJ's skill set, but he seriously doubted JJ would see it that way. Not in her current predicament. She'd simply think they were bringing someone on to take her place.

While they waited for the others to join them, Reese went into the kitchen, scrounged through the cabinets until he found the bottle of aspirin. He popped two pills in his mouth, downed them with water. As it was, the cut on his head was burning like the fires of hell, and he figured while he didn't have a headache yet, why risk it?

Reese was returning to the main room when his cell phone rang.

Snatching his phone from his pocket, he glanced at the screen, saw Baz's number.

"Hey," he answered quickly. "How's JJ doin'?"

"Better. And you? I heard you took a hard hit."

Reese peered at Brantley, who was walking to the door to open it for their new arrivals.

"It's nothin'. Just a scratch. About to head over to the governor's mansion, let them know what's goin' on."

"You've got confirmation the blood and the finger belonged to Dante?"

"No, unfortunately. But I think it's safe to say somethin' happened to him from what little we do know."

"And the crime scene…? Gone, huh?"

"All of it," Reese confirmed. "There was nothin' left to salvage at JJ's." Reese exhaled, turning away from the people filing in. "Even her SUV's a total."

"Fuck."

Reese echoed that sentiment, but he kept it to himself.

"Unfortunately, we can't worry about any of that right now. We have to find Dante. He's somewhere, and since he hasn't come to one of us, we have to assume he's been kidnapped."

And that was assuming the man was alive, something else Reese kept to himself.

"I checked all the hospitals and clinics in the area," Baz relayed. "Dante hasn't received medical care."

"Son of a bitch," he muttered under his breath. "I think we have to assume the injury's not as bad as it looks."

"So all that blood…"

"Unless they gutted Dante from neck to navel, they wouldn't get that much blood," Reese told him. "And since we only had a finger…"

"Point taken. What else do you want me to do?" Baz inquired.

"Well, since we can't rule out that JJ was the target and they used Dante to get to her, I'd say it's best if you keep her there. At least until we know more."

"JJ the target? Then why not take her instead of Dante?"

"Good question. One of many."

"I guess it might explain why Dante made her get her gun," Baz said.

"What're you talkin' about?"

"She told me he insisted she get her gun from the safe, said she needed to keep it on her at all times."

"I didn't find it at the scene," Reese said, thinking back. "Why would they take her gun?"

"Another good question. I need some time to process this, and we need to talk to Governor Greenwood. So for right now, sit tight. We'll let you know when we have somethin', Baz, I promise."

"Easier said than done. You know JJ. Once she starts feelin' better, she's gonna want somethin' to do."

"Understood. I'll let you know as soon as we know."

He could tell Baz wasn't happy with that answer, but at least the man had the decency to hold his tongue. For now.

When the call ended, Reese tucked his phone back in his pocket, turned around to find Brantley was standing over Luca, watching as the man's fingers flew over a keyboard.

Reese didn't know much about Luca Switzer, aside from the fact his family had been in Coyote Ridge almost as long as the Walkers. And by family, Luca's father and uncle had been the terrors of the county back in the day. At least according to rumor. Luca had a wild streak himself, but everyone said he managed to keep it under control because of Holly. Since their father was a grade A asshole, Luca had been responsible for raising her, and in order to do so, he couldn't get into too much trouble.

"Hey, Tavoularis," Luca called out, eyes never leaving the computer screen. "How's it goin'?"

"It's goin'. We appreciate you doin' this."

This time Luca did look over, his navy-blue eyes intense. "Anything for a friend."

"Hey, Reese," Holly said with a small wave.

"Hey. He wrangle you into this?"

She smiled. "I didn't give him a choice."

"She's bossy like that," Luca joked, eyes on the screen.

"What is it you're doin', anyway?" Reese asked, coming to stand beside Brantley and Trey.

"I'm makin' friendly with some of the cameras at the local businesses."

"Makin' friendly?" Reese laughed. "What you mean to say is you're hackin' into them."

"Call it what you will." Luca continued to stare at the screen. "What time frame are we lookin' for?"

Reese glanced at Brantley, waited for him to answer.

"Try around twenty-one hundred last night. Baz said he was at the diner with JJ. He got to Moonshiners shortly after that."

"Nine o'clock," Luca said. "Got it."

They stood there for several minutes, watching images play across the screen. Nothing worth noting happened, unfortunately. Thanks to it being New Year's Eve, there were a lot of people out and about. Even small towns celebrated holidays like this one.

Not that Reese expected them to get lucky enough to catch Dante and his captor chatting it up on the street.

"What about JJ?" Luca asked. "Doesn't she have cameras?"

"She did," Brantley confirmed. "House blew up."

Luca whistled long and low. "Heard about that." His fingers moved faster on the keyboard. "Shouldn't matter, though. If I know JJ, she's got them recordin', and that information would be saved in the cloud."

Brantley peered over at Reese, forehead wrinkled to reflect his confusion.

Reese merely shook his head, letting him know they'd get into that later. While Brantley was good at a lot of things, technology wasn't his strong suit.

"All right. Here we go." Luca's fingers stopped, his hand moving to the mouse. "Anyone ever tell JJ she's paranoid? She's got half a dozen cameras rollin' twenty-four seven. Might be considered overkill."

Reese didn't respond to Luca's musings.

Luca pointed at the monitor. "That looks to be JJ pullin' into her driveway. Parkin'. Gettin' out."

They watched on the screen as JJ walked up to the front door, unlocked it.

"That's Dante," Brantley noted, stepping closer.

Sure enough, that was Dante Greenwood joining her on the porch. The camera was a bit grainy and a little glitchy, so every move they made looked pieced together, but it was easy to discern what was going on. Once inside, they watched as Dante gave one more look out the door before closing it.

"Pull up another camera," Brantley ordered, his impatience beginning to bleed through.

Luca skimmed the other camera recordings until he found the one that overlooked the living room.

For the next ten minutes, they watched things play out just as JJ had said. Dante moved from room to room, they shared a brief conversation, then JJ disappeared down the hall in the direction of her bedroom. When she returned, she held up her gun, clearly showing Dante she had it. They spoke again and then JJ was walking off. Then the camera feed blipped and went fuzzy.

"What happened?"

"Looks like it got turned off."

"Why'd she have her gun?" Brantley asked.

"She said Dante told her to get it," Reese answered. When Brantley shot a questioning look his way, he added, "I just got off the phone with Baz. She doesn't seem to know why. He just told her to keep it on her."

"Maybe he was hopin' she would protect him?" Holly pondered.

"She have a view of the kitchen?" Reese asked.

Once again, Luca was skimming the recorded feeds, but this time he was shaking his head.

"She does," Luca confirmed, "but not from that time period. Looks like it had a critical system failure."

"Meaning?"

Luca shrugged a shoulder. "Could be anything."

"Someone disabled it, too?"

"Possibly, but not likely. I'd say old equipment. Doesn't look like she's upgraded these in a while."

Of course it couldn't be they'd get lucky enough to see who else was in JJ's house.

"You think whoever set this in motion is skilled?" Luca asked, twisting in his chair to look at them.

"They're somethin'," Brantley bit out, pivoting and pacing.

Reese remained where he was, staring at the screen that showed a list of files.

"Go back to the camera at the front of the house," he instructed Luca.

Luca spun around. "What're you lookin' for?"

"To see if they disabled the other cameras after Dante arrived."

Luca keyed in a few things, then they were watching from JJ's front porch once more.

"What time is that?" Reese asked when the porch light was flipped off.

"Nine thirty-seven," Luca noted.

They continued to watch, although it was nearly impossible to see. JJ clearly hadn't invested in night-vision cameras, because this one reflected nothing more than a dark screen with a few pinpoints of light every now and then.

"Hold up. Is that…?"

There was a sliver of light, and Dante appeared in the doorway, then he stepped back and another figure stepped inside.

"Son of a bitch," Brantley grumbled. "Dante opened the fucking door. That motherfucker."

Reese peered at Luca. "Any chance you can get into any other camera feeds nearby?"

"Like what? This is Coyote Ridge. Not like we're spyin' on the residents."

"What about doorbell cameras?" Holly suggested.

All eyes shifted to her.

"Damn good thinkin'," Reese told her.

She smiled, a light blush infusing her cheeks.

Before Luca could get to work, Brantley's cell phone rang.

"It's the governor's wife," he said, his gaze swinging from one face to the next.

Reese moved a step closer. "Answer it."

Brantley did, and for a few seconds, he was silent before saying, "Hold on, Trina. Slow down." He pulled his phone from his ear, tapped the screen so the call would come through the speaker. "All right. Tell me what happened."

"It's Dante," the frantic woman explained. "He's been kidnapped!"

"Trina, I need you to calm down."

"Please, Brantley. Please. You have to come over. They … they said they would call back with instructions."

Reese looked over at Brantley, saw the anger flash in his gaze, and knew he was thinking the same thing Reese was: Dante Greenwood had stooped to an all new low.

AFTER JJ FINISHED HER COFFEE, SHE EXCUSED herself back to the room Baz had brought her to, crawled back in bed, and slept. If it hadn't been for Baz's poking and prodding her every hour—doctor's orders, he reminded her when she'd all but bitten his head off—she would likely still be snoozing.

Maybe. Her stomach was grumbling loudly enough to wake the dead. And since the clock on the bedside table said they were inching toward dinner in the very near future, her grumbling stomach was requesting sustenance even if she was hesitant to feed it. Now that the nausea was gone, she didn't want to risk it coming back.

On the plus side, the sleep had helped to alleviate the majority of her headache. However, once she started to feel more human, she'd started sulking, pacing, and trying to wrap her head around everything. Only she wasn't letting Baz know that, because if she had time to sulk and pace, she knew she had time to work. Which meant she needed to help the team figure out who had Dante and where they'd gone. It was the only way she would figure out how she'd come to be a pawn in this and what it really meant for her.

Sadly, she couldn't muster the energy to care.

Well, that wasn't entirely true. She cared. In fact, she was worried about Dante, but right then she felt helpless.

Sure, it was probably another pity party, brought on by the fact that she had smelled perfume on Baz's shirt. Something flowery and fruity, which was making her brain work overtime trying to imagine the type of woman who wore shit like that. It wasn't sexy, but it wasn't something a grandmother would wear, either. Maybe young? Flirty?

Was that who Baz had been with last night? A young, flirty woman who'd had the pleasure of his company, gotten close enough to transfer her scent? Did JJ know her? Did she live or work in Coyote Ridge? Would JJ be subjected to seeing Baz with another woman from here on out? Was it serious?

All the questions had her stomach roiling, her heart cracking open just a little more.

He'd been with another woman.

And yes, her entire world had literally been blasted apart a short time ago, her ex-boyfriend was possibly lying dead somewhere, and whoever took him clearly had it out for her since they'd blown up her house. Hell, she could've been inside at the time. Had it not been for Baz whisking her away, she very likely would've been.

And despite all that, all JJ could think about was Baz and some floozy.

As she stood at the French doors that led out onto a small private patio overlooking what she'd normally consider a rather lovely pond, the only thing she could do was imagine what Baz looked like in the throes of passion with another woman.

It would've been easier if she could scrounge up some anger, but since this was all her fault, the only thing she managed was a few tears leaking down her cheeks.

JJ didn't want to cry about it. She didn't want to think about the fact she had effectively pushed Baz into the arms of another woman by being ... her.

"It was inevitable," she whispered under her breath.

From the beginning, JJ had known she would fuck this all up. Every time she found something she gave a shit about, it was ripped right out of her life. And her actions or words were generally at the epicenter of the explosion that leveled things around her.

Interesting metaphor considering that was exactly what had happened to her house.

She closed her eyes, took a deep breath, but when she did, her mind conjured up the image of Baz standing in the kitchen admitting to her that he'd been with another woman last night. He'd looked so guilt-ridden it had pained her to see it.

But he shouldn't feel guilty. JJ had all but ordered him to move on with his life, not to wait for her. And it wasn't like she was mad about it. No, that wasn't the right word. It was more along the lines of heartbroken.

A soft knock sounded from behind her, drawing her out of her thoughts.

When she turned around, gripping the blanket she'd pulled over her shoulders to ward off the chill, JJ found Baz standing in the doorway. His dark blond hair was still wet from his shower, his hard-angled face clean-shaven. But his eyes were what she noticed most. Not the intense color this time, either. It was what was in them that had her heart pinching in her chest.

"Can I get you anything?" he asked, facing off with her from across the room.

She wanted to move toward him, to simply walk into his arms and let him hold her until the cold seeped out of her bones, but she knew she couldn't. Not anymore.

"I'm good," she lied. "Did Brantley and Reese find anything?"

He shook his head, stepped forward. "Nothin' yet. Do you know a Luca Switzer?"

JJ frowned. "Yeah. Why?"

"Trey said he's helpin' them with some research."

That cold that had filled her marrow flashed hot for a moment, then froze over again.

"That rat bastard," she muttered, turning away from Baz, and for the first time since she woke up in her blood-sprayed house, something other than fear slammed into her.

"You don't like Luca?"

"I'm not talkin' about Luca," she snapped back, staring out the window as though that might possibly help. "I'm talkin' about Brantley, the rat bastard traitor. I should've known he'd do this."

Baz's voice sounded closer when he said, "Do *what* exactly?"

"Replace me."

"I ... uh... JJ, I don't think that's what he's doin'."

She spun around, grateful for the energy that came along with all those emotions beginning to churn through her. "I am damn good at what I do, Baz. No, I'm *better* than damn good. I'm ... I'm brilliant."

A smile pulled at his mouth. "Modesty'll get you everywhere in life."

JJ ignored his teasing. "And I know a lot of brilliant people who can't quite do what I do."

"Okay. We've established you're brilliant. What's the point here?"

JJ narrowed her eyes and pursed her lips. "Luca Switzer is ... the asshole's a freaking genius."

Baz's eyebrows dipped low. "I'm confused. You're brilliant, but Luca's a genius."

"Yes, damn it. And Brantley traded me in for an upgraded model."

Now Baz laughed, a sharp echo in the enormous room. "I seriously doubt that's what happened. I think he's just trying to figure out what's goin' on, and he doesn't want to put that burden on you."

"I deserve that burden," she argued, her tone that of a petulant, bitter child. "It's mine to have if I want it."

Baz continued to stare at her, amusement glittering in his otherworldly eyes. "And I assume this means you're gonna take it?"

"Damn right I am." JJ yanked the blanket off her shoulders, tossed it onto the bed as she strolled toward the door. "I need a computer."

Chapter Eighteen

IT WAS DÉJÀ VU.

The first and only time Brantley had come to the governor's mansion had been when Dante called at his mother's request because Katrina Greenwood believed her daughter had been kidnapped.

She'd been right.

When William Dugan felt the Off the Books Task Force was getting too close to figuring him out, he'd resorted to drastic measures. Corinne had been taken right out of her apartment by a man who had a penchant for keeping young women, sometimes girls, against their will, brainwashing them into believing he was their husband, then murdering them when they were no longer of use.

Katrina's instincts had been spot on, and because of that, they'd managed to find Corinne as well as Lauren Tyler, a girl who'd gone missing from Coyote Ridge ten years earlier.

"It sucks that we're doin' this again," he muttered to Reese and Trey as the three of them stepped into the house using the back entrance. Brantley had brought his brother along to ensure someone was able to stay with the Greenwoods throughout the ordeal.

"That it does," Reese replied.

Instead of Dante greeting them, this time they were met by Corinne. She looked tired, not even close to her usual vibrant twenty-four-year-old self.

Brantley could see the concern and fear etched on her pretty face as she greeted them with hugs.

"My parents are in the living room," she said softly. "My mom refuses to move away from the phone."

"Do you know what happened?" he asked, wishing to get a little insight before he joined them.

"She's a bit erratic," Corinne said, her face a ghostly white, "so I didn't understand much. A man called. At least she thinks it was a man. She said his voice was disguised with one of those robot-sounding things."

"Did he say what he wanted?"

Corinne shook her head. "He asked if my dad was here. She told him no, and he said the governor needed to be here when he called back or"—she swallowed hard and a sheen of tears clouded her eyes—"or he'd kill Dante."

Reese was instantly there, putting his arm around Corinne's narrow shoulders, pulling her close as he started toward the living room, muttering to her softly. "Let's go in here, talk to your mom and dad. Get this figured out."

Brantley sighed, then nodded his chin in their direction, a silent instruction for Trey to go with them.

Once he was alone, Brantley took a deep breath, scanned the large, modern kitchen, and prepared himself for what was to come.

He recalled what he'd seen on that grainy security camera. Whoever was calling … whoever was likely going to demand a ransom … they were doing this with Dante. And he knew that as certainly as he knew his own name.

The question he and Reese and Trey had pondered on the drive over was whether or not they should tell Gerard and Katrina. He damn sure had no intention of letting Dante get away with this, but he also wasn't willing to let the Greenwoods fork over whatever ungodly amount of money was requested in order to get their son back safely when he was already safe.

The only reason they hadn't decided on outing Dante's plan was that damned finger. Deep down, he knew that finger belonged to Dante. Which meant one of two things: either Dante was a complete idiot and had cut off his own finger in an effort to make this plausible—highly unlikely considering his vanity—or something had gone cross between Dante and the person he was working with.

Because of that, they agreed they would let the fake kidnapper remain in control for now. They would change the narrative to work for them, but in order to do that, they needed the ransom demand to be made and the Greenwoods to buy them a little time.

When he joined the others in the living room, he cataloged the scene before him.

Katrina was sitting on a salmon-colored couch, Corinne at her side. Both women were huddled close, arms around one another as though holding each other together.

In one of the two straight-backed armchairs patterned in flowers the color of the couch was Gerard. He looked like a defeated man, his eyes rimmed in red, his body language rigid. When Brantley stepped into the room, the man pinned him with a distraught gaze.

Trey and Reese were nearby, doing their best to blend in with the furniture and failing miserably.

As he stared at the overwrought family, Brantley knew he needed to come clean about what had happened at JJ's before they heard it elsewhere. He didn't know quite where to start, so he decided ripping off the Band-Aid was likely the most respectful means.

Brantley stepped around to stand so that all three of them could see him, but he refused to sit down when Gerard motioned toward the other armchair.

"Sir, before the kidnapper calls back, I'd like to have someone on my team run a trace on the call." Brantley motioned toward the cordless receiver on the table. "To do that, I need to know the number."

When Corinne rattled it off, Brantley shot a text to Luca asking him for the trace. The response he got was immediate and affirmative.

He kept his focus on Gerard, finding it difficult to look at Katrina or Corinne. The last thing he wanted was to see pain on the women's faces.

"Also," he said as he was tucking his phone back in his pocket, "there was an incident we need you to be aware of."

Gerard was immediately shaking his head. "The only person I'm worried about right now is Dante. So your incident'll have to wait until later."

"The incident involves your son," he added, his tone harder than before, not appreciating the governor giving him the brush-off regardless of the topic.

When no one spoke, Brantley continued. "This mornin', one of my investigators called me to come over to JJ's house to deal with an urgent matter."

"JJ?" Katrina's eyes widened with worry. "Is she all right?"

"She is, yes."

"What incident? And what does it have to do with anything?" Gerard hissed, his eyes reflecting his confusion and his anger with the entire situation.

"Sir—" Brantley began heatedly but was cut off.

"Sir, last night, your son reached out to Jessica James," Reese relayed, his tone matter-of-fact and far more calm than Brantley's. "From her account, he was upset, lookin' for help. We're not certain why he reached out to her rather than one of us, or even you, but we're lookin' into the matter."

Gerard's eyes had rounded like saucers while Katrina's face was now ashen, fear glittering in hers.

"Are you telling me…?"

"What we're tellin' you, sir," Brantley stated firmly yet sympathetically, "is that we've spent the past few hours lookin' into this. We were about to come over to discuss with you when Katrina received that call."

Brantley opted not to tell them that he believed Dante was involved in his own kidnapping. Probably would get him kicked out on his ear.

"You knew?" Gerard exclaimed. "You *knew* and you didn't think it was urgent enough to come right here? Who the hell do you think you are, Walker? I have every right to know——"

"Gerard," Katrina's voice was soft yet powerful. "They're doin' their jobs. It's not our place to question their methods."

Governor Greenwood took a deep breath, stared Brantley down.

When no one else laid into him, Brantley decided to share what he could. He explained all that they knew for fact, how Dante had called, the amputated finger, the state of JJ's house both before and after the explosion.

"An explosion?" The governor had the decency to look contrite. "Was anyone injured?"

"No, sir. Reese, Trey, and I were the only ones there at the time, and we'd gone outside to speak with my cousin Travis."

"Someone was after him," Trina said, clearly processing what she'd learned. "Someone was after my son, and he went to JJ for help."

Brantley figured that was a logical conclusion. Likely incorrect, but still logical.

"Because JJ was unable to seek help until this mornin', we assume whoever took Dante had enough time to take him somewhere safe until they can negotiate with you."

"But they have to come out at some point," Corinne noted, her tone pleading. "If they want a ransom, they'll have to come get it, right?"

"Or they'll have us take it somewhere, leave it," he told them, watching all three of them. "That's why we're here. We want to help you negotiate Dante's safe return."

"You think this is only about money?" Gerard asked. "Or do you think it's retaliation against me?"

"It could be the latter, but you have to consider there were likely many opportunities for someone to take Dante if they were simply lookin' to get back at you. What we don't understand is why he would go to JJ. She hasn't spoken to him in months, and they didn't end things on good terms."

"You think he reached out to her because someone made him?"

More like he thought it was the best way to manipulate the situation. But Brantley kept that to himself and said, "It's a good possibility."

"Where's JJ now?" Katrina asked, still looking shocked and stricken.

Thinking on his feet, Brantley said, "We have her lyin' low, in the event this had somethin' to do with her. She was attacked last night and possibly drugged, so there's a chance she's still in danger."

Katrina's hand went to her heart. "Oh, God."

Her exclamation was cut off by the ringing of the telephone.

Trina instantly looked down at where the cordless receiver lay on the table, her hand shaking as she reached for it.

"Put it on speaker," he instructed Katrina while at the same time he texted Luca to let him know the call was coming in.

"H-h-hello," Katrina greeted, her voice thick with tears.

"Put the governor on the phone," a deep, robotic voice demanded.

Brantley nodded at Gerard, approving him to answer.

"I'm here. Where's my son?"

There was an almost demonic chuckle that sounded thanks to the voice synthesizer they were using. "I had a feeling you would follow instructions."

"I'm here," Gerard repeated. "Let me talk to my son."

"Uh-uh-uh. Not until I get the money."

Brantley glanced at Reese, wondering if they'd already discussed an amount and they simply weren't privy to it.

"How much do you want?"

Well, that answered *that* question.

"I think one million will be good."

Gerard looked up at him and Brantley mouthed, "Proof of life."

"I need to speak to Dante first. I'll get your money," he tacked on quickly, "but I need to know Dante's alive."

"Oh, he's alive. In a little bit of pain, but he's alive." Another demonic laugh.

Katrina sobbed in response and Corinne held her mother tighter.

"Let me talk to him."

"I don't think you're in any position to make demands," the caller countered.

Gerard's eyes were pleading when he looked up at Brantley this time. He mouthed the words again. They had to have proof of life before they could agree to any demands.

"How do I know you haven't"—Gerard swallowed hard, his eyes slamming closed as he spit out the rest of the words— "killed him yet?"

"Fine."

There was some rustling, and a second later, Dante's pained voice came on the phone.

"Mom? Dad?" His words were slurred, and Brantley didn't think it was all for show.

"Dante!" Katrina cried out.

"Are you all right?" Gerard asked, keeping his cool. "Have they hurt you?"

"I'm okay, Dad."

"That's enough!" the original caller shouted, clearly having taken the phone back. "Now you've got two hours to get me the money."

Brantley shook his head, then mouthed for him to ask for more time.

"I…" Gerard inhaled. "It'll take me longer to get that much money together. It's a holiday. The banks are all closed."

"Good point."

Brantley shot a look at Reese. Seriously? The guy sounded sincerely baffled, as though hadn't considered today was a holiday. Who the fuck was this idiot?

"I'll get it, I swear to you," Gerard added in a rush. "I just need a little time."

"So you can get it today?"

Brantley was dumbfounded by this true moron. How the fuck did he get through the day on his own? Clearly not a criminal mastermind.

"I can, yes," Gerard blurted.

Brantley closed his eyes so the governor couldn't see him rolling them. They could've bought time until tomorrow if he hadn't said that.

"When can you get it?"

Gerard looked up at him and Brantley held up four fingers.

"Four hours."

"Fine, but it'll cost you. The price has gone up to two million," the caller huffed. "Two mil in four hours. You better have it."

"I will. Where do you want me to bring it?"

Another chuckle and this time Brantley glanced at Reese. He saw in his eyes the same morbid curiosity. Who the hell had Dante gotten to help him with this plan? Whoever it was … they were about as smart as a box of rocks.

"I'll call you with instructions in four hours."

The call ended abruptly.

Instantly Reese was making a call, most likely to Luca to see if he managed to get the trace.

"What do we do now?" Katrina asked, getting to her feet.

Brantley moved closer to the family. "Right now, I've got my entire team lookin' at this. Give me a little time to work it." He looked at Gerard. "I want Trey to stay here with y'all, and I'll keep you updated when I have something. You bought us a few hours, and we'll use 'em wisely."

"What about the money? It's not like we've got that kind of cash. Investments, sure."

Although he had no intention of letting the Greenwoods hand over that kind of money, he figured it would give them something to do. "Figure out where it'll come from, and I'll let you know."

Dante glared at Marcus when the call disconnected. "Two million," he snapped. "We agreed we'd ask for *one*."

Marcus's grin was pure evil. "My price went up."

"They don't have that kinda money," he argued.

"Well, they better take out a loan. That or they'll never see their sweet little boy again."

"Didn't you hear him? It's a holiday."

Marcus shrugged. "They do it in the movies all the time. I'm sure your dear old dad will figure it out."

Not for the first time since they'd made this arrangement, Dante felt real fear. This time he feared for his own safety. He got the feeling Marcus was willing to sacrifice him for money. Which meant, if his parents did fork over two mil, Marcus was going to take it and split. But probably not until he'd killed Dante first.

Marcus let out an evil laugh. "You should see your face right now. Looks like you might piss your pants. You scared, Dante?"

He schooled his expression, watching and wondering how the hell he was going to get himself out of this mess.

Chapter Nineteen

AFTER GIVING HIS STATEMENT TO SHERIFF ENDSLEY and promising Brantley he'd keep his nose out of the investigation, Travis played the dutiful husband for the majority of the day, ringing in the new year in the best way possible, spending time with Kylie, Gage, and the kids.

They'd started off with lunch as a family, then watched a movie with Kate, who was back on board with the idea that *Frozen* was the greatest movie of all time. At six years old, he could see how she might think that. Travis would admit, he hadn't minded the animated singalong. The first time. The six or seven dozen times after had been hell.

After the movie, he'd played a couple of rounds of video games with four-year-old Kade, who would be content with a controller in his little hand all day if they'd let him.

He'd then built a block fort with Haden, who was two and a half but, based on his little attitude, believed he was five. Moving on from that, he'd spent the better part of an hour with three-year-old Avery, coloring pictures of Disney princesses.

Plus he'd managed to spend some quality time with nineteen-month-old Maddox, who was content to put his chubby little legs to use by wobbling nonstop from one end of the house to the other.

Being here with them wasn't a hardship by any means. In fact, Travis considered himself truly blessed. He had the greatest roles life could offer: husband to both a beautiful, amazing woman and a ridiculously sexy man, as well as father to five wonderful kids. Some would probably say he had more than he deserved, and he wouldn't have an argument for that.

However, every time he sat down to enjoy that little bit of family time, it felt as though he was sitting on pins and needles, his entire body eager to move, to do something to eliminate the noise brewing in his head. As much as he loved his wife, his husband, his children, Travis wanted to contribute to the hunt for Juliet Prince. Regardless of whether she was responsible for what had happened to JJ, she needed to be found. Dead or alive, he no longer cared, as long as she was no longer a threat to his family.

And as of an hour ago, Brantley had confirmed that this was a legit kidnapping, one that had resulted in a two-million-dollar ransom for Dante Greenwood's safe return. He had also informed him that Juliet Prince was not part of that plan, but no one seemed to have an answer for who lured Travis over to that house. They only knew that it wasn't JJ.

Was he disappointed that this incident wasn't spearheaded by Juliet Prince? Yeah, he figured he was. While he didn't wish harm on anyone, he figured the only way he was going to get any sort of closure was for the woman to make another move. She would. He knew that much.

Which, for him, meant that crazy, psycho bitch was out there waiting, probably watching, preparing to pounce. The very reason Travis was in his office, scouring the internet, looking for anything and anyone who could help him find her.

And yes, he'd gone back on his promise to Gage. But in his defense, he'd been on his best behavior for the past three weeks, and he'd promised himself he wouldn't allow this to fuck up his relationship with his family. Not this time. But he couldn't sit on his hands any longer. Not if he was expected to maintain his sanity.

His cell phone rang, the sound startling him enough that he flinched before glaring down at the device sitting on his desk. He saw his dad's name and picture on the screen, so he picked it up, answered.

"Hey, Pop."

"How's it goin'? Any news on that house fire today?"

"Not yet," he said with a sullen sigh. "Brantley's still workin' to figure it out."

"They'll find him," Curtis said reassuringly.

Him. Right. His old man was worried about Dante Greenwood while he was an afterthought for Travis.

"You talk to Governor Greenwood?" Travis asked.

"I did not, no. I tried but had to leave a message."

He turned in his chair, stared out the window to the front of the house. It was already dark out but not quite six o'clock.

"What's on your mind, boy?" Curtis asked, his tone sympathetic.

"Nothin'," he lied.

"What'd I tell you about that?" his father said, his tone stern. "Lyin' ain't gonna solve the problem."

Travis felt the same wash of shame he'd felt when he was a kid and his father had caught him in a lie. He had a deep love and respect for his father, which meant being admonished by the man had the same effect it'd had as a child. Even at the ripe young age of forty-two.

"If Dante was kidnapped," he wondered aloud, "who texted me to send me over there? And why?"

"You think she had somethin' to do with it?"

"I don't know what to think," he admitted. "I just need this to be over. I need them to find her so my life can get back on course. With her out there, I can't..." *Eat, sleep, work. Breathe.* "There's this feelin' I've got. I don't know what it is, but it..." Travis lowered his voice. "It scares me, Pop."

"It scares all of us, boy. But you're doin' what needs to be done. Spendin' time with your family is most important right now. Be there for them and they'll be there for you."

"Always the philosophical one."

Curtis chuckled, that deep, gruff laugh Travis had heard all his life.

Someone spoke in the background before his father said, "Your mama wants to know if you'll be goin' to the Fantasy Festival next Saturday."

"Fantasy Festival? Who came up with that name? Y'all are aware that sounds kinky, right?"

Another laugh. "Trust me, it's not. Somethin' about fairy lights and a winter wonderland for the kids. All the businesses on Main Street are participatin'."

"Yeah, I've heard all about it. Kate can't stop goin' on and on. And the answer's yes. Kylie intends to take the kids for the festivities. We'll stay with 'em."

Curtis relayed that information to Travis's mother, then said, "Kaden and Keegan'll be there to help out. Sounds like Bristol's helpin' your cousin Violet with one of the booths, so she'll be there."

There was more talking in the background, followed by, "Evidently your mother invited Jared and Hope. Sounds like Hope's sisters'll be taggin' along."

Another pause, more talking.

"Hey, Pop," Travis interrupted, "why don't you just put me on speaker?"

He chuckled again. "I would, but I don't know how to do all that fancy nonsense."

"Give the phone to Mom."

There was some rustling, then his mother said, "Hi, honey."

"Hey, Mom." Travis smiled, unable to help himself. He seemed to do that whenever he talked to her.

"I was tellin' your dad that Wolfe's comin', too. Bringin' his better…" Lorrie giggled. "I guess you can't call 'em a half when they're a third."

Travis grinned, feeling lighter with his mother's laughter. "Rhys and Amy'll be there?"

"They will, yes. As will Lynx and Reagan."

"Any reason you've invited two towns to this festival?"

"It's for a good cause," she said, although he suspected that was her go-to answer.

When it came to these things, Lorrie was the town's biggest supporter, usually wrangling up all the help needed whether it was for the church coat drive or the spring pet festival. Whatever the occasion, his mother had a way of bringing people together.

"I'm sure it is," he told her.

"And don't you worry," she added, her voice softer. "We'll all be lookin' out for each other."

Travis didn't respond to that because he wasn't sure what to say. His throat constricted whenever he thought of what Juliet Prince was capable of, and he wondered if his life would ever be the same again. He didn't like the fact he had to keep his kids locked up in the house, his wife, too.

What if they never found her? Would he spend the rest of his days looking over his shoulder, expecting the worst?

KNOWING THERE WAS NOTHING HE COULD DO by waiting around, Brantley took Reese back to HQ, hoping to get some good news from Luca.

"Sorry we couldn't get you a location on that call," Luca said when Brantley stepped into the barn.

"Yeah, well. That would've been too easy, right?" Brantley offered a curt nod to Charlie and Holly on his way to the desk Luca was sitting at. "Tell me you got somethin' though?"

"Well, the doorbell cams were a bust. We got a little movement, but nothin' from your bad guy."

"What about Dante? Did you happen to catch who dropped him off?" Reese asked.

"We caught a glimpse of a four-door compact comin' through around eight thirty. They stopped in front of JJ's and someone got out. But the cam we saw it on had a narrow scope. Can't really see who it is."

The entire time Luca was talking, he was keying something into the computer, his fingers moving rapidly over the keys.

"What're you workin' on?"

"He's helpin' *me*," came a female voice projected from a phone sitting on the desk.

"Hello, JJ," Brantley said cautiously. "How're you feelin'?"

"My back hurts a little," she said, her tone far too sweet for the JJ he knew.

"Your back?"

"Yeah. You know, from the knife you put in it."

Brantley knew he would have to have a conversation with her at some point about Luca, but he couldn't afford for it to be now.

"Understood," he said. "We'll talk about it later. What else you got?"

"You're not gonna like it," Luca said, his voice low.

"He's a no-good bastard," JJ announced.

For a second, Brantley thought she was talking about him, but he refrained from making a comment. Good thing, because she'd been talking about Dante.

"He did this, B. Dante set this whole thing in motion."

"You're sure of that?"

"Positive. For one, the call that came into the governor's mansion came from the same burner phone that Dante called me on last night. I mean, seriously. What does he take me for?"

"JJ, stay on track."

"Right." She huffed. "But my first clue that somethin' was wrong was when you said they called the governor's mansion. Who calls that number? It's a private line and I seriously doubt Gerard or Trina hand it out. They've both got cell phones." She sighed. "Dante really is an idiot."

Brantley couldn't argue with that.

"If Gerard and Trina were thinkin' clearly, they would've wondered the same thing," JJ went on. "But I'm sure it's natural to automatically worry about your kid, to give him the benefit of the doubt. Especially if someone claims they're holdin' him for ransom. What I wanna know is how much did he ask for? How much does Dante think his life's worth to his parents?"

"It started at a mil, then went up to two mil by the end of the call."

Luca whistled long and low. "He does think pretty highly of himself, huh?"

"It's easy for us to sit here and talk shit," Reese inserted, "but we do have to consider the fact that Dante's finger was left at JJ's. While he might be desperate, I don't see him as the type to chop off his own finger to prove a point."

"No," JJ agreed, her tone smoothing out. "You're right. He's not."

"The Greenwoods did get proof of life," Brantley explained. "We heard Dante's voice. He doesn't sound good. I'd say he's in tremendous pain and likely needs medical attention."

"At least he's not dead," Charlie noted.

"Serves him right," JJ admonished.

"JJ," Brantley warned.

"Did his co-conspirator turn on him, maybe?" Charlie asked, coming to stand beside them. "They have an argument?"

Charlotte Miller, a.k.a. Charlie, was the newest member of the task force. She'd been referred to him by Baz, who'd had the pleasure of working with Charlie at some point over the years. Charlie had officially joined the task force the first week of December, and in the past few weeks, she was proving to be a valuable asset.

"It's possible," Brantley told her. "Certainly more feasible than thinkin' Dante would cut off his own finger."

"Our first priority is to get a bead on Dante before our four hours is up," Reese stated. "But I think it's important we figure out his motivation. It could be he was desperate for money and he came up with this plan. He obviously had help, and it wouldn't be the first time someone's greed got the best of them. Dante'll be a small consolation if this person can get two mil out of it."

Brantley considered that, then turned his attention to the phone. "JJ, do you know if Dante was involved in anything?"

"Like what?"

"Anything that might put him in debt," Reese chimed in.

"Ah, that's sweet of you, Reese. Thinkin' he'd only rip off his own parents to pay off—"

"The mob," Brantley said, remembering Reese's original theory.

"Along those lines, maybe," Reese agreed. "JJ? Can you think of anything?"

"He's spoiled," she said, her tone irritated. "I'm pretty sure he lives above his means. And that's with his parents payin' for everything."

"What about gamblin'?" Luca asked.

"Or maybe the stock market?" Holly offered.

"Funny." JJ huffed a laugh. "I remember him makin' some dumb-ass comment about how he should invest in powder. Said he'd be rich. Idiot doesn't even use powder."

Brantley glanced at Charlie, Reese, Holly, then Luca. They were all looking at him and based on their expressions they were thinking the same thing he was.

"Hey … uh … JJ," Luca said, his tone low and even. "Does Dante … uh … do you know if he does drugs?"

"Drugs?" This time JJ snorted. "Guy couldn't do drugs. He spends all his time with a sinus infection. It's part of the reason I didn't want to be around him this last go-round. Every time I saw him, he was sniffin' and snortin'. It got…"

They heard JJ inhale sharply.

"Oh." She sucked in more air. "Oh, my God! Dante's a drug addict?"

"Sounds like cocaine is his drug of choice," Charlie said.

Brantley agreed. It was known to do significant damage to the sinus cavity.

"There's a good chance he's in debt to a dealer," Luca said, looking up from his chair.

Charlie exhaled heavily. "Great. Because that's something we can easily narrow down."

"We could hack his email and his phone. The one you recovered at the scene," Luca offered. "JJ, it'd be worth a look. See if we can find any communication between him and a dealer."

"We didn't recover the phone," Reese said. "I left it on the table. Alongside the finger."

Luca considered that. "Email, then. We can also see if he kept anything from his phone in the cloud. It's possible he utilized the automated backup."

"What the fuck is a cloud?" Brantley asked, glancing from one face to another.

Like the last time, Reese shook his head. Brantley was really getting tired of that response.

JJ ignored his question, too. "I agree. We'll have to do a scan, though. I doubt he'll openly use phrases that would call attention to it." She snorted, then muttered, "Then again, he's provin' to be a world-class idiot."

"Which do you want me to take, boss?" Luca asked her.

There was no response on the phone.

Brantley grinned, knowing JJ thought Luca was asking him. "JJ, he was talkin' to you."

"Me?" she squeaked. "Oh. I … uh … I'll take the email since I've already got a path in. The phone'll be a bit trickier. I know how you like a challenge, Luca."

Luca grinned. "Your wish is my command."

Brantley wouldn't lie, he felt a little bit useless, but at least they had a string to pull on.

While they started on that, he stepped outside to make a call to the governor. Not exactly news he wanted to relay, but he'd promised to keep the family in the loop.

AFTER BRANTLEY AND REESE LEFT, TREY HAD politely excused himself to the kitchen, giving the Greenwoods a bit of privacy. He had taken a seat at the small dinette table, doing his best not to eavesdrop on the conversation taking place in the next room. Not an easy feat when the family was on edge and louder than they likely intended.

He wasn't sure why Brantley thought it a good idea to leave him behind. He had absolutely no experience in this sort of situation. He didn't know what to say to possibly ease their fears and worries. He had no idea what he would do if they asked for a status update, either.

But the one thing he'd learned about his brother: Brantley didn't much care about his comfort level. At every turn, Trey found himself in an awkward situation, usually of Brantley's design.

At least this was keeping his mind from wandering to last night.

It was still hard to believe it had only been hours and not days since he'd boldly gone back to his place with Magnus and spent hours indulging in the sinfully delicious man. Like this one, that wasn't a situation Trey generally found himself in, either. He wasn't a man-whore like so many would like to believe. He didn't go around hopping from one man's bed to the next. Nor did he invite them into his bed frequently.

If anything, Trey figured he was a serial monogamist. He preferred to be in a relationship, to have someone to talk to, laugh with. It was rare for him to go without an exclusive commitment. And he knew that wasn't a good thing. It didn't make for an appealing quality. Not as far as most men he'd been with recently were concerned, anyway.

Last night, he'd told Magnus that was all he wanted from him. One night of mind-blowing orgasms. With the light of day, they would move on, pretend it never happened. And while Magnus had slipped out like a thief in the night, here Trey was, violating his own rule. He shouldn't be thinking about the sexy man or how good Magnus had felt moving beneath him while they both chased that elusive release.

Realizing sweat was forming on his brow, Trey forced the thoughts away, cleared his throat, and sat up straight.

He had damn good timing, because Corinne stepped into the room. She looked a bit worse for wear, tears streaking down her face.

"I'm so sorry we left you in here," she said softly. "Can I get you somethin' to drink? We've got water, tea, sodas. I was gonna make some coffee."

"I'll take coffee if you're makin' it," he replied, keeping his voice low and even. "Thank you."

Trey's phone buzzed on the table.

He peered down, saw it was a text from Brantley: *Tugging on a few strings to see where they lead. Will keep you updated.*

That told him nothing really. Certainly not enough to relay to the Greenwoods, which he hoped was not something he was supposed to do.

Chapter Twenty

BAZ LOVED WATCHING JJ WORK.

It had been a fascination of his since the very beginning. With each case they handled together, he would learn more little details about her in the way she worked. The way she would move her fingers over the keys even without depressing them. As though she was typing up her thoughts as she had them. Or the way she would chew on her bottom lip while she toggled between screens. And every now and again, she would blow her hair back from her face, which rarely did any good because those stray strands would simply fall forward again.

As he sipped coffee, Baz unabashedly admired her, listening to her mutter to herself as her fingers flew over the keyboard, this time with intent. He'd been listening to her for an hour, learning her true feelings for Luca Switzer, a man she clearly respected but secretly despised. Baz wanted to believe that was due to the man's superior abilities—JJ's words, not his—and not a previous relationship the two of them had.

If only Baz had the right to care or be jealous of JJ and her past relationships, then he might just ask her. Unfortunately, he'd given up that right last night when he had…

He shook off the thoughts of last night. It made him sick to his stomach to think about, to know he was capable of being with another woman when only one held his heart. It didn't matter that he'd overindulged, that he'd drowned his sorrows in whiskey. That was no excuse.

"Why would you do this, Dante?" JJ grumbled to herself.

Forcing himself back to the present, Baz got to his feet. He grabbed JJ's lukewarm coffee, poured it in the sink, and got her a fresh cup, adding milk and sugar, just as she preferred.

He passed it back to her without a word, not wanting to intrude.

She muttered a thanks but didn't look up from her computer screen.

"Most of his email correspondence is work related," JJ said absently. "Probably be more beneficial to hack his social media accounts."

He listened as she worked through the problems, her eyes continuing to scan the screen. Although sitting idly wasn't his favorite thing to do, Baz knew better than to offer to help.

Baz had just sat down when his phone buzzed. It was lying on the kitchen island, right by JJ's computer, so she was the first to see the name on the screen.

"Is Molly the woman from last night?"

Frowning, he picked up his phone, saw Molly Ryan was the caller.

Problem was, Baz didn't know a Molly.

Answering anyway, he greeted with a clipped, "Hello."

"Hey," a sugary-sweet voice sounded on the other end. "I was hoping you'd answer."

He had no idea who she was, but she sounded completely comfortable with him, so Baz had to assume he knew her. "Yeah, hey."

"I thought for sure you'd call me today. I expected you to come by after I got back from brunch."

Ah, hell.

Baz's stomach roiled, his eyes shooting to JJ.

Nope, no way was she too preoccupied to notice. She was staring back at him, clearly waiting for him to say something.

Because he had no explanation for either woman, he stepped out of the room, opting for a little privacy. "How'd you get my number?"

"I called myself from your phone. Then I programmed mine into yours, silly. I didn't want you to forget to get it. Which you did," she said in a singsong voice. "So, would you like to come over?"

He was able to answer with a resounding, "I can't."

"You can't? Or you won't?"

Yeah, this wasn't good.

"Look, Molly, last night…"

"Was amazing," she filled in. "So amazing. I know you felt it too, Sebastian."

Sebastian? No one called him that.

"And I think we owe it to ourselves to explore this, see where it goes."

Before he could object, she blasted him with news that nearly took him out at the knees.

"After all, there's a good chance I'm pregnant." She giggled. "I mean, we did have sex without a condom."

"What?"

Instantly the night was on replay in his head. He recalled Moonshiners, going home with her, on the couch. He specifically remembered her rolling a condom on him because—

Oh, fuck.

She had rolled a condom on him, but she'd been so aggressive it had broken.

Had they had sex without it? Seriously?

Oh, Jesus.

"It's okay, Sebastian," Molly said sweetly. "I know you think we don't know each other well enough to have a baby, but if it happens, then it must be kismet, right? Divine intervention and all that?"

Oh, hell.

Baz was going to be sick.

JJ FORCED HERSELF TO FOCUS ON SEARCHING Dante's emails for anything that might lead them to his drug dealer.

Normally this would've been a relatively easy task, something she could probably do in her sleep.

That was not the case when Baz was taking calls from women, then disappearing out of the room to talk in hushed tones.

There was no doubt in her mind that this Molly was the woman he was with last night. And clearly they'd connected on at least some level for him to have given her his phone number. One-night stands generally didn't result in the exchange of digits.

Was he in there right now promising to come see her as soon as he could? Would he spend the night with her again? Take her to dinner? Coffee?

Speaking of coffee… The little bit she'd had gurgled in her stomach.

JJ narrowed her eyes on the computer screen. Dante. That was the only thing she needed to worry about right now. Finding the man before someone decided he was a loose end after they managed to swindle the Greenwoods out of two mil.

God, he was such a douche. Why in the world would he think hitting his parents up like this was a good idea? And heaven help him if he thought cutting off his own finger would net him more. She'd always known he was a spoiled brat who thought he was God's gift to women, but this…? This was beyond ridiculous.

JJ paused to modify the search she was running. The first couple had come back with nothing. Using words like *drug*, *dealer*, *cocaine*, and *buy* wasn't getting her the results she wanted.

JJ had just kicked off another search parameter when Baz stormed through the kitchen, then disappeared down the hallway. She craned her neck, trying to see where he went and briefly wondered if she should go after him. She hadn't gotten a good look at his face, but from his profile, he'd appeared a bit green.

Probably from the alcohol he'd indulged in last night. When she'd asked, he had told her after she left the diner, he'd gone over to Moonshiners and hung with Brantley and Reese for most of the night. Obviously his agenda had consisted of more than that, but JJ was doing her best to avoid getting those details even if her curiosity was getting the best of her.

She didn't really want to know.

Just the thought of Baz with another woman…

Now *she* was feeling a bit green.

Thankfully, her cell phone rang, Luca's number popping up on the screen.

"You're done already?" she asked by way of greeting.

"I think I've found somethin' that might be helpful in your search."

"Give it to me," she said, cheerfully engaging in the task.

"It's a phone number I came across. It was actually in his contacts. He had a meeting scheduled two weeks ago to meet with MH. I skimmed his contacts for someone with those initials and came across Marcus Harris. I didn't do a lot of research, but from what I found, the guy's a little shady. He works as a collector."

A collector? What the hell was a collector?

JJ used the information to do a search on Dante's messages. She looked for the initials, then by first name, and finally by last and came up with nothing.

"I don't suppose he's got a number for that contact."

Luca chuckled. "As a matter of fact…" He rattled off the number.

"Bingo!" she exclaimed when it brought up an instant messenger conversation. "In his email, the contact name is Book. Looks like Dante was promising to give him the money for his last purchase as soon as he got paid." JJ frowned. "Since when does Dante buy books?"

Another laugh from Luca, followed by, "Book? Like Bookie? Dante's gamblin'."

"At least it's not his drug dealer," she muttered.

"Hate to break it to you, but I found his contact for that, too," Luca said, sounding sincerely bothered by it.

Ah, Jesus. It pained her to know that Dante had gone down that path, but honestly it didn't surprise her that he had. This last time they'd attempted to make a go of it had been the worst yet. He'd always seemed so distracted and so energetic. He wanted to go places and do things, never slowing down.

She probably should've seen it at the time, recognized the signs, but the truth was, her heart hadn't been in it.

"Did you find something?" Baz asked when he walked into the room.

JJ's gaze shot to his face, scanned it with concern in her heart. He looked better, more color in his cheeks.

"We've got a number." She turned back to her computer to ping the phone, see if she could get a location. "If we're right, this is the guy his bookie sent to collect his debt."

"There's a damn good chance," Luca said, his voice echoing from the phone's speaker.

"Anything I can do?" Baz offered.

"We're good for now, but thanks." She grinned wide when the ping delivered results. "Luca, I've got a location!"

"Seems too easy," Luca said.

"Too easy?" JJ snorted. "Speak for yourself. I'm the one with the mild concussion and the scent of copper baked into my brain."

"Touché."

"And who says it's always gotta be a twisty-turny mystery," she told him. "This is Dante. He obviously didn't think this one all the way through."

"No, probably not."

"Brantley still there with you?"

"He is," Luca confirmed, then shouted for Brantley.

She heard Brantley's familiar grumble as he moved closer to the phone.

JJ was quiet while Luca gave a quick rundown of what they'd done, what they'd found.

"We've gotta move on this now." Brantley's tone was no-nonsense once again. "We're gonna head over. Charlie, you'll go with us. We'll call Trey on the way, let him know what's goin' on. JJ, you're a rock star, as always."

"Keep me in the loop," she told him. "I wanna talk to Dante once you've got him."

"Figured you would."

When the call disconnected, she was left with nothing to do but look at Baz. She had no idea what to say to him, how to make this incredibly awkward situation any better. For either of them.

"I guess I'll get to go home soon," JJ told him, not meeting his gaze.

"Your house, JJ. It's…"

Her heart instantly plummeted at the reminder that she'd lost everything she had. It was easy to pretend it was still there, still intact. But it wasn't.

She had nothing to her name. No house, no car.

What was she going to do now?

Chapter Twenty-One

"THIS SEEMS TOO EASY. EITHER HE REALLY is stupid or we're gonna royally fuck this up," Reese told Brantley as they drove toward Taylor, a small town just northeast of Coyote Ridge.

Reese couldn't remember the last time he'd been out this way. Probably back when he'd assisted Travis with a situation his cousins Wolfe and Lynx were involved in. Although that time he'd ventured a little farther to the even smaller town of Embers Ridge, which seemed to be another hub for those related to the Walkers.

Brantley's eyes remained on the road. "I know you like a challenge, but I don't think that's what's goin' on here."

Reese would have to take his word for it. In his experience, when things seemed too easy, there was usually a catch. It was difficult for him to believe they would close this case in a matter of a day.

"Do you know Dante?" Charlie asked, glancing sideways, her question directed at Reese.

He answered with a shake of his head, although neither Brantley nor Charlie could see him from the front seat. "Never officially met him. Only time I encountered him was the night he brought a woman to Moonshiners, back when he was datin' JJ."

He still remembered that night, but it had nothing to do with Dante or his infidelity. That night had been a low point in his relationship with Brantley. They'd been at an impasse—Brantley wanting something Reese wasn't sure he could give him—and they'd taken a bit of a break. Enough of one that Reese came to terms with the fact he was in love with Brantley.

"What a douche," Charlie murmured, staring at the side window.

"He absolutely is," Brantley agreed. "Pretty much always has been."

"Then how'd JJ end up with him?" Charlie inquired.

"Young and dumb, like the rest of us back in high school. He was popular with the ladies, the self-proclaimed bad boy. Buckin' the rules, mouthin' off to the teachers, spendin' a good amount of time in detention."

"I remember guys like that. A couple of girls, too," Charlie said wistfully.

"Early on, he set his sights on JJ, and when she played hard to get for a little while, I'm pretty sure he fell in love. Unfortunately, teenage love lasts about as long as the chase. They were together for years, on and off. Mostly off."

Reese glanced at Brantley. "I'm surprised she'd date an entitled, pompous ass."

"I'm not sure he's always been quite as bad as he is now. But I think there's reason to worry about him. If he's gone to these lengths to get money, he's in deep. While I don't have a high opinion of him, I honestly didn't think he'd do somethin' like this."

"People surprise you." Charlie sighed. "And not always in a good way." She pointed out the windshield. "You're gonna want to take a left on Main. According to the GPS signal, they're holed up in an industrial area close to the rail yard."

"You're familiar with the area, then?" Brantley asked.

"I don't live too far from there. Taylor's a small town. Those of us who live or work here know our way around."

Reese remained quiet, half listening to Charlie's instructions. While they focused on the navigation, he shot a text to Trey, asking for an update.

Luckily for him, Trey didn't mince words, responding quickly. The update: Gerard and Katrina were still waiting for the phone call. They'd scraped together the full two million and were more than willing to pay it to get their son back.

If all went well, they wouldn't have to pay. The only concern Reese had was whether or not Dante's partner was going to do things the hard way. Money was a significant motivator, and for those driven by greed, they'd do pretty much anything to get it.

"Just outta curiosity, what charges will they be brought up on?" Charlie asked.

"Destruction of property, assault, attempted murder by blowin' up the house," Brantley rattled off.

"Sure. Those I can see. I guess what I mean is, Dante's not bein' held against his will. Does kidnapping still apply?"

"That we know of," Reese added. "It could've started out that way. We don't know the status of their workin' relationship at the moment."

"I'm not a DA," Brantley said, "so it's anyone's guess. I figure Marcus Harris will be charged with kidnappin'. He's the one who made the ransom call, therefore he's stated his intent."

Reese still couldn't wrap his head around the reason for cutting Dante's finger off. They'd watched Dante willingly open the door for someone—they now assumed that someone was Marcus—then let him in. They'd done enough damage to warrant some attention. That and the blood they'd covered the house in. What was the point of leaving a finger? It seemed like overkill. The only thing that made sense was the pair had a falling-out.

"True." Charlie looked at Brantley. "What about Dante? Will he be charged with anything? Extortion? Coercion?"

"Plus the aforementioned assault, etc. He's damn sure guilty." Brantley glanced at Charlie. "But you have to remember what this'll do to the governor's reputation if people find out his son staged his own kidnapping for a payday. I figure he'll have this swept under the rug. Can't afford for it to get out."

Reese had to agree there. He didn't see Governor Greenwood watching his son go down for extortion. The best they could hope for was that they got Dante into rehab for his addiction.

"This is it," Charlie said, her voice lowering. "It's around the corner. Since this is a sparsely traveled area, I suggest we move closer on foot. They see your truck, who knows what they'll do."

Brantley nodded, then shot a look back at Reese as though seeking his input.

He nodded his agreement, retrieved his weapon from its holster, thumbed off the safety. Because they weren't sure what they were walking into and Tesha wasn't far along in her training, Reese had opted to leave her back at HQ with Luca and Holly, so he was rolling without his four-legged backup today.

Once Brantley stopped the truck, the three of them got out. They moved as one, Reese keeping close to Charlie, letting her lead the way while Brantley covered their six.

Charlie began using hand signals the closer they got to the building, splitting them up. They'd tested their comms earlier to ensure they could communicate between them if necessary, so Reese moved away, heading for the south entrance.

He kept close to the building, scanning his surroundings as he moved. This looked to be a deserted area, mostly three-story corrugated metal buildings surrounded by pitted gravel lots and old chain-link fence.

The big metal door he came to was once red but had faded with time and gotten a few colorful graffiti paint jobs over the years.

As quietly as possible, he opened it, peeked inside before moving into the interior. The inside was damp and dark except for the sunlight peeking in through the large windows that ran the length of the building on all four sides. If it wasn't for the grime clouding the glass, the space would've been well lit. Thanks to it, Reese had to move in the shadows, keeping an eye out for someone or something lurking.

Every twenty feet or so, there was a trio of pylons holding things up above. What had once been a three-story building appeared to have been reduced to two if the crumbling and rotting piles of wood and concrete were any indication. Above him, the holes left behind from the falling debris.

The main floor was littered with old wooden pallets and a few large blue barrels. Whether or not anything was in them was a good question, but Reese decided it wasn't worth finding out.

He made his way through, weaving between the piles of rubble and doing his best to keep his noise to a minimum. It wasn't until he was halfway up the south-end staircase that he heard voices.

Reese keyed his mic, said, "Sounds like two males in the south end of the second floor."

"Ten four," Brantley responded, his voice coming in clear through his earpiece. "Movin' your way."

Holding until Brantley and Charlie joined him, Reese attempted to hear what the men were saying. Every now and then he'd catch a word, but nothing that made much sense. If the raised voices were anything to go by, they were arguing.

A loud crash sounded from behind him, and everything came to a standstill.

"What was that?" came a muted shout.

Reese peered back, saw Brantley looking behind him, Charlie's expression one of apology.

Didn't look like they had the element of surprise on their side anymore.

BRANTLEY WINCED WHEN CHARLIE HIT THE BOARD that had been propped up against a rail. He hadn't thought to warn her it was dangling precariously over the edge. Or it had been. Now it was on the ground, having made enough noise to alert the pair that someone was there.

"I'll kill him!" came the angry shout from the second floor.

Brantley continued up the stairs, stopping behind Reese.

"Come through that door and I put a bullet in his head!"

"You did this, you know," Brantley muttered to Reese.

Reese's *what the fuck* expression was priceless.

"You said it was too easy."

Brantley held back a smile when Reese rolled his eyes.

"Marcus, it's over," Brantley shouted up to him. "The building's surrounded. You need—"

The gun's report was loud in the metal building, the first bullet slamming into the wood door that separated them from the room the two men were holed up in, no more than ten feet above them.

The second bullet whizzed past, way too close for comfort.

"Fuck," Brantley bit out, urging Charlie back down the stairs. They were sitting ducks out here in the open.

Stealth no longer a concern, the three of them hightailed it back to the main floor, taking cover—pathetic as it was—behind a row of blue plastic barrels.

"Any suggestions on what to do now?" Reese snapped, gun aimed at the second floor.

Brantley glanced around, looking for options. That had been their best chance of getting to the men without being seen or heard. Now that they knew they were here, Brantley feared Marcus was going to do something stupid.

"You better have my goddamn money!" Marcus shouted. "Otherwise, I kill this idiot."

"You don't want to hurt him, Marcus. He's leverage," Charlie called out.

Nice thinking.

Brantley glanced over, nodded for her to continue.

"He's your ticket out of here," she added. "Our job is to get him home safely. Only you can help us do that. Which means you hold all the cards."

"I do, don't I?" he shouted back, sounding relieved.

"Keep him talkin'," Brantley told Charlie, motioning for Reese to move with him.

While they shouted back and forth, Brantley moved to the staircase at the other end of the building. It took longer than he would've preferred but moving slowly was necessary. The second floor had a direct line of sight to the area, which meant they were open and exposed if Marcus decided to open fire.

They stuck to the shadows until they reached their destination, then paused to come up with a plan.

Marcus was in the process of shouting a list of demands when suddenly he stopped.

Well, hell. That whole *this is too easy* bullshit just went right out the window.

Brantley had enough time to look up and realize they'd been spotted. A second later, a shot rang out, sending both of them diving for cover. As he was about to crouch behind a concrete pylon, a blaze of heat speared his right shoulder, the impact powerful enough to have him pitching forward, a foot shy of being clear.

Another shot hit a foot from his head, then another a few inches to the left of that.

Brantley gritted his teeth, fought the blinding pain, and tried to lever himself behind the protective barrier. Any second, one of these bullets was going to hit its mark—

Three rapid-fire shots echoed in the space, followed by complete silence and a ringing in Brantley's ears.

Brantley looked over, saw Reese standing out in the open, his gun aimed at the second floor. He'd broken cover to save Brantley's life.

"Dante?" Reese shouted.

"I'm here!" came the response. "You killed him! He's dead!"

Brantley waited until Reese looked his way. It was then he saw the fear in his eyes, knew Reese had thought he'd gone down for good, so he'd taken out the shooter.

"I'm all right," he assured the man. "Flesh wound."

Another eye roll from Reese.

"Charlie, call an ambulance," Reese ground out, still looking directly at Brantley. "You stay there. I'm gonna lock it down up there."

Because he could tell Reese was still on edge, perhaps a little brittle, Brantley could do nothing but nod in agreement, pushing himself up with his good arm. He took a seat on the bottom step while Reese pounded up to the second floor.

"You're shot," Charlie snapped when she joined him.

"Flesh wound," he told her. He hadn't confirmed that with his eyes, but based on his experience with bullets slamming into his flesh, this one was minor.

"Shooter down!" Reese called out from the second floor. "Scene secure."

Brantley looked at Charlie, grinned. "Damn good end to the first day of the year, huh?"

The look on her face said she thought he'd lost his damn mind.

He couldn't help but grin.

That grin didn't last too long, though. It died shortly after Reese insisted that Brantley go to the hospital to have his bullet wound treated. He'd argued but ended up overruled. Both Charlie and the EMT had agreed with Reese, and in an effort to avoid an ensuing argument, he had reluctantly climbed into the ambulance.

Now, two hours later, he was waiting for Reese to return to the house. After he'd gotten a handful of stitches, he'd been released, practically as good as new. At Reese's insistence, he had come home—via an Uber—only to find himself in a perpetual state of waiting.

Not easy considering the only thing he'd been able to think about for the past couple of hours was finding somewhere private where he could strip Reese bare and have his wicked way with him, and moving was the only way he knew to deal with the adrenaline.

Sure, sex with Reese was probably an inappropriate train of thought while having a bullet wound stitched, but it was all he could do to keep from running out of the hospital. He despised the place, the overwhelming smell of antiseptic, knowing the sick and dying were behind closed doors. In order to avoid going postal, Brantley had allowed his Reese-fueled fantasies to play out in his head.

Good thing Reese proved to be a damn fine mental distraction when he needed one. Then again, Reese was a damn fine distraction *all* the time. Brantley would say he thought about Reese a good ninety-five percent of the day. Longer when he had nothing to do. Thankfully, those times were few and far between because Brantley wasn't good at being idle.

The sound of tires on gravel had him strolling to the front window and peering out, watching as Brantley's Chevy came pulling down the dirt drive, Reese behind the wheel. Planting his hands on his hips, he stared out, waiting for that moment when he would see Reese for the first time after they'd been apart. He wasn't sure what it was about the man that kept him riveted, but Brantley had been awestruck since day one.

And there he was. All six feet five inches of grade A prime male. It sometimes surprised him that it was still a shock when he saw Reese. There was something about him—perhaps it was everything—that tripped him up and made him ache for things he'd never ached for before. He'd experienced it the first moment he'd laid eyes on Reese and every day thereafter. Reese had changed him in so many ways, brought out a side of Brantley he hadn't realized existed. And yes, the man he loved had tested his patience a few times, but it was so fucking worth it.

Speaking of patience…

Brantley remained where he was, continuing to stare out even as Reese made his way up to the door. When the door opened, Tesha came lumbering over, tail wagging as she greeted Reese. Brantley allowed Reese to give her the requisite pat on the head, scratch behind the ears, but then when Tesha trotted off to find her bone, he was on Reese. Hell, he didn't even give him time to shut the front door before he was slamming him up against the wall, lips colliding.

"You're injured," Reese growled.

Brantley didn't stop kissing him, taking what he wanted. "Good as new," he mumbled as he plundered Reese's mouth.

Reese grunted, but his hands gripped Brantley's hips firmly, holding him in place as their tongues mated.

Oh, yeah. Just what he'd needed.

The kiss ignited into a firestorm right there in the entryway. It was a wonder their clothes didn't disintegrate from the heat they generated.

"Christ Almighty, you taste good," he whispered against Reese's mouth.

It was that familiar taste of peppermint—inspired by Reese's addiction to Altoids—and man that revved his engine even more.

"Great minds…" Brantley groaned when Reese flipped the button on Brantley's jeans open.

The zipper followed and Brantley's lungs seized up as an overwhelming pleasure mixed with his ever-increasing adrenaline.

"Been thinkin' 'bout this all day," Reese breathed against his mouth, continuing to work Brantley's jeans open.

The heat of his hand against his lower stomach had Brantley sucking in a breath, his cock pounding in earnest, all the blood in his body making a detour south. The anticipation built, his nerves growing more chaotic as he waited not so patiently for that moment when Reese would touch him.

But then Reese moaned in his mouth and Brantley nearly lost it.

"Don't. Move," he warned Reese before the man could get his hand around his aching cock.

"Your shoulder hurt?"

Brantley shook his head. This definitely wasn't pain he was feeling.

Reese's fingers brushed against the sensitive head of his dick, but he stopped pursuing, which gave Brantley a moment to rein himself in.

They were both breathing hard when Brantley nipped Reese's lower lip, bringing their hips together.

"You get me too worked up." He panted, tightening the metaphorical leash on his control. "Don't wanna come."

Well, he did. Just not yet.

Good thing he knew of a way to distract himself.

It was his turn to do the unbuckling and unzipping, freeing Reese's cock before stepping back so he could watch as he took the man's steel-hard length in his hand.

A guttural moan escaped Reese as he stared down between them, the sound vibrating straight through Brantley.

The guy had a phenomenal cock. Thick and heavy, the shaft curved slightly to the left, with a wide head and an intricate design of veins running along the length. At the moment, it was a dark purple thanks to the blood flowing through it, and the sight made Brantley's mouth water.

Continuing to admire, Brantley stroked Reese firmly. Up, down. Up, down. Slow and easy, enjoying the way the thick head peeked out of his fist, glistening with pre-cum.

The more he worked him, the more Reese panted, letting the wall hold him up.

Brantley leaned in, trapping Reese's cock between them as he sucked on Reese's lower lip.

"You like that?" He nipped him, continuing to stroke, wrenching his wrist, running his thumb over the head, then teasing the sensitive spot just below.

The only response he got was a grunt when Reese bucked his hips.

"You do. You wanna come in my hand, don't you?" Brantley kissed him, licking the inside of his mouth, tongue lapping at tongue, keeping the pace with his stroking.

"Want…" Reese licked Brantley's lower lip, groaned. "To … oh, *fuck*…" His head fell back against the wall, his hips pumping faster.

"Tell me, baby," Brantley whispered. "Tell me what you want."

"Want to ride your cock."

Those words went straight through him, making his cock kick in his jeans and his hand to still momentarily.

Fucking hell.

He never knew what to expect from Reese, but he was certainly never disappointed.

He managed to resume his steady pace rather than race to a flat surface, leaning down and licking Reese's neck. "Let me get this straight." He nipped his ear lobe. "You want to sit on my cock?"

Reese nodded.

"And ride me—"

"Like a bull," Reese inserted.

"—until I come deep inside you?"

"Fuck, yes."

Brantley felt Reese's cock swell in his hand.

"What're you waitin' for?" he challenged, nipping Reese's jaw.

It took effort, but Brantley managed to step back, reluctantly releasing Reese so they could head to the bedroom. He was all for getting down and dirty anywhere in the house, but for this, a bed would do nicely.

There was no hesitation on either of their parts once they were in the room. While hands and mouths continued to roam, clothing began to fall away until Reese's warm body was pressed perfectly against him.

The fall into bed took no time at all, and then Brantley found himself pressed into the mattress by Reese's weight.

He loved this part, when he was awash with sensation. Every single inch of him was aware of Reese. From his smooth, firm lips to his calloused hands, the crisp hair on his legs. Brantley had never paid much attention to those things. For most of his adult life, an orgasm had been the end goal. Relief until the next time the urge overcame him. With Reese, it was about the journey. Getting there was as important as the grand finale.

Because he knew Reese had ventured out of his comfort zone with his request, Brantley figured he could ease him into it. No doubt about it, the thought of Reese looming over him, riding his cock was something he'd fantasized about. Many, many times. But when it came to their lovemaking, Brantley let Reese set the pace, make the suggestions.

Oh, sure, eventually they would be on the same page, and Brantley would have free rein to give and take exactly what he wanted, but he wasn't willing to rush things. Being that he was the only man Reese had ever been with, he was sensitive to Reese's hesitation.

Sliding his hands down Reese's sides, he skimmed his fingers over all the hard muscle and warm skin, over his hip bones, then changing direction and pausing to squeeze the firm globes of Reese's ass as he ground his hips upward, their cocks aligned almost perfectly. It would've been so damn easy to simply dry hump him to completion—something they enjoyed on occasion—but Reese's request had Brantley holding off.

He let his hands trail down to the backs of Reese's thighs, then urged Reese to bend his knees until he was straddling Brantley's hips. His adrenaline was spiking once again, his body and mind already anticipating the hedonistic pleasure he would be shrouded in momentarily.

Luckily, Reese was as eager as he was. The next thing Brantley knew, Reese was sitting astride him, the lube in his hand as he began generously coating Brantley's cock while they both watched. Sensations assaulted him as that wicked hand stroked firmly, gliding effortlessly up and down, over and over.

Unable to help himself, he reached for Reese's cock, stroking lightly, ensuring he remained right there on the precipice along with him.

Brantley was pumping his hips before he realized Reese was looking at the bandaged wound on his shoulder.

"It's fine," he assured him. "I'm lettin' you do all the work."

Reese's gaze moved to his face.

"But if you keep that up," he warned, "I'll come in your hand. I don't care."

Reese grinned, those wonderful fingers prying open, releasing him.

When Reese leaned down, Brantley slid his hand behind Reese's neck, urging his mouth closer.

Damn, but he loved Reese's mouth.

"Never done this before," Reese whispered, his breath fanning Brantley's lips.

"I know." Brantley nipped Reese's chin. "And I fuckin' love that I'm your only."

And boy did he. Brantley had never known a high quite as great as knowing the man he was with had never been with another man before. Every single one of their experiences was new for Reese. In turn, it made it all the hotter.

When their mouths fused once more, Brantley took over. He shifted lower while jerking Reese's hips to nudge him up his body. Then finally, he was right where Brantley needed him to be.

"Put your hands beside my head," he said when their lips parted. "And lift your hips."

The position allowed Brantley to see Reese's face, which was exactly what he wanted.

With a firm grip on his cock, he guided Reese with a hand on his hip.

"Sit on me, baby," he groaned when the head of his dick pressed against Reese's puckered hole.

Time became nonexistent as Reese eased downward, that tight ring of muscle stretching to take him fully. Brantley never looked away from Reese's face as their bodies joined intimately.

Fucking perfection. That was what this was. With Reese, it was both heaven and hell. So fucking good it was damn near painful.

His cockhead finally breached the tight ring of muscles, and he held firm, pushing inside the blistering heat of Reese's body. His breath lodged in his throat momentarily as the pleasure consumed him.

When Reese's eyes squeezed shut, Brantley ran his hand down his thigh. "Slow. I want you to take all of me."

And then he did.

Reese's body enveloped him, wicked heat sending shards of electricity lighting up his spine. He focused on breathing while Reese shifted forward, rocked back. Once, twice.

Then Reese settled into a rhythm that had the hair on Brantley's arms standing on end, the sensations overwhelming.

"Good?"

He smiled up at Reese, still watching him. "Better than good. Fuck me. Take exactly what you need."

When he did, when Reese began rocking forward and back, taking his cock to the hilt, Brantley had to clamp his teeth together to keep from coming.

He knew it wasn't merely physical, their joining. And that was what made it so intense. They weren't only two bodies coming together. This was more. So very much more.

Minutes ticked by as Reese rode him. All the while, Brantley let his hands roam over Reese. Up his thighs, over his stomach, higher. He pinched Reese's nipples, grazed his cock with a brush of his hand. He wanted to push him higher than he'd ever been before.

"Oh, fuck," Reese ground out, slamming his hips down before rocking forward, slamming down again. "More."

"Two choices," he said with a smirk.

Reese's eyes narrowed.

"You can jerk your cock while I fuck you. Or I'll jerk you and you can fuck yourself on my cock. Your choice."

Reese reached between his legs, gripped his cock with one hand, and leaned forward, propping himself on the other. "Fuck me."

Brantley did.

He bent his knees, dug his fingertips into Reese's hips, holding him still while he drove his hips up from underneath, fucking him hard and deep, faster and faster, he drove them both toward release. It didn't take long before he was emerging on the crest, gearing up to soar over the edge, but he somehow managed to hold off until Reese shouted his name.

The feel of Reese's cum spurting over his belly and chest was the trigger. He drove up, at the same time pulling Reese's hips down, and came with a guttural roar.

Chapter Twenty-Two

Saturday, January 2, 2021

THE FOLLOWING MORNING, WEARING CLOTHES SHE HAD borrowed from Baz's father's guesthouse, JJ walked the halls of the hospital.

She'd convinced Baz to drive her here in order to check on Dante and his family, but they both knew she had really wanted to have a chat with the man responsible for the epic disruption in her life. According to the update from Trey, the Greenwoods had met him at the hospital last night and were utilizing the governor's security to keep the press at bay.

While JJ would've preferred to move on, to let Dante and his family reconnect and find him the help he needed, she found she couldn't let it go. Not until she understood why he'd used her to carry out this stupid plot of his.

"You want me to go in with you?" Baz offered when they came to a stop outside of Dante's door.

JJ glanced up at him, shook her head. "I'd prefer to do this alone."

He nodded, his blue eyes reflecting his concern for her. "If you need me, I'll be right out here."

Taking a deep breath, JJ stepped up to the door, rapped her knuckles on the metal trim. It drew the attention of Katrina and Corinne, both women hovering over Dante as though he'd been through a horrific ordeal when, in reality, the stupid ass had masterminded the whole thing.

Katrina was the first to come over, greeting JJ with a firm hug. "I'm so glad you're all right."

JJ couldn't find words, so she nodded and smiled, hoping that was enough assurance that she really was. As far as her physical condition was concerned, she was all right. Mentally and emotionally … well, only time would tell.

Corinne hugged her next, then traded a look with JJ before suggesting she and her mother go get coffee, leaving JJ alone with Dante.

As she walked into the room, she took stock of the man in the bed.

Dante was reclining, head and injured hand propped on pillows. He looked a little worse for wear, his skin pale, his hair a mess, but he looked like he would make a full recovery.

"How's the finger?"

He lifted a fully bandaged hand. "Gone."

"Does it hurt?"

He lifted his other hand, which held a button that she assumed gave him pain meds when he needed them. "They've got me set."

Clearly the family was in the denial phase of his addiction. Otherwise JJ doubted they would have him hooked to a morphine pump.

She ignored the urge to chastise him, opting for, "Your mom and sister are happy you're back."

"I'm just glad *you're* all right," Dante said dramatically. "I didn't know what was goin' on or who—"

JJ cut him off with a hissed, "Cut the shit, Dante. We know you were behind it all."

His eyebrows slammed down. "What're you talkin' about? I was kidnapped."

She took a deep breath but didn't move closer, fearful she would strangle him if she did. "My house was monitored by cameras," she informed him. "Those recordings are managed in the cloud, so the explosion didn't destroy them."

And that was only a partial lie. She did have cameras that recorded to the cloud, but she also had hidden cameras that only she knew about, ones that she recorded straight to a cloud server even the best of hackers couldn't access.

At least Dante had the decency to keep his mouth shut.

"We saw you open the door and let Marcus in." In fact, JJ had watched in horror as Dante had let that bastard in her house, had seen him stroll across the room and grab one of her metal statues off the shelf by the kitchen before disappearing. As for the camera that was set up in there, JJ didn't know why it had failed, but she wasn't sure she really wanted to see that man bash her over the head anyway.

"He made me."

"He didn't," she countered. "This was your plan, Dante. I just need to know why? Why'd you feel the need to extort money from your parents?"

Dante took a few deep breaths, and she saw the moment he accepted he'd been caught. His face fell, his defensiveness shifting into a whine. "Because I owe too many people. I had no choice. They were gonna kill me if I didn't pay them back."

"So, what? You thought it'd be fun to include me? Was it your idea to have Marcus hit me on the head?" She fought the urge to reach up and touch the knot that was still there.

"Of course not," he hissed. "He was supposed to drug you. That's all."

"Drug me?" Her voice was louder as she took a step forward. "You agreed to let him *drug* me, Dante?"

"It needed to look real, JJ. It was nothin' personal. I just needed my father to believe it. I knew if you were involved, they'd do somethin' about it."

"I was out cold, Dante," she said, remembering the other video she'd seen, the one from the camera in her bedroom. The one Luca had come across but had kept to himself when he realized what it showed. Rather than watch it, Luca had called her on the phone, told her she might want to see if it had any clues. "Unconscious, Dante. Do you understand what I'm sayin'? Out cold, in my bedroom. Defenseless."

Just thinking about what she'd seen, the way Marcus had loomed over her, made her sick to her stomach.

"I didn't let him touch you," Dante choked out.

No, he hadn't. She'd witnessed Dante attempting to hold open the door, and that was when she realized exactly what had happened. Dante had been keeping Marcus from closing himself in the room with her. In turn, Marcus had chopped off his finger. The guy was lucky it hadn't been his whole hand.

"I protected you, JJ. You have to know that."

"What I know is that you need help. Professional help."

Dante was nodding his head furiously. "I know. I'll get it, too. Once I get out of here, I'm gonna turn my life around. I'll find a meeting or something to go to."

JJ shook her head. "That's not gonna happen."

He was frowning again. "My mother—"

"Brantley and Reese are talkin' to your parents right now. They're tellin' them everything that happened."

Dante's head tilted up in that way that said he was tired of the subject and too good to put up with her any longer.

"What you did was illegal," she added. "You won't be able to simply walk out of here without some sort of punishment."

"My father's the governor, JJ, in case you hadn't noticed."

"I noticed." JJ exhaled, tucking her hands in her pocket. "I just have one last question for you."

"What's that?"

"Why'd you blow up my house?"

Dante held her gaze. "I didn't. That was Marcus's idea. I didn't even know about it until we were back at the warehouse."

"Why'd he do it? What did it accomplish?"

Dante shrugged. "He was talkin' to some woman he met online. Well, actually, I met her online. Anyway, he said she wanted him to make a big statement."

JJ's eyes widened as his explanation sank in. "What's this woman's name?"

"Katherine," he said easily. "Katherine King."

Katherine King? Was it a coincidence that the name was the same as Travis's daughter?

"Did she go by Kate?"

"No. Kat. Why?"

JJ ignored the question. "How'd she find you?"

He smiled. "How'd you know she found me and not the other way around?"

"I'm serious, Dante. How'd she find you?"

"Online dating app, okay? But it's not what you think. I don't have to use an app to meet women. It's just—"

"How'd you communicate with her?" she asked, interrupting his tirade. "Email? Phone?"

"Yeah," he said. "All of the above. But I stopped talkin' to her. She bored me. But I guess Marcus was being nosy. He got my phone one day, texted her back on it. They started talking."

Shit. JJ spun around to leave. She needed to get those phones, needed to figure out where the hell Katherine King—a.k.a. Juliet Prince—was.

"Hey!" Dante called out. "Where're you goin'?"

JJ found Baz in the hallway. "Where's Brantley and Reese?"

"They left a few minutes ago. Why?"

"Because I just got some new information from Dante that might lead us to Juliet Prince."

"From Dante?"

JJ nodded, started walking. "I'm pretty sure it really was a coincidence that she's involved in all this, but not so much that Travis was lured to my house shortly before it blew up."

"She blew up the house?"

"She had Marcus do it, but yes."

"Marcus? The dead guy?"

"Yep. That one."

BAZ DROVE JJ BACK TO HQ WHILE she spent the majority of her time on her phone texting someone. He wasn't sure if it was Brantley or Reese or Luca, but whoever it was, they were quick with their responses, and JJ seemed happy with the replies.

No sooner had he pulled into the driveway than she hopped out of his truck, making a mad dash for the barn. Based on the other vehicles, it looked as though the gang was all there. Brantley, Reese, and at least two others.

By the time he walked around to the back of the house, JJ had disappeared, leaving him to stroll by himself. As he was approaching the keypad to unlock the door, his cell phone chimed.

He glanced at the screen, swallowed a frustrated groan when he saw that it was once again Molly. She'd been texting him almost once an hour since yesterday afternoon, asking when she was going to see him again. Each text that went unanswered earned him another, more demanding one.

This one: *I think it's best you come by so we can talk about the other night. I'll need to know what to do about the pregnancy.*

Baz didn't want to be a dick to the woman, but even he knew she didn't know for sure she was pregnant after twenty-four hours. She definitely could be, yes, but he would prefer they wait to have this discussion once she knew for certain. If she was, Baz had every intention of doing what was right by the child. But from the texts he was getting, Molly was expecting more for herself than the baby, and unfortunately, Baz knew that wasn't going to happen.

The door to the barn opened and JJ poked her head out. "Hey, you comin'?"

Tucking his phone back in his pocket, he nodded, held the door, and followed her inside.

"Luca Switzer, meet Sebastian Buchanan. Baz, meet Luca," JJ introduced.

Baz took a single step back when the big man got to his feet, thrusting out his hand to shake.

He returned the gesture, added a "Nice to meet you," and earned a smile in return.

"You look good, darlin'," Luca told JJ, openly eyeing her. "How long's it been?"

"Not nearly long enough," she said with a chuckle. "Aren't you married yet?"

"Haven't met the ol' gal who can wrangle me," he teased. "You up for the challenge?"

Baz couldn't help it, he stared at JJ's face, watched as she smiled, eyes glittering. Clearly she wasn't bothered by Luca's flirtatious manner, but Baz would honestly admit he didn't care much for it.

She was laughing merrily when she said, "Not in this lifetime, you old coot."

"Well, then if you ever meet her, send her my way, will ya?"

"I wouldn't do that to any woman, Luca. You know that."

Baz turned away, reminding himself he had no right to be jealous and he had absolutely no say in who JJ flirted with.

"I talked to Brantley," JJ explained. "He said we should get started without him."

"Hit me, woman. Whatcha got?" Luca asked.

JJ went on to explain what she'd learned from Dante about the woman she referred to as Katherine King, who she was insistent was Juliet Prince.

"Brantley told me he had the phones they were usin' at their hideout," JJ told Luca. "All we need to do is find out her IP address, trace it, and see where she was messagin' from."

"Easy-peasy," Luca agreed.

Baz took a seat and fought the urge to roll his eyes.

Two hours later, after JJ and Luca had worked their magic, the entire team was watching while the Grand Rapids Police Department went to the Lakeside Motel to find Juliet Prince.

He hadn't believed it was possible for them to track her so easily, but they were absolutely certain that was where she'd been as of three o'clock yesterday afternoon, when she'd sent the last text to Marcus asking him how things were going.

"Please, God, let her be there," JJ muttered to herself, her shoulder brushing Baz's as they watched a live feed from the scene.

On the screen, a SWAT officer walked up to the door, knocked. When there was no answer, he motioned for someone to come over. A short, middle-aged man stepped over, swiped a key card, then was ushered back out of the way.

The next couple of minutes were chaos as they rushed the room, checking under the bed, in the closet and the bathroom. But it hadn't taken but a second for everyone to realize that the room was empty.

If Juliet Prince had been there, she was gone now.

Chapter Twenty-Three

Friday, January 8, 2021

ONE WEEK AFTER THE SHOWDOWN AT THE warehouse, finding Dante, and ending up with another dead end on the whereabouts of Juliet Prince, things had returned to normal.

Well, as normal as they could be, considering.

After they'd secured Dante Greenwood, returned him to his parents, Brantley had given him one night to recover before relaying the details of what had really happened to Gerard and Katrina. A discussion that went exactly as Brantley had predicted it would: not well at all.

Needless to say, Brantley was not on Governor Greenwood's good side. The man did not want to believe his son had masterminded—a term Brantley used loosely when referring to Dante—the kidnapping in an effort to extort one million dollars to cover his gambling and drug addictions. Evidently, Dante had taken out a "loan" with his bookie *and* his dealer and had been unable to cover the balance and interest of either. When Marcus had been sent to collect the gambling debt, Dante had been able to appeal to his greed, coming up with the plan that would net Marcus five hundred thousand as payment for helping and allow Dante to pay off his debt with the other half.

When asked why they'd decided to cut off his finger, Dante had explained that hadn't been the plan. He'd insisted Marcus had gone completely crazy and chopped it off in a fit of rage when he really did take Dante hostage. Of course, that tale had lasted all of five minutes, because Dante's pain meds had kicked in and he revealed, with a spooky smile, that he'd been the knight in shining armor and had sacrificed himself in order to keep Marcus from raping JJ while she was unconscious.

Such a *fucking* gentleman.

But the worst part had come when Brantley asked Governor Greenwood how he wanted to proceed with Dante's charges. In no uncertain terms, the governor informed him he would be handling Dante's punishment personally and there was no need to share the details with the police. Marcus Harris would go on record as having kidnapped Dante, assaulted JJ, blown up her house, and attempted to blackmail him. And since Marcus was dead, there was no one to argue those facts.

Awfully *fucking* convenient.

That had been the icing on the cake for Brantley, and he had refused to listen to any more. Probably the reason he hadn't gotten as in depth as JJ had with his questioning. If he had, perhaps he would've been the one to uncover Juliet Prince's part in all of this. But like usual, they'd been just a little too late to catch the woman in that shitty motel in Michigan.

He'd managed to get Governor Greenwood to agree to hold off on cutting off their access, using the excuse that they needed it to find Juliet Prince. After he'd explained that she had played a partial role in Dante's scheme, the governor had given them until the end of the month.

In truth, it hadn't done much more than buy Brantley some time to explain to Reese and the team what was going on.

Now, as he sat with his back to the wall in a corner booth at the diner, his attention on the man sitting across from him, he pondered just how to reveal the news that they were currently in limbo when it came to employment.

Brantley had been playing it out in his head for a while now. Days, in fact. And it wasn't so much the revelation that bothered him. More so the questions he would be asked, such as *What's next?* For which he wasn't exactly clear on the answer.

He and Reese had taken a break to grab some dinner, opting for the diner because it allowed them to get out of the house. It was probably the perfect place to give bad news since it was a controlled environment, restricting an overreaction.

Hopefully.

Yeah, he should probably suck it up and tell Reese now.

"You don't think you jumped the gun offerin' Luca a job?" Reese asked, pulling Brantley from his reflective thoughts.

He took a sip of his sweet tea. "I figure it'll take him a few weeks to get around to makin' a decision. Luca's not the kind to commit to anything quickly."

"Probably the reason he's still single and what? Goin' on forty?"

Grateful for conversation that didn't involve Juliet or Dante, Brantley smiled. "Word is, he's got a thing for my cousin, Honor. They met at that auction Bianca did back in October."

Reese grinned. "I remember that. Kaden and Keegan were up in arms about it. They were auctioned off to Kate."

"That they were." Brantley grinned, remembering the horrified look on their faces when they thought Gage was the one bidding on them. They'd been relieved when they learned they were serving at the whim of a six-year-old who wanted to go to McDonald's for her "date."

"Luca and Honor... It serious?"

Brantley let his gaze scan the room. "Who knows with him. Or her. Honor's never been all that big on relationships, either." Shifting topics, he looked at Reese again. "What do you think about hirin' Holly to be JJ's assistant?"

Reese's dark eyebrows shot down into a V. "You really are tryin' to piss her off, huh? You don't think she can hire her own assistant?"

"I think she's a procrastinator. Plus, she's got enough on her plate, what with her house explodin' and all." Brantley broke eye contact, worried he'd be unable to hide his guilt. "I think we need to get things movin'. We already agreed we'd be on the hunt for warm bodies to fill all those vacancies on the task force by the first of the year. We're there. I don't have time to wait for JJ to get with the program."

He could tell Reese was surprised by his response. And truthfully, he was, too. Perhaps it had to do with all the stress he was under. Most of it having to do with the fact the task force was on borrowed time. Which meant hiring *anyone* was something Brantley had to shoulder all on his own. And when one didn't have a firm plan of action, that was a lot to deal with.

"I like her," Reese said, watching him intently. "Holly. I think she'd be good at it. Plus, she's probably used to her brother's quirks, so she's equipped to deal with JJ's as well."

Brantley took a drink of his tea, sitting back when the waitress delivered their food. "Good. Because I offered her the job this afternoon. She accepted."

Reese exhaled roughly, shaking his head in disbelief. "Of course you did."

No, it probably hadn't been his place to make a decision like that without consulting Reese first, but he was serious when he said he needed to fill those vacancies. Even if the task force wasn't exactly what it had once been.

Brantley understood the politics behind Governor Greenwood's decision, something he'd endured during his time in the military. It was all one big political chess game, and while the governor had been quick to bring them on, he did get a lot of push back from a lot of people. Turned out, they didn't make decisions in a vacuum, and when they did, they were held accountable.

The thing was, Brantley wasn't willing to let the task force go, but at the same time, he wasn't opposed to going off the books entirely. If they went into the private sector, they could focus on what they'd banded together to do in the first place: find missing people. From the moment the governor had said they would be loaned out to help with homicide investigations, Brantley had been having second thoughts.

Which was partly why he'd asked RT and Z for a tour of Sniper 1 Security when they'd been in Dallas for Christmas. And why he'd kept in touch with both of them since. Without funding from the state, they would need to get it from somewhere. And while Travis was giving them money when they asked for it, he was only one man.

"What's on your mind?" Reese asked, interrupting his thoughts.

He recentered his focus, realizing Reese was eating, but Brantley had yet to pick up his fork.

"Been a long week," he said, reaching for the utensil.

"The good news is, Dante's safe and secure in a rehab facility," Reese said with a smile.

"For now."

"Ever the optimist." Reese grinned. "One of the reasons I love you."

Brantley stared, his brain processing the words.

It wasn't the admission of love that caught him off guard. Reese had spoken those words numerous times already. But what he hadn't done was say them in public, loudly enough for anyone to hear. He hadn't whispered or looked away or appeared embarrassed by it in any way.

And while that made Brantley's heart fuller than it had ever been, it also made him feel incredibly guilty.

"I … uh…" He sighed, set his fork down. "I should probably mention…" He swallowed, overwhelmed by nerves.

"Somethin' wrong?"

Brantley figured that depended on how Reese looked at it, so he spit out the words. "We're unemployed."

Reese's expression fell. "We're *what?*"

"The … uh … the task force. It no longer exists."

"The governor *fired* us?"

"You could say that, sure." Brantley reached for his tea. "But it's cool."

"Cool?" Reese leaned forward, lowered his voice. "You think it's cool that we're unemployed?"

Brantley exhaled and blurted out, "No, I think it's cool that we're gonna literally go off the books. You know, do this on our own."

"I THINK MAYBE YOUR BLOOD SUGAR'S LOW," Reese told Brantley, staring back at him.

He wanted to take the task force private? As in run it like a business? On their own?

Brantley set down his glass. "Hear me out."

Reese lowered his fork, forcing himself to relax as he waited to hear Brantley's big reveal.

"Let me preface this by sayin' the governor made the decision, not me."

"The decision to what?"

"Disband the task force."

Reese frowned, sitting up straight, trying to understand what Brantley was saying. "What do you mean disband? I thought you said we were fired."

That was something he would understand. The being fired part. After all, Reese had been privy to the conversation with the governor after they'd recovered Dante and returned him home. The man had not accepted that Dante had come up with the plan on his own, insisting his son was incapable of such an egregious act, accusing Brantley of reaching. They hadn't exactly left the hospital in the governor's good graces.

"This was a decision the governor made before the incident with Dante."

Before? "How long *before*? And why's this the first time I'm hearin' about it?"

The waitress chose that moment to swing by to check on them, but rather than wave her off, Reese held up a finger, asked for two coffees. If he had to guess, this was going to be a long night. Might as well fuel up now.

"The Monday before Christmas, I got an email from Governor Greenwood tellin' me there's a good possibility he'll have to officially disband the task force. Somethin' about gettin' pushback regardin' the allocation of the budget. Accordin' to those in opposition, the governor should've been dedicatin' the money bein' used for us to the law enforcement agencies already in place."

Reese nodded. "Makes sense."

It was one of the questions he'd had from the beginning but never voiced: why would the governor want to create something on the side when he could invest more in what he already had?

"It does," Brantley continued. "But Governor Greenwood truly believed the task force provided somethin' the other agencies couldn't. We didn't have to deal with the bureaucratic red tape, we could focus our attention on whatever we needed to focus on, and so forth."

Reese had no argument there. They did have more leeway than the police and sheriff departments.

"You're sayin' all this in past tense. So it's real. The task force no longer exists?"

"Technically, we'll have access for the remainder of the month, but those opposed to his decision accused him of doin' it for personal gain, so yeah. It's a done deal."

"Personal? Because we found his daughter," Reese mused.

"Her and Lauren Tyler. Since she was a direct connection to the governor before she went missing, and our first official case, they argued that he was keepin' the task force in his pocket."

Probably didn't matter that they'd made the decision to make that their first case. They hadn't consulted with the governor when they had.

Reese studied Brantley's face as a few dots connected. "That's why you were talkin' to Z and RT."

Brantley exhaled and Reese could see his concern. Likely worried Reese would be angry that he'd been left out of the loop. And fine, maybe he was a little frustrated that Brantley hadn't bothered to share this with him. After all, Brantley was the one who continued to claim Reese was his equal, not just another member of the team.

"That's the part that isn't past tense," Brantley noted.

They paused while the waitress delivered their coffee, bringing a small metal canister of cream and a glass bowl with sugar and sugar substitute to go with it.

"Thanks," Brantley told her before turning his attention back to Reese. "I've given it a lot of thought, and this last case … with Dante … it solidifies my decision. It's best we do separate ourselves from the governor, take the team private. And yes, we're gonna keep the task force together."

Reese nodded, understanding. "Work for hire."

"Yes." Brantley exhaled again. "For the most part. But I wanted to design it so we can take pro bono cases when necessary. The most critical ones."

"Missing kids," Reese acknowledged.

Brantley nodded.

There was no denying the fact that Reese found he loved this man more because of little things like that.

"I didn't know how to tell you. I was hopin' to come up with a foolproof plan before I had to."

"It's your task force, I'm just—"

"Don't even," Brantley snapped. "You are not *just* anything. This task force came about because of both of us. Not just me."

Maybe, but that didn't mean Reese had to be in a position of power. Truth was, he didn't want to deal with all the politics and bullshit. He wanted to find missing people. He wanted to solve cases. And he wanted to partner with Brantley to do it, but he didn't care about all the added responsibilities.

"Obviously you've come up with somethin'," Reese said, redirecting to avoid an argument. "Otherwise, you wouldn't've hired Holly and offered Luca a job."

He watched as Brantley sipped his coffee, clearly preparing his response.

"Just spit it out," he said softly. "Whatever you've decided to do, I'm on board."

Brantley's blue-gray eyes were wary when he looked at Reese. "We've got a meetin' with Ryan Trexler and Hunter Kogan in the mornin'."

"RT and Hunter? As in the heads of Sniper 1 Security?"

"Yes."

"In Dallas?"

"They're comin' to us this time."

Reese let the news tumble around in his gray matter.

"As much as I want to believe we could do this on our own," Brantley explained, "I think we'd have more success if we were absorbed by a company with a reputation that can sustain us."

"You've given this a lot of thought."

"I want what's best for everyone involved. You, me, the team. And I truly believe this is our calling. We're good at what we do."

Reese couldn't argue with that. They had proven they were a valuable asset as a team.

But there was one thing he did have a problem with. "I can't see us relocatin' to Dallas."

Brantley quickly shook his head. "No. Definitely not. That's why they're comin' here. RT mentioned lookin' at property in Austin and Houston. I told him to hold off on makin' a purchase until we talked."

"They're on board with this?"

"They're probably more excited about it than we are."

Well, that was reassuring.

Chapter Twenty-Four

JJ STOOD IN HER FRONT YARD, STARING at the charred mess of what used to be her house.

It was a mess. A big, stinky pile of ashes and bricks and a few partially constructed walls. It was even worse than what Brantley had said. Evidently, the water from those fire hoses had demolished anything that might've remained.

The truth was, JJ wasn't as torn up about losing the house or the contents as she'd thought she would be. Then again, she'd long ago stopped attaching sentimental value to objects. The house was a house. It provided shelter. The furniture gave her a place to sit or lay her head. The knickknacks had given it some flair, but there wasn't anything she would shed a tear for. Her books were about the only things she would miss, but thankfully, those could be replaced for the most part.

On the other hand, and what she hadn't told a single soul, JJ was almost grateful this had happened. While the team hadn't questioned why she had so many cameras in her house, she knew they were thinking she was paranoid. And they were right. She was. But thankfully she didn't have to explain herself, because she wasn't sure if they would ever understand. After all, *she* didn't really understand.

But she did have to find a new normal, one that included a place of her own. What worried her most was how long it would take to get to that new normal. Building a house would take time, but how much time was the question. Six months, a year? Longer? And where was she going to stay during that process?

She felt more than saw Baz standing beside her. He'd offered to drive her here so she could see what she was dealing with. Ever since he'd taken that phone call from the Molly woman he'd spent the night with, he'd been acting strange. Six days and counting. Definitely not his usual laid-back, fun self. And if she was being honest, it worried her.

"We got lucky," she said under her breath.

It had been a stroke of luck that no one had been in the house when it had blown up. Based on what they'd ascertained, Juliet Prince had convinced Marcus to set that bomb to do the most damage, then she'd texted Travis Walker pretending to be JJ so that he would arrive just in time to go up in flames. Juliet would've wiped them all out in one fell swoop.

It was another reason JJ hated that bitch.

But now she was also questioning Juliet's skill set. The woman would've had to hack her phone to send that text. How had she done it? It wasn't an easy thing to do. Where'd she acquire that skill set? Or was she working with someone?

So many questions, not nearly enough answers.

"You're welcome to stay at my apartment until it's completed," Baz said, his voice soft. "I've got the second bedroom. I can clean it out, get you a bed and whatnot."

The old JJ would've immediately refused the offer of help. But that was the JJ who'd had something of her own. This woman, the one staring at the charred rubble of her existence, wasn't in a position to refuse anyone.

"I'd appreciate it," she said softly, glancing over at him. "I'll pay you rent. Split the utilities."

Baz nodded, his gaze never quite meeting hers.

"Are you sure you're okay with it?"

His pretty blue eyes lifted, but the luster that was usually in them was dim. "What? Of course, JJ."

Although she wasn't sure how she was going to manage living with Baz, especially if she had to endure him dating this Molly person—or any other woman for that matter—she wasn't disappointed. She knew Baz, she trusted Baz. Most importantly, she felt safe with Baz, and right now, she didn't feel safe anywhere. And she definitely didn't want to be alone.

After taking one last look at what was left of her house, JJ turned around, started back toward Baz's truck.

"You ready to go home?" JJ realized how that sounded. "I mean, you know, to your apartment?"

"It's home," he said in that monotone she was getting used to. "For now."

Yeah. For now.

That seemed to be where everything in their lives was currently positioned: right between somewhere and nowhere.

She only hoped this was the worst of it.

Stay Tuned

I hope you enjoyed the fourth installment of the Off the Books Task Force. There's definitely more to come for Brantley and Reese, JJ and Baz, Trey and Magnus, and the rest of the task force. Each book in this series is a full-length novel involving a new case and the continuation of the relationships between them all. And I promise not to keep you waiting long for each installment.

If you enjoyed *Deadly Coincidence*, please consider leaving a review.

WANT TO READ ABOUT THE OTHER CHARACTERS?

If you haven't had a chance to read about **RT and Z**, you can find their story in the Sniper 1 Security series. Their story unfolds in *Never Say Never*, which is available on all retailers. There is also a follow-up story in *Naughty Holidays 2015*, which includes the recipe for the Jack Daniel's pecan pie.

ABOUT NICOLE EDWARDS

New York Times and *USA Today* bestselling author Nicole Edwards lives in the suburbs of Austin, Texas with her husband and their youngest of three children. The two older ones have flown the coup, while the youngest is in high school. When Nicole is not writing about sexy alpha males and sassy, independent women, she can often be found with a book in hand or attempting to keep the dogs happy. You can find her hanging out on social media and interacting with her readers - even when she's supposed to be writing.

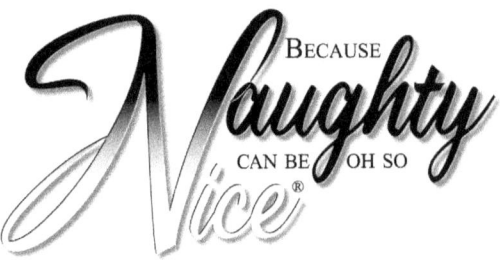

CONNECT WITH NICOLE

I hope you're as eager to get the information as I am to give it. Any one of these things is worth signing up for, or feel free to sign up for all. I promise to keep each one unique and interesting.

NIC NEWS: If you haven't signed up for my newsletter and you want to get notifications regarding preorders, new releases, giveaways, sales, etc, then you'll want to sign up. I promise not to spam your email, just get you the most important updates.

NICOLE'S HOT SHEET: A couple of years ago I produced a weekly hot sheet that gave a summary of what I'd done and what I had in the works, and I have decided to bring it back. This is a more personal newsletter that I send out for those who are curious about me, my family, my dogs, and all that goes along with the daily author life.

NICOLE'S BLOG: My blog is used for writer ramblings, which I am known to do from time to time. I will keep these separate from the newsletter updates or what I post in the Hot Sheet so that I don't duplicate in your inbox.

NICOLE NATION: I created Nicole Nation on my website to provide exclusive content to my readers including, First Look notifications, sneak peeks, A Day in the Life character stories, exclusive giveaways, cards from Nicole, Join Nicole's review team. It's free and gets you access to exclusive content you won't find anywhere else!

NN ON FACEBOOK: Join my reader group to interact with other readers, ask me questions, play fun weekly games, celebrate during release week, and enter exclusive giveaways!

INSTAGRAM: Basically, Instagram is where I post pictures of my dogs, so if you want to see epic cuteness, you should follow me.

TEXT: Want a simple, fast way to get updates on new releases? Sign up for text messaging. If you are in the U.S. simply text NICOLE to 64600. I promise not to spam your phone. This is just my way of letting you know what's happening because I know you're busy, but if you're anything like me, you always have your phone on you.

NAUGHTY & NICE SHOP: Not only does the shop have signed books, but there's fun merchandise, too. Plenty of naughty and nice options to go around. Find the shop on my website.

Website:	NicoleEdwardsAuthor.com
Facebook:	/Author.Nicole.Edwards
Instagram:	NicoleEdwardsAuthor
BookBub:	/NicoleEdwardsAuthor

ACKNOWLEDGMENTS

Of course, I have to thank my wonderfully patient husband who puts up with me every single day. If it wasn't for him and his belief that I could (and can) do this, I wouldn't be writing this today. He has been my backbone, my rock, the very reason I continue to believe in myself. I love you for that, babe.

Chancy Powley – You continue to come through for me in every way. You even tolerate my inability to answer my text messages in a timely manner. I will apologize for that now and for all future instances because we all know, I'm horrible at it. Just keep in mind, you are the absolute best friend I have and I am forever grateful for your friendship.

Jenna Underwood — Because you continue to be my friend despite the fact that I am the world's worst friend. Thank you for always being there for me and for the postcards. They make me smile.

I also have to thank my street team – Naughty (and nice) Girls – Your unwavering support is something I will never take for granted.

I can't forget my copyeditor, Amy at Blue Otter Editing. Thank goodness I've got you to catch all my punctuation, grammar, and tense errors.

Nicole Nation 2.0 for the constant support and love. You've been there for me from almost the beginning. This group of ladies has kept me going for so long, I'm not sure I'd know what to do without them.

And, of course, YOU, the reader. Your emails, messages, posts, comments, tweets... they mean more to me than you can imagine. I thrive on hearing from you, knowing that my characters and my stories have touched you in some way keeps me going. I've been known to shed a tear or two when reading an email because you simply bring so much joy to my life with your support. I thank you for that.

By Nicole Edwards

The Walkers

Alluring Indulgence
Kaleb
Zane
Travis
Holidays with The Walker Brothers
Ethan
Braydon
Sawyer
Brendon

The Walkers Of Coyote Ridge
Curtis
Jared (a crossover novel)
Hard to Hold
Hard to Handle
Beau
Rex
A Coyote Ridge Christmas
Mack
Kaden & Keegan
Alibi (a crossover novel)

Brantley Walker: Off The Books
All In
Without A Trace
Hide & Seek
Deadly Coincidence
Alibi (a crossover novel)

Austin Arrows
Rush
Kaufman

CLUB DESTINY
Conviction
Temptation
Addicted
Seduction
Infatuation
Captivated
Devotion
Perception
Entrusted
Adored
Distraction

DEAD HEAT RANCH
Boots Optional
Betting on Grace
Overnight Love
Jared (a crossover novel)

DEVIL'S BEND
Chasing Dreams
Vanishing Dreams

MISPLACED HALOS
Protected in Darkness
Salvation in Darkness
Bound in Darkness

OFFICE INTRIGUE
Office Intrigue
Intrigued Out of The Office
Their Rebellious Submissive
Their Famous Dominant
Their Ruthless Sadist
Their Naughty Student
Their Fairy Princess
Owned

PIER 70
Reckless
Fearless
Speechless
Harmless
Clueless

SNIPER 1 SECURITY
Wait for Morning
Never Say Never
Tomorrow's Too Late

SOUTHERN BOY MAFIA/DEVIL'S PLAYGROUND
Beautifully Brutal
Without Regret
Beautifully Loyal
Without Restraint

STANDALONE NOVELS
Unhinged Trilogy
A Million Tiny Pieces
Inked on Paper
Bad Reputation
Bad Business

NAUGHTY HOLIDAY EDITIONS
2015
2016